AN EVELYN WAUGH CHRONOLOGY

AUTHOR CHRONOLOGIES

General Editor: Norman Page, Emeritus Professor of Modern
English Literature, University of Nottingham

J. L. Bradley
A RUSKIN CHRONOLOGY

J. R. Hammond
A ROBERT LOUIS STEVENSON CHRONOLOGY

John McDermott
A HOPKINS CHRONOLOGY

Norman Page
AN EVELYN WAUGH CHRONOLOGY

Peter Preston
A D. H. LAWRENCE CHRONOLOGY

An Evelyn Waugh Chronology

Norman Page
*Emeritus Professor of Modern English Literature
University of Nottingham*

First published in Great Britain 1997 by
MACMILLAN PRESS LTD
Houndmills, Basingstoke, Hampshire RG21 6XS and London
Companies and representatives throughout the world

A catalogue record for this book is available from the British Library.

ISBN-13: 978-0-333-63894-1

First published in the United States of America 1997 by
ST. MARTIN'S PRESS, INC.,
Scholarly and Reference Division,
175 Fifth Avenue, New York, N.Y. 10010

ISBN 0-312-17417-9

Library of Congress Cataloging-in-Publication Data
Page, Norman.
An Evelyn Waugh chronology / Norman Page.
p. cm. — (Author chronologies)
Includes index.
ISBN 0-312-17417-9
1. Waugh, Evelyn, 1903-1966—Chronology. 2. Authors,
English—20th century—Biography—Chronology. I. Title.
II. Series: Author chronologies (New York)
PR6045.A97Z749 1997
823'.912—dc21   96-53540
                                                                                    CIP

© Norman Page 1997

All rights reserved. No reproduction, copy or transmission of this publication may be made without written permission.

No paragraph of this publication may be reproduced, copied or transmitted save with written permission or in accordance with the provisions of the Copyright, Designs and Patents Act 1988, or under the terms of any licence permitting limited copying issued by the Copyright Licensing Agency, 90 Tottenham Court Road, London W1P 9HE.

Any person who does any unauthorised act in relation to this publication may be liable to criminal prosecution and civil claims for damages.

The author has asserted his right to be identified as the author of this work in accordance with the Copyright, Designs and Patents Act 1988.

This book is printed on paper suitable for recycling and made from fully managed and sustained forest sources. Logging, pulping and manufacturing processes are expected to conform to the environmental regulations of the country of origin.

10 9 8 7 6 5 4 3 2 1
06 05 04 03 02 01 00 99 98 97

Contents

General Editor's Preface	vii
Introduction	ix
AN EVELYN WAUGH CHRONOLOGY	1
The Evelyn Waugh Circle	89
Index	203

General Editor's Preface

Most biographies are ill adapted to serve as works of reference – not surprisingly so, since the biographer is likely to regard his function as the devising of a continuous and readable narrative, with excursions into interpretation and speculation, rather than a bald recital of facts. There are times, however, when anyone reading for business or pleasure needs to check a point quickly or to obtain a rapid overview of part of an author's life or career; and at such moments turning over the pages of a biography can be a time-consuming and frustrating occupation. The present series of volumes aims at providing a means whereby the chronological facts of an author's life and career, rather than needing to be prised out of the narrative in which they are (if they appear at all) securely embedded, can be seen at a glance. Moreover, whereas biographies are often, and quite understandably, vague over matters of fact (since it makes for tediousness to be forever enumerating details of dates and places), a chronology can be precise whenever it is possible to be precise.

Thanks to the survival, sometimes in very large quantities, of letters, diaries, notebooks and other documents, as well as to thoroughly researched biographies and bibliographies, this material now exists in abundance for many major authors. In the case of, for example, Dickens, we can often ascertain what he was doing in each month and week, and almost on each day, of his prodigiously active working life; and the student of, say, *David Copperfield* is likely to find it fascinating as well as useful to know just when Dickens was at work on each part of that novel, what other literary enterprises he was engaged in at the same time, whom he was meeting, what places he was visiting, and what were the relevant circumstances of his personal and professional life. Such a chronology is not, of course, a substitute for a biography; but its arrangement, in combination with its index, makes it a much more convenient tool for this kind of purpose; and it may be acceptable as a form of 'alternative' biography, with its own distinctive advantages as well as its obvious limitations.

Since information relating to an author's early years is usually scanty and chronologically imprecise, the opening section of some volumes in this series groups together the years of childhood and adolescence. Thereafter each year, and usually each month, is dealt with separately. Information not readily assignable to a specific month or day is given as a general note under the relevant year or month. The first entry for each month carries an indication of the day of the week, so that when necessary this can be readily calculated for other dates. Each volume also contains a bibliography of the principal sources of information. In the chronology itself, the sources of many of the more specific items, including quotations, are identified, in order that the reader who wishes to do so may consult the original contexts.

NORMAN PAGE

Introduction

The principal sources for an Evelyn Waugh chronology are the writer's own diaries and letters, and I have made extensive use of *The Diaries of Evelyn Waugh*, edited by Michael Davie (1976) and *The Letters of Evelyn Waugh*, edited by Mark Amory (1980). The latter has been supplemented by *Mr Wu and Mrs Stitch: The Letters of Evelyn Waugh and Diana Cooper*, very helpfully edited by Artemis Cooper (1991). Though materials of this kind survive from all phases of Waugh's life, from childhood and youth to his last years, the record is inevitably far from complete: he kept a diary only intermittently (though at times regularly and fully), and it also seems likely that diaries kept during certain sensitive periods were subsequently destroyed, while the letters are as usual subject to the laws that determine the preservation, suppression or destruction of documents that pass from the writer's hands into those of other people. Inevitably, therefore, some parts of Waugh's eventful life are covered more fully than others by the existing evidence and, accordingly, in this chronology.

Another problem that arises for the chronologist is the repetitiveness inherent in certain aspects of the subject's life. Waugh's social life was an unusually full one, but a complete record of his luncheons and dinners, his visits to his clubs or to other people's houses, would be tedious and even pointless: and though Waugh himself regularly recorded the occasions on which he got drunk or had his hair cut, few readers will care to have this information set down in full. I have, therefore, made a selection from these items so as to convey the flavour of his existence at various times and at the same time to record both the shifting patterns of his friendships and any particularly notable encounters with individuals. In the same way, the complexity of his wartime activities and movements would demand an excessive proportion of space if they were to be noted with anything approaching completeness; as it is, even a selective record communicates a vivid impression of the muddles, inefficiencies and confusions, occasionally illuminated by high drama or broad farce, of his military experiences.

Waugh was not only a prolific novelist but a highly productive journalist, and no attempt has been made to record every article or review he published, though a selection of the more significant items has been given. A substantial number of his shorter non-fictional pieces are reprinted in *The Essays, Articles and Reviews of Evelyn Waugh*, edited by Donat Gallagher (1983), which also contains as an appendix a useful 'Chronological List of Occasional Writings Not Printed in this Volume'. Again, Waugh's extensive travels were often intricate in their itineraries, and his movements are not always easy to date with precision; consequently the account of them given here, though reasonably full, leaves a few unavoidable gaps. Space has, however, been found to record many of the books he read, the films and plays he saw, and the exhibitions he attended.

Waugh has been fortunate in having as a biographer Martin Stannard, whose two volumes – *Evelyn Waugh: The Early Years 1903–1939* (1986) and *Evelyn Waugh: The Later Years 1939–1966* (1992) – are not only thoroughly researched and lucidly narrated, but possess a wit, shrewdness and stylishness worthy of their remarkable subject. My own debt to Martin Stannard's exemplary biography is considerable and gratefully acknowledged.

As is customary in this series, a few significant historical events have been included, as well as a few references to major writers who were Waugh's contemporaries or near-contemporaries. Information concerning the more important figures associated with him appears in the section 'The Evelyn Waugh Circle'; others who played a lesser part in his life are briefly identified when they appear. Throughout, 'EW' refers to Evelyn Waugh, and he must be understood to be the subject of verbs for which no other subject is given. 'Tells' usually indicates that the reference is to one of Waugh's letters.

An Evelyn Waugh Chronology

Early Years (1903–21)

1903 (28 Oct) Arthur Evelyn St John Waugh born at 11 Hillfield Road, West Hampstead, London, second child and younger son of Arthur Waugh (1866–1943), publisher and man of letters, and his wife Catherine (née Raban), daughter of a magistrate in the Bengal Civil Service; they had married in 1893. Their first child, Alexander (Alec), who also became a writer, had been born in 1898 (died 1981).
(17 Dec) Orville and Wilbur Wright make a successful flight in an aeroplane with a petrol engine.
Among the year's publications are Samuel Butler's *The Way of All Flesh* and Henry James's *The Ambassadors*; G.B. Shaw's *Man and Superman* is produced; the building of Liverpool Cathedral, to designs by Gilbert Scott, is begun; the first motor taxis appear in London.

1904 (26 Aug) Christopher Isherwood born.
(2 Oct) Graham Greene born.

1906 (12 Jan) The Liberal Party wins a landslide victory in the General Election.

1907 For the next three or four years, receives his first lessons at home from his mother; they are shared with Stella Rhys, daughter of the writer Ernest Rhys.
(21 Feb) W.H. Auden born.
(Sep) The Waugh family move to a newly-built house, 'Underhill', 145 North End Road, Golders Green. EW's brother Alec goes to a boarding preparatory school and is very unhappy there.

1908 (28 May) Ian Fleming born.

1909 At about this time, writes his first literary composition, a short story titled 'The Curse of the Horse Race'.
(10 Apr) A.C. Swinburne dies.
(18 May) George Meredith dies.

1910 (15 Jan) In the General Election, the Liberals retain power with a reduced majority.
(6 May) Death of Edward VII and accession of George V.

(Sep)   Begins to attend his first school, Heath Mount preparatory school, Hampstead, as a day boy. (The headmaster, J.S.G. Grenfell, has been at Sherborne School with Arthur Waugh.) During this year EW also begins to attend St Jude's, Hampstead Garden Suburb, with his parents and is attracted by the Anglo-Catholicism of the vicar, the Rev. Basil Bourchier.

1911 (Sep)   Begins to keep a diary, continued intermittently until August 1916. Notes that his brother Alec has just gone to Sherborne.

1912   During the summer, has his appendix removed.

1913 (11 Aug)   Angus Wilson born.

1914 (28 Jun)   Assassination of Archduke Franz Ferdinand of Austria and his wife at Sarajevo.
(4 Aug)   Britain declares war on Germany.

1915   EW's diary contains a reference to a Zeppelin raid on London which he has witnessed.
   At the end of the summer term Alec Waugh is asked to leave Sherborne after being caught engaging in homosexual acts; the matter is discreetly handled by his father, and EW does not learn the details until 1962.
   During this year, serves briefly as a War Office messenger.

1916 (28 Feb)   Henry James dies.
(29 Jun)   Is confirmed as a member of the Church of England (see also 29 June 1920).
(12–19 Aug)   On holiday at Westcliffe-on-Sea, Essex (described in his diary).
   During this year, devises, edits and contributes to a school magazine, *The Cynic*, and writes a long poem in the *Hiawatha* metre, *The World to Come: A Poem in Three Cantos*, on the subject of Purgatory (privately printed).

1917   Leaves his preparatory school in the spring, and on 9 May enters Lancing, a minor public school on the Sussex coast with a strong High Church tradition.
(20 Jul)   Publication of Alec Waugh's novel *The Loom of Youth*, written in a few weeks, based on his experiences at Sherborne,

and containing allusions to public school homosexuality; it becomes a best-seller, but results in both his and his father's names being removed from the list of old boys at the school. Though EW has been originally destined for Sherborne, his brother's withdrawal in 1915 (see above) and the impending publication of his book have made this impossible.
(Nov)   'In Defence of Cubism', EW's first published article, appears in *Drawing and Design*.

1918 (29 Jul)   Alec Waugh marries Barbara Jacobs.
(11 Nov)   The Great War ends.
(14 Dec)   In the General Election a Coalition government is returned.

1919 (23 Sep)   Begins to keep a diary, continued until he leaves Lancing in December 1921.
(20 Dec)   During the school holidays, visits a Matisse exhibition at the Leicester Galleries, London and is unimpressed.
(21 Dec)   Attends High Mass at St Jude's, Hampstead Garden Suburb.

1920 (18 Apr)   During the school holidays, attends High Mass at St Mary's, Primrose Hill.
(29 Jun)   On the fourth anniversary of his confirmation, reflects that at that time he must have been 'rather a prig'.
(16 Aug)   Attends an exhibition at Hampstead Art Gallery and admires paintings by Mark Gertler.
(11 Sep)   Visits Oxford for the day and is overwhelmed by its beauty. His name has been put down for New College, and he will try to win a Christ Church scholarship.
(6 Dec)   Hears that his mother has undergone an operation and writes to her at once to express his deep concern.
   During the Christmas holidays, begins a novel.

1921 (10 Jan)   Has already abandoned the novel on which he has been working.
(31 Mar)   Strike of British miners.
(8 Apr)   Railway and transport workers announce their intention of striking in sympathy, and the next day EW notes that the situation is 'fiercely exciting'; his wish to join the strike-breakers is, however, frustrated.

(13 Jun) Tells his father that he has won a school prize for literature, and that he is reading some philosophy with enjoyment: he plans to start on Bergson soon.
(19 July) Writes a long diary entry concerning his thoughts about suicide.
(16 Oct) Is 'hating' school. Two days later his father gives him permission to leave at the end of the term and either go up to Oxford at once or spend some time in France.
(28 Oct) EW's 18th birthday. He is now working hard for an Oxford history scholarship.
(Nov) EW's review of *The Poetic Procession* by J.F. Roxburgh (a master at the school) appears in the *Lancing College Magazine*. His 'Editorial' in the same issue is responded to in the next month's issue in a letter written by EW himself under the pseudonym of Lavernia Scargill.
(5 Dec) Goes to Oxford to sit the scholarship examination, but is pessimistic about his chances.
(9 Dec) Returns to London.
(15 Dec) Hears that he has won a £100 scholarship at Hertford College.
(16 Dec) Leaves Lancing 'without regret'.

1922

January

Goes into residence at Hertford College, Oxford. (There are no surviving diaries for EW's Oxford period, but letters written to Dudley Carew in 1924 hint at experiences that would make 'strange reading'.)
 During this term, speaks in a debate at the Oxford Union.

February

13 (Mon) Tells his schoolfriend Tom Driberg that he has been to hear W.R. Inge, Dean of St Paul's, preach at the University Church.

April

16 Kingsley Amis born.

May

31 (Wed) Tells Dudley Carew that he has spoken again at the Union but has suffered from nervousness and has not spoken well.

October

23 Conservatives gain power after the fall of Lloyd George's coalition government.

November

15 Marcel Proust dies.
Joyce's *Ulysses* and Eliot's *The Waste Land* are among this year's publications.

1923

December

6 General Election, in which the Conservatives retain power with a decreased majority.

1924

January

23 Ramsay MacDonald forms the first Labour government.

June

21 (Sat) Resumes his diary. Returns home from Oxford: he has left the university heavily in debt.
23 Lunches with Tony Bushell; devotes great pains to the purchase of a new walking-stick: dines with Alastair Graham.
24 Goes to Kew Gardens and Hampton Court with Tony Bushell.
25 Spends the day with Alastair Graham, who is shortly leaving for Kenya.
27 Again spends the day (and the next three days) with Graham, who stays the night at the Waugh home. Joyce Fagan joins them for dinner.
30 Goes with Graham to the Empire Exhibition at Wembley.

July

1 (Tue) Attends a performance of *The Merry Widow* at the Lyceum Theatre.
3 Bank refuses him a further overdraft. Attends a party at which a speech is made by J.C. Squire, whom he dislikes.
5 Sees Shaw's *Saint Joan* from the gallery.
6 Attends a service at Westminster Cathedral and hears Ronald Knox preach.
20 Begins a novel, *The Temple at Thatch* (never completed).
27 Goes with Alastair Graham to the Abingdon Arms, Beckley, Oxfordshire (a favourite resort of theirs at this time, and of EW's subsequently), staying until 1 August.
29 Attends a viva (oral examination).
Filming of *The Scarlet Woman*, scripted by EW, begins during this month; it is not completed for over a year.

August

1 (Sun) Goes with Graham by train to Barford House, near Warwick, the Graham family home, where EW is a frequent visitor between 1924 and 1932. There they borrow some money and set off for Dublin, later returning to Barford.
3 Joseph Conrad dies.
Is back at his parents' home by the end of the month.

September

8 (Mon) Goes with Dudley Carew to Covent Garden to see Pavlova (from the gallery).
14 Goes to Mass with Alastair Graham, who has stayed overnight at the Waughs'.
15 Visits Oxford with Graham for an overnight stay.
18 Alastair Graham leaves for Kenya.
21 Attends St Alban's Church with his parents. Is still working on *The Temple at Thatch*, but has lost confidence in it.
22 Begins course at Heatherley's Art School, Newman Street, London.
30 Goes to the Soane Museum and, with his father, to the film of *The Hunchback of Notre Dame*.

October

1 (Wed) Is given £80 by his father.
3 Rereads, with great pleasure, Drummond of Hawthornden's *Cypresse Grove*.
9 Lunches with Tom Driberg.
12 Goes with his brother to lunch with E.S.P. Haynes and gets very drunk.
19 Meets the actor Ernest Thesiger.
25 Goes to an exhibition of Eric Kennington's work at the Leicester Galleries.
28 EW's 21st birthday; he lunches with Tony Bushell, then goes alone to a cinema. Joyce Fagan comes to dinner.
29 In the General Election the Conservatives win a landslide victory.

31 Dines at his brother's flat and meets G.R. and Naomi Mitchison among other guests.

November

7 (Fri) Goes to stay at Barford House (Alastair Graham is still in Africa).
10 Goes to Oxford and attends a lunch party given by John Sutro at which the other guests include Harold Acton, Robert Byron, Hugh Lygon and Richard Pares. The next day he sees many other Oxford friends before returning to London.
14 Goes to Oxford for the weekend, where he sees many friends, including Roy Harrod, Brian Howard and Peter Quennell, and meets Henry Yorke.
16 Goes to Mass at Pusey House, and later in the day returns to London.
30 Notes in his diary that during the past week he has made a number of visits to the National Gallery and is acquiring a taste for Velasquez, Rubens and Poussin.

December

Early in the month, goes to Oxford on an impulse, remains there for five days, and drinks a great deal. On returning to London, contacts James Guthrie, who runs the Pear Tree Press, asking to be taken on as a pupil, and also seeks employment as a teacher in various private schools. Is trying at this time to revise *The Temple at Thatch*.
19 Visits Guthrie, whom he has already met in London, at his press in the village of Flansham, near Bognor Regis, Sussex, and stays overnight.
24 Suspects he may be falling in love with Olivia Plunket Greene.
25 Spends Christmas Day at home. Decides to grow a moustache (the plan is abandoned within the week).
30 Lunches with Olivia at a pub, then they go to Maskelyne and Devant's conjuring show.
31 Olivia comes to lunch at the Waughs'.
During this month, visits an exhibition of the paintings of Marie Laurencin, greatly admires the paintings of William T. Woods, and reads the *Discourses* of Sir Joshua Reynolds.

1925

January

1 (Thu) Sees Olivia and meets her mother.
3 Goes to a performance of G.B. Shaw's *The Philanderer* at the Everyman Theatre, Hampstead, and later sees Olivia and her brother.
4 Goes to a nightclub with Olivia.
5 Meets Mr Banks, headmaster of Arnold House preparatory school, Denbighshire, who offers him a job as assistant master at £160 a year. Alastair Graham returns unexpectedly from Kenya.
6 Spends the evening and most of the night at a series of restaurants and nightclubs with Alastair, Olivia and others.
13 Goes to stay at Barford House.
17 With Alastair, spends the day in Oxford, lunching with Claud Cockburn and others.
18 Returns to London and dines with his brother, the Greene family being among the other guests; later they go on to a theatre and a nightclub, and EW gets drunk.
19 Gets drunk again, this time with Tony Bushell and Bill Silk.
20 Raises £4 by pawning a ring, a snuffbox and a watch.
21 Olivia and her family visit the Waughs' home.
22 Travels by train to Chester, where he is joined by a number of boys on their way to school, and escorts them to Arnold House, Llanddulas, Denbighshire, where his teaching and other duties begin the next day and continue until term ends on 31 March. (The journey and the ensuing term are described at length in the diaries and in *A Little Learning*.)

February

18 Tells Harold Acton how much he has enjoyed reading his volume of poems, *An Indian Ass*.

April

2 (Thu) Returns to London, spends all his money on clothes, and then goes to his parents' home in Hampstead.

3   Goes to an exhibition, meets John Rothenstein and John Sutro, dines with Tony Bushell, and gets very drunk.
4   Goes to a musical comedy with Olivia and his mother.
5   Olivia spends the day at the Waughs' home. Dines at the Savile Club with his brother.
6   Helps to organize a party at Olivia's urging, but while collecting the drink with a friend, decides to pub-crawl, is arrested in Oxford Street on a charge of being 'drunk and incapable', and spends several hours in a police cell before being bailed out. By the time he reaches the Greene home in Hanover Terrace, the party is over.
7   Spends the day with Olivia.
8   Goes to Lundy Island for a holiday with the Greene family and some of their friends.
24 Leaves Lundy, spends the night at Exeter, and the next day, after viewing the cathedral and other sights, travels to Stratford-upon-Avon, where he is met by Alastair Graham and taken to Barford House.
26 Attends Mass in Warwick, then goes to Oxford with Alastair and meets numerous friends, including Harold Acton, Tony Bushell, Robert Byron, Claud Cockburn and John Sutro.
28 They go to Oxford again and lunch with Harold Acton; Alastair gives a dinner at the George, then EW returns late to London, spending the night at the Greenes' home in Hanover Terrace.
29 Goes to an exhibition of Max Beerbohm's work ('quite marvellous') and then takes Alastair to lunch and tea at the Greenes'. Later they all go to the Globe Theatre (Peter Quennell joining their party) to see Noel Coward's *Fallen Angels*.
30 Travels to Denbighshire for the start of the new term at Arnold House, where W.R.B. (Richard) Young, a new master who later becomes the prototype of Captain Grimes in *Decline and Fall*, has joined the staff. Notes that his financial situation is 'desperate' and that he is deeply depressed.

May

5   (Tue) Diary contains references to suicide and to buying a revolver. Is reading the essays of Bertrand Russell.

14 Has concluded that he has been suffering from caffeine poisoning and is now feeling less depressed. Has not heard from Olivia.

June

Early this month, hears from his brother Alec that C.K. Scott Moncrieff, the translator of Proust, who lives in Pisa, is willing to employ him as a private secretary, and, on the strength of this news, resigns his teaching position and is for several weeks in good spirits. On the 30th, however, he learns that Scott Moncrieff does not want him, and the news plunges him into despair.

July

1 (Wed) or 2 (or possibly on 30 June) Attempts suicide (the episode is recounted at the end of *A Little Learning*).
3 A fairly ebullient diary entry notes that he is now feeling less depressed. On the 1st he has received a visit from Professor Dawkins, and presumably on the 2nd has got drunk with Young, who has told him the story of his very chequered career.
4 Is encouraged to apply for a job at Heath Mount, his old preparatory school; by the 10th, however, he has been turned down.
27 At the end of term, goes to London, dines with his brother at the Ritz, and sees Tony Bushell.
28 Writes letters seeking employment in the London art galleries and art magazines.
29 Lunches at the Sutros (and again the next day), dines with the Greenes, who are now living in Sumner Place, drinks with Tony Bushell and meets the composer Richard Addinsell.

August

1 (Sat) Sees Pirandello's *Henry IV* at the Everyman Theatre. During the following week, spends much time applying for jobs and being interviewed by the directors of art galleries.

6   Sees Chekhov's *The Cherry Orchard* and then goes to a music-hall. Notes that he is suffering from insomnia (a chronic problem in his later years).
9   Goes to Aston Clinton, Oxfordshire, where there is a possibility of a schoolmastering job, but is not optimistic. He is, however, offered the job on the 14th.
15 Orders a morning coat, needed for his new job, and lunches with Alastair Graham at Kettner's; later they go to see Ernest Thesiger in a revue, *On with the Dance*.
19 Lunches with John Rothenstein, then travels to Barford House to stay with Alastair Graham, who is now acting as guarantor for his overdraft.
22 Goes with Alastair to visit David Talbot Rice at Oddington.
23 Attends Mass in Leamington.
25 Finishes a long short story, *The Balance*: after rejection by the Hogarth Press (see 18 September) and other publishers, it subsequently appears in *Georgian Stories* (1926), edited by Alec Waugh and published by Arthur Waugh's firm of Chapman & Hall.
26 Goes to Stratford-upon-Avon, lunches with Alastair, and attends a performance of *The Two Gentlemen of Verona*.
29 Leaves Barford House with Alastair intending to go to London via Oxford; but changes his mind and spends the night at Beckley.
30 Alastair rejoins him and they drive to Tring, where EW stays with the Cockburns; after dinner his hosts read *The Balance*, which EW has had typed in Leamington.
31 Returns to London.

September

1   (Tue) Goes for a week's holiday with the Greenes to Happisburgh, Norfolk, visiting Norwich Cathedral on the way. On the 7th they visit Great Yarmouth.
8   Returns to London and immediately goes to Oxford, where he is met by Alastair Graham; together they go to Beckley and then to Barford House.
10 Goes to Birmingham (to meet Mrs Graham, who is returning from Harrogate), and dislikes the city.

12 Goes with Alastair to Droitwich, Ludlow and Bridgnorth (where they spend the night).
13 They visit Wenlock Edge and Church Stretton, then return to Barford, EW catching an evening train to London and proceeding to his parents' home.
14 Sees (and dislikes) Chaplin's *The Gold Rush*.
16 Begins to read Plato's *Republic*.
17 Goes with his mother to see Barry Jackson's modern-dress production of *Hamlet* at the Kingsway Theatre.
18 Sends *The Balance* to Leonard Woolf at the Hogarth Press (it is returned on the 29th). Goes to see Noel Coward's *Hay Fever*.
19 With Alastair Graham and Claud Cockburn, meets Christopher Hollis off the boat-train at Victoria (he has been in America); they spend the rest of the day together, joined for a time by Alec Waugh, and a good deal is drunk.
20 Again spends the day with Graham, Cockburn and Hollis; they are joined for lunch by Harold Acton.
23 Alastair Graham leaves after spending some days at the Waughs' home. Lunches with Harold Acton at Claridge's.
24 Is driven to Aston Clinton, where the new school year is beginning, by Richard Plunket Greene, who is also a master at the school. EW's first impressions of the place are not favourable. However, the proximity of Aston Clinton to Oxford and London means that his social life flourishes much more vigorously than during his time in Denbighshire.
26 Is taken by Claud Cockburn to dinner at his home in Tring.

October

1 (Thu) Goes to London for the day with Richard Plunket Greene, but finds Olivia is away.
3 Spends the weekend in Aylesbury with Alastair Graham and other friends.
8 Goes to London, drinks with John Sutro, dines with his mother and Olivia, goes to a party given by Richard Plunket Greene at the Café Royal, and is not back at the school until 3 a.m.
10 Is visited by Elizabeth Russell (see 24th below) for the weekend; they go to see a Harold Lloyd film.

12 After the day's teaching, spends the evening in Oxford dining and drinking with friends.
15 Is reading Dostoevsky's *The Brothers Karamazov*. Gives a dinner for friends (some of whom fail to turn up) at the local pub.
16 Receives a visit from Olivia Plunket Greene, Robert Byron and others; they dine at the George in Oxford.
20 Goes to Oxford, reading Dostoevsky on the bus, and visits Harold Acton, later going with him to a party at Christ Church and getting drunk; returns to the school at 4 a.m.
22 Spends the day in London, sees his mother, and visits the Greenes.
24 Elizabeth Russell and Alastair Graham come on a visit; the next day is spent with the latter. (The former, who is engaged to Richard Plunket Greene, makes frequent visits to Aston Clinton at this time.)
28 EW's 22nd birthday.

November

7 (Sat) Goes to Oxford during the half-term holiday and sees Tom Driberg and others.
8 Goes to London and spends a few days with his parents.
12 Returns to Aston Clinton. By this time, has decided he wishes to write a book about the Pre-Raphaelites, whom he has been studying while at 'Underhill'.
15 Goes to Oxford and sees Olivia and others.
19 Visits the Cockburns and other friends. *The Balance*, which has been rejected by another publisher, is sent off to yet another.
21 Dines with Alastair Graham and Claud Cockburn at the local pub.
26 Spends the day in London.

December

In the middle of the month, receives two visits from Alastair Graham, and also sees much of Claud Cockburn at this time.
17 (Thu) Term having now ended, goes to London and lunches at the Ritz with Olivia and Claud Cockburn.

18 Lunches with Christopher Hollis at the Café Royal.
21 Is best man at the wedding of Richard Plunket Greene and Elizabeth Russell.
25–6 Spends Christmas at Alec's London flat in Earl's Terrace; John Rothenstein and Audrey Lucas are also there.
27 Goes to Paris with Bill Silk, whom he has invited to accompany him on the spur of the moment. There it rains and the Louvre and other galleries are still closed for the Christmas holiday.
28 They visit a male brothel.
29 Leaves Silk asleep at the hotel and visits the Louvre.
30 To the Louvre again.
31 Goes to the Musée Rodin and ascends the Eiffel Tower. They return home overnight by train and boat.

1926

January

2 (Sat) Visits the Greenes.
4 Visits the Greenes again, then goes to see a Harold Lloyd film, afterwards meeting Alfred Duggan in a Soho club he has gone to with Richard Plunket Greene.
5 Resumes his course at Heatherley's.
8 Goes to Barford House.
9 Goes with Alastair Graham to East Hendred, where Alastair has rented a house; on the way they stop in Oxford and EW buys a copy of T.S. Eliot's poems, by which he is greatly impressed.
10 Goes to Mass with Alastair.
16 Leaves Barford and goes with Alastair to Oxford, where they lunch with Claud Cockburn, and then travel by train to London, dining at Kettner's with Richard Plunket Greene and his wife. With Alastair, spends the next two nights at the Greene home in Sumner Place, lunching with his parents on the 17th.
18 Alastair leaves. Richard buys EW a motorcycle and he spends the next two days learning to ride it.

24 Visits Lancing.
25 Returns to Aston Clinton for the new term.
28 Spends the day in Oxford, seeing Alastair Graham and Claud Cockburn and dining with Harold Acton and Brian Howard.
30 Has a disastrous journey to Barford, during which his motorcycle suffers much mechanical trouble.

February

2   (Tue) Receives a visit from Richard and Elizabeth Plunket Greene, who come again on the 6th.
4   Receives a visit from Harold Acton; they lunch at the village pub and dine at Thame.
6   With the Greenes to Oxford, where they have tea with Acton; later EW gets drunk and gatecrashes a party at Christ Church.
11 Goes to London for the day and visits his parents. Has now acquired a new motorcycle.
13 Dines at Tring with the Cockburns.
16 Visits Oxford, sees Claud Cockburn and John Sutro, and goes to a party at Merton College.
23 To Oxford, where he sees Cockburn, then to Shenley, where he dines with his brother Alec.
25 Spends the day in London and takes his mother to tea at the Greenes'.
26 Goes with Cockburn to a dance in Tring.

March

2   (Tue) Goes to London (and again on the 4th, when he dines at his brother's flat and sees Tony Bushell).
9   To London, to a cocktail party at his brother's.
14 To London, to see Olivia – a disillusioning experience.
26 Receives a visit from Young (see 30 April 1925).

April

3   (Sat)–4 Spends the weekend at Barford House.
7   Term having ended, returns to London in time to see Alastair Graham off for Constantinople.

8 Visits the Greene home in Sumner Place.
9 Feeling already tired of London, spends the night at a pub in Hungerford and the next day goes on to stay with his aunts at Midsomer Norton.
13 Spends the day in Wells with Roger Hollis and gets very drunk.
14 Visits Clevedon with Hollis.
18 Has read and enjoyed L.H. Myers' novel *The Orissers*.
20 Visits Sherborne School.
22 Travels by motorcycle to Taunton and thence (23rd) to Fowey, Cornwall, where he stays with a family named Poole.

May

1 (Sat) Miners' strike begins.
2 Attends a political meeting in Hyde Park.
3 General Strike begins (lasts until the 12th). Goes to the Royal Academy, then to a series of pubs, several restaurants, a club, a cinema and a pawnbroker's, getting very drunk in the process.
6 Term begins at Aston Clinton. Before travelling there later in the day, goes to Limehouse with his brother, who enrols as a special constable; they then lunch at the Berkeley and drink port at the Savile Club.
9 Goes to London and enrols as a special constable, chiefly in order to escape the boredom of the school, to which few boys have returned. The next two days are spent in futile journeys across London and much waiting for orders. On the 12th, joins the Civil Constabulary Reserve at a barracks in Camden Town, but within a few hours the strike ends. On the 13th, receives his discharge and returns to Aston Clinton.

In the latter part of the month, visits London and Oxford, dines with the Cockburns in Tring, and is visited by Richard and Elizabeth Plunket Greene.

June

At the beginning of the month, is visited by his brother Alec, and on the 4th by Richard and Elizabeth Plunket Greene.

5 (Sat)–6 Spends the weekend at Barford House, and goes with Alastair Graham to see a Harold Lloyd film in Warwick.
Later in the month there are other visits to London, Oxford and Tring.
27 Goes to London to see his parents.
29 Is visited by Claud Cockburn.

July

4 (Sun) Receives a visit from his parents.
8 Goes to London and sees Alastair Graham; they both stay overnight at the Waugh home.
10 Dines with the Cockburns.
About the middle of the month, spends a weekend in London with Alastair Graham and sees Tony Bushell, both of whom return with him to Aston Clinton. On the 18th, goes with Alastair to Windsor. During the next few days, in the intervals of marking examination papers, writes an essay on the Pre-Raphaelite Brotherhood (finished on the 23rd).
28 Term ends; returns to London, where Arthur Waugh reads and approves of the essay.
31 Goes to Barford House, where they are joined the next day by Christopher Hollis.

August

3 (Tue) To Bassenthwaite Lake, Cockermouth, Cumberland, with Alastair Graham and his mother. The next day, takes part in an otter hunt.
5 They continue to Preston Hall, near Edinburgh; the next day, explores Edinburgh with Alastair.
Later they visit Braemar, Killin and other places in the Highlands, and on the return journey stay near Glasgow and in York, where EW attends Holy Communion at the Minster. They return to Barford on the 20th and the next day, after a quarrel with Mrs Graham, EW returns to London and sees Olivia Plunket Greene.
22 Goes to Paris with Alastair, and on the 24th goes to Tours, where he visits various châteaux, meets the bibliographer

John Hayward, and rereads I.A. Richards' *Principles of Literary Criticism*.

September

4   (Sat) Spends the night at Blois, then returns to Tours before going on to Chartres on the 7th, to Rouen on the 9th, and thence to Le Havre, Southampton and London.
20 Alastair Graham arrives at the Waugh home, and together they go to a lesbian party, see Harold Lloyd in *For Heaven's Sake* and lunch with Tony Bushell. Has been given £150 by his mother to pay his debts, and resolves to live a sober and chaste life.
22 Sees Gilbert & Sullivan's *The Mikado* and, the next day, Sybil Thorndike in *Henry VIII*.
23 Goes shopping with his mother, pays some of his bills, and redeems some possessions he has pawned.
27 Returns to Aston Clinton for the new term.

Towards the end of the month, on the strength of his mother's gift, has his diaries bound and tours Oxford paying his debtors. Is also occupied in proof-reading his essay on the Pre-Raphaelite Brotherhood, a privately printed edition of which Alastair Graham is producing at the Shakespeare Head Press.

October

5   (Tue) Goes to London, where he sees his parents and Alastair Graham. There are various other excursions to London during this month, on one of which he visits an exhibition of Henri ('le Douanier') Rousseau's paintings.
28 EW's 23rd birthday.

Towards the end of the month, successfully proposes a book *Noah; or, the Future of Intoxication* to the publishing firm of Kegan Paul for their series 'Today and Tomorrow'. Has written about 2000 words by 7 November, and it is finished and submitted within a few weeks. At this time, is assisting Harold Acton in the search for a publisher for Acton's poems.

November

At this time, tries unsuccessfully to obtain a job as tutor in order to earn money during the school holidays.

20 Is taken by Richard and Elizabeth Plunket Greene to Oxford for the weekend; they dine at the George and he stays at the Randolph Hotel and sees Harold Acton, Robert Byron and other friends. The next day, sees Roger Fulford and Henry Yorke. (At some point during this year he has written to Yorke to express his great admiration for his first novel, *Blindness*.) Lunches at Christ Church with Roy Harrod, and returns to Aston Clinton.
25 Visits Claud Cockburn at Tring (and again on the 30th).

December

10 (Fri) Term ends; returns to his parents' home.
11 Goes with his father to see a performance of Wycherley's *The Country Wife*.
24 Sets off for Marseilles, from where he sails to Athens, reading during the voyage William James's *Varieties of Religious Experience*.
29 Arrives in Athens and is met by Alastair Graham (now working at the Embassy there), with whom he stays.

1927

January

4 (Tue) Visits the National Museum in Athens.
5 Embarks at Piraeus for the return journey, regretting that the visit has been a 'failure'. Stops off at Olympia, then sails to Corfu and Brindisi, from where he takes a train to Rome, arriving on the 10th. There he visits St Peter's, takes a Cook's sightseeing tour, and goes to a music-hall.
15 Arrives home after an exhausting journey from Rome via

Paris. Spends most of the next week resting, but pays two visits to an exhibition of Flemish art at the Royal Academy.
22 Dines with the Sutros.
24 Returns to Aston Clinton for the new term. *Noah* has been rejected by Kegan Paul.

In the early part of the term, is visited by Claud Cockburn and by Richard and Elizabeth Plunket Greene; also goes to London, lunches at the Ritz and buys clothes and cigars.

February

20 (Sun) Is abruptly dismissed from his teaching job – according to Christopher Hollis's later statement (*Oxford in the Twenties*, p. 80) for 'trying to seduce the matron' – and returns to his parents' home.
21 Starts looking for another job, but feels that it is time to become a 'man of letters'.
24 Sees Olivia and later visits a Father Underhill, who seems unimpressed by his stated desire to enter the Anglican priesthood.
25 Claud Cockburn comes to stay at the Waugh home, and the next day they have tea with Harold Acton.
28 Accepts a temporary job, at £5 a week, at a school in Notting Hill, London.

March

4 (Fri) Is offered employment on three weeks' trial at the *Daily Express*, to begin at the end of term.
5 Dines at the Ritz with his brother (who has just returned from America) and Harold Acton; they then visit E.S.P. Haynes and go on to a party at Oliver Messel's.
9 Dines with Harold Acton and Sacheverell Sitwell. During the rest of this month there are numerous other social engagements. At about this time he meets the Hon. Evelyn Gardner, whom he later marries, and is encouraged by the publishing firm Duckworth to write a biography of D.G. Rossetti.

April

Early this month, begins work on the *Daily Express*.

May

During this month, spends a day in Paris and a weekend in Plymouth, and goes to a number of parties, including one given by Evelyn Gardner and her friend Pansy Pakenham at their Ebury Street flat. Has received a £20 advance from Duckworth and spent it within the week. By the 23rd, has been dismissed by the *Daily Express*.

June

Is unemployed during this month; visits Wiltshire and later goes to France with his brother, joining his parents (who are already on holiday there) and visiting Nîmes, Tarascon, Les Baux, Arles, Avignon and other places, later accompanying Alec to Marseilles.

July

1 (Fri) Has begun work on the biography of Rossetti, and by the 22nd has written about 12,000 words.
22 Sees Olivia and goes to the ballet with John Sutro and to a party given by Brian Howard.
24 Lunches at the Sutros' and sees Roy Harrod there; later visits Olivia.

August

4 (Thu) Has felt ill for ten days and done no work, but has seen Olivia often.

Towards the middle of the month, after a drunken evening with Alastair Graham, goes to the Abingdon Arms at Beckley and spends the days working on the Rossetti book in the library of the Oxford Union (40,000 words have been completed by the

23rd). During this time, pays several visits to Francis Crease, who now lives in Marston, near Oxford.
26 To Barford House until 30th, when he goes with Alastair to the Waughs' home.

September

3 (Sat) Has begun *Decline and Fall*.
4 Has been reading his Lancing diaries.
8 Sees Anthony Powell (and again on the 11th).
9 Interviews Hall Caine, who has known Rossetti.
12 Goes to the Bell, Aston Clinton, to work on the Rossetti book. Writes 20,000 words during the week, then returns to London, where he sees Powell, Evelyn Gardner and others and is interviewed (and rejected) for a teaching position. Returns to Aston Clinton, then pays another visit to Barford House.

October

At this time, writes a preface for *Thirty-Four Decorative Designs by Francis Crease* (privately printed).
6 (Thu) Visits Kelmscott Manor and meets May Morris, daughter of William Morris.
Later in the month, returns to London and continues to see Evelyn Gardner.
25 Begins to attend classes in cabinet-making at the Central School of Arts & Crafts, Holborn, London.
28 EW's 24th birthday.
30 Goes to church and sees Tom Driberg there.

November

4 (Fri) Has tea with Evelyn Gardner, Pansy Pakenham, Henry Lamb, Lord and Lady Dunsany and others.
18 Dines at the Ritz with Evelyn Gardner and others. During this month is meeting Evelyn frequently and also seeing Olivia.

December

12 (Mon) Dines at the Ritz with Evelyn and proposes to her: the outcome is 'inconclusive'. Tells Olivia, and seeks advice from Pansy Pakenham. Evelyn accepts him the next day.
The surviving diary breaks off at this point and is not resumed until 22 June 1928: it seems clear that EW subsequently destroyed large portions of his diary for 1928.
Spends Christmas with his parents at 'Underhill'; Evelyn is also with them.

1928

January

11 Thomas Hardy dies.

April

During the spring, lives for a time at the Barley Mow, Colehill, two miles from Wimborne, Dorset. At this time Evelyn Gardner is staying at a nearby boarding-house with her friend Pansy Pakenham. There, by the end of April, he finishes *Decline and Fall* (at this stage titled *Untoward Incidents*). *Rossetti, his Life and Works* is published during this month. At about this time Henry Lamb paints a portrait of EW (now lost).
7 Thanks Anthony Powell for sending an advance copy of *Rossetti* and tells him that *Decline and Fall* will be completed in a week.

May

Returns to London, as do Evelyn and Pansy.
14 Peter Quennell writes to EW defending his review of the Rossetti book (published in the *New Statesman* two days earlier), to which EW has evidently objected.

17 *The Times Literary Supplement* publishes an ironical letter from EW, complaining that in its review of his book on Rossetti he is referred to as 'Miss Waugh'.

June

22 (Fri) Goes with Evelyn to buy a marriage licence.
27 The marriage of EW and Evelyn Gardner takes place at St Paul's, Portman Square; Harold Acton is best man, Robert Byron gives away the bride, and Alec Waugh and Pansy Pakenham are witnesses. (The bride's family are not present and know nothing of the event.) Later the couple go to Beckley for their honeymoon. While at Beckley they visit Barford House.

July

Returning to London, they spend a week at 'Underhill' and EW writes to inform his mother-in-law, Lady Burghclere, of his marriage; she is not pleased by the news. The marriage is subsequently announced in *The Times*. At this time they dine with Osbert Sitwell, have tea with Pansy Pakenham and lunch with John Sutro; EW has an interview with Lady Burghclere. Designs the jacket for *Decline and Fall*, proofs of which he is correcting. The couple move into 145 North End Road, Hampstead.

September

At about this time the Waughs move to 17a Canonbury Square, Islington.
  8 *Decline and Fall* is published (an American edition follows in 1929). At this time EW is working on a life of John Wesley (soon abandoned) and a detective story (likewise nevercompleted).

October

6 (Sat) They are visited by Harold Acton.
7 Visits his parents and reads Aldous Huxley's *Point Counter Point*.

8 Lunches at the Savile Club with Harold Acton, Raymond Mortimer and Reginald Turner.
10 Reads Harold Acton's novel *Humdrum*.
11 Is pleased to learn that Arnold Bennett has reviewed *Decline and Fall* in today's *Evening Standard*. Lunches with his father; goes to an exhibition of Giorgio de Chirico's paintings (and again on the 17th).
12 His wife is suffering from a severe attack of German measles.
15 Is reading Virginia Woolf's *Orlando*.
16 Has tea with Olivia.
19 A 'second edition' of *Decline and Fall* is being printed. Is now receiving invitations to write articles for newspapers.
22 Goes to an exhibition of Aristide Maillol's sculptures.
24 To Oare House, near Marlborough, Wiltshire, where they have been lent a house to assist in his wife's convalescence.
28 EW's 25th birthday.
29 They dine with Robert Byron at his house in Savernake.

November

5 (Mon) They leave Oare House, where EW has managed to do a certain amount of work, and return to London a few days later.
8 Meets Henry Williamson, whose *Tarka the Otter* (1927) has been a success.
23 They go to a cocktail party given by Cyril Connolly and Patrick Balfour.
24 They dine with EW's parents. The diary breaks off at this point and is not resumed until 19 May 1930.

1929

February

Leaves England with his wife for a voyage on MY *Stella Polaris*: he has been commissioned to write a travel book (eventually titled *Labels*). His wife, who has recently been ill, falls ill again on the train between Paris and Monte Carlo, and they are detained in the latter place for two days before sailing to Naples, Haifa and Port Said. She is seriously ill on the voyage, develops double pneumonia, and at Port Said is taken to hospital. A plan to go to Russia by Turkish cargo boat is abandoned. In response to an appeal from EW, Alastair Graham travels from Athens to visit them for two days in Port Said. When she recovers they move to a hotel near Cairo for her convalescence (staying there from 29 March to 12 April), then travel to Malta, where they rejoin the *Stella Polaris*. The cruise continues to Crete, Athens (where they see Alastair Graham and Mark Ogilvie-Grant) and Constantinople; in Constantinople they lunch at the British Embassy (as EW tells Henry Yorke in a letter of 4 May), Osbert and Sacheverell Sitwell also being present. They then continue to Venice, Ragusa (now Dubrovnik) and Barcelona, and are back in England by June.

May

30 In the General Election, the Labour Party retains power by a narrow majority.

June

Soon after his return to England, tells Henry Yorke of his high esteem for his new novel, *Living*.

Goes to spend six weeks at Beckley (see 27 July 1924) in order to work on *Vile Bodies*; during this time Nancy Mitford moves into their London flat as a companion for his wife.

July

9 His wife writes to tell him that she has fallen in love with John Heygate. EW returns to London for two weeks, and they agree to try to save their marriage but fail to do so. Engages in many social activities during this period, and attends an exhibition of paintings by D.H. Lawrence. During this month the 'Bruno Hatte' hoax is perpetrated by Bryan

and Diana Guinness and their friends, EW having written the notes for the catalogue of an exhibition of paintings allegedly by a German avant-garde painter (actually by Brian Howard).
The precise circumstances of the Waughs' separation are unclear, but it may have taken place towards the end of this month.

August

In the middle of the month, goes to Belfast to see motor-racing, then stays with Bryan and Diana Guinness at Knockmaroon, the Guinness home on the edge of Phoenix Park, Dublin. While there he meets W.B. Yeats and goes to the Abbey Theatre.

September

3 Files a petition for divorce.
9 Attends the solicitor's office in order to fulfil the legal requirement of serving the petition on his wife; Heygate, as co-respondent, is also present.
Vile Bodies is probably finished by the end of this month.

October

28 EW's 26th birthday. Wall Street Crash precipitates world economic crisis.
Towards the end of the month, pays a short visit to Paris.

November

During this month, pays a longer visit to Paris, spending two weeks at the Guinness family flat at 12, rue de Poitiers; Nancy Mitford is also there.

December

24 Attends a High Anglican Midnight Mass with Tom Driberg.
25 Spends Christmas with his family at 'Underhill', and on Christmas Day visits the Guinnesses at their London flat.

Towards the end of the year, meets Max Beerbohm at a dinner-party given by E.S.P. Haynes; Hilaire Belloc and Maurice Baring are also present.

1930

In the early part of this year, spends much time with the Guinnesses (to whom, on 4 January, he presents the manuscript of *Vile Bodies*), and is at work on *Labels*.

January

14 (Tue) *Vile Bodies* is published and is an immediate success.
17 Is granted a *decree nisi* (provisional divorce).
23 Tells Harold Acton that he has read Ivy Compton-Burnett's *Brothers and Sisters* twice with great admiration.

February

19 (Wed) By this date, has written 30,000 words of *Labels*.

March

2 (Sun) D.H. Lawrence dies.

Early in the month, finishes *Labels*. In the middle of the month, joins his brother Alec in France; they spend five days together at Villefranche, then EW goes to Monte Carlo for an assignation (Stannard conjectures [*Early Years*, p. 214] that this may have been with Audrey Lucas).

During this month Jonathan Guinness is born; EW stands

godfather, and at the christening meets (possibly for the first time) the other godfather, Randolph Churchill.

May

19 (Mon) Resumes diary. Is invited by the *Daily Mail* to contribute articles on a regular basis. Dines with the Yorkes and later sees Nancy Mitford and meets the film actress Anna May Wong.
20 His agent, A.D. Peters, has negotiated a payment of £30 per article from the *Daily Mail*, bringing his annual income up to about £2500. Lunches at the Ivy with two publishers; later goes to a cocktail party given by Cyril Connolly, where he sees Logan Pearsall Smith, Christopher Sykes and others.
21 Goes to a cocktail party given by Cecil Beaton.
23 Goes to a cocktail party given by Francis Meynell.
24 Has tea with Edith Sitwell; Harold Acton is also there.
25 Goes to church, then works for the rest of the day.
26 Sees Paul Robeson in *Othello*, then goes to a supper party given by Frank Pakenham at which the guests include John Betjeman and Peter Fleming.
27 Sees Nancy Mitford and Olivia Plunket Greene among others.
28 Is reading, disapprovingly, Harold Acton's *History of the Later Medici*.
29 Receives the proofs of *Labels*. Goes to a cocktail party given by Harold and William Acton.
30 Goes to see Frank Dobson's sculpture 'Truth', then to a lunch given by Edward Marsh at which the other guests include the actor Robert Speaight and Bryan and Diana Guinness. Later attends a lecture given by Robert Byron.
31 Goes twice to the cinema, works on the proofs of *Labels* and begins to read a study of Joyce's *Ulysses* (perhaps the monograph by Stuart Gilbert, published this year). Begins to contribute book reviews to the *Graphic*, often dealing with up to six or seven books at a time, and continuing until 25 October.

June

6 (Fri) Gives a luncheon party at the Ritz: among the guests are Cecil Beaton, Bryan and Diana Guinness, Nancy Mitford, Frank Pakenham and Sacheverell and Georgia Sitwell. Later, drives with the Guinnesses to their Sussex home, Poole Place, for the Whitsun weekend.

7 Visits Bramber Museum and Bramber Castle.

10 Returns to London and sees a performance by the American *diseuse* Ruth Draper, whom he finds 'brilliant' but sentimental rather than satirical.

11 Writes his regular articles for the *Daily Mail* and *Graphic*.

12 Goes to a cocktail party at Sacheverell Sitwell's.

15 Goes to Oxford, where he sees Randolph Churchill, John Betjeman and others and dines with the Pakenhams.

18 Lunches with Harold and William Acton and has tea with Nancy Mitford.

19 Goes to a cocktail party given by Diana Guinness, where he sees Cecil Beaton and others; dines with Audrey Russell; later meets Carl van Vechten, popular American author and music critic.

21 Lunches with Olivia, spends the weekend in the country, then goes (23rd) to Birmingham, where he visits the art gallery and is given a tour of his factory by Henry Yorke; returns to London later in the day.

24 Attends a dinner held at the Savoy for members of the Odde Volumes dining-club and meets the popular novelist Ethel Mannin.

25 Meets Carl van Vechten again, also Rebecca West; later goes to a cocktail party given by Cecil Beaton and dines with Audrey Lucas.

26 Lunches with Frank Pakenham and dines with Audrey Lucas.

27 Dines with Olivia Plunket Greene, then goes to a party given by Diana Guinness at which he fights with Randolph Churchill.

28 Spends the weekend with Henry and Pansy Lamb at Coombe Bissett, Wiltshire.

30 Dines with the Duke and Duchess of Marlborough and sits next to Edith Sitwell; Dame Nellie Melba is also there.

July

1. (Tue) Meets Noel Coward.
2. Sees Olivia and asks her to find a Jesuit priest who can give him instruction.
3. Lunches with Nancy Mitford and meets Clough Williams Ellis.
4. Attends a dinner of the Railway Club, which travels by train from Charing Cross to Folkestone; Harold Acton and Bryan Guinness are also present. Later goes with Guinness to Brighton and the next day to Poole Place, where they are joined by Diana Guinness, the Lambs and others.
7. Lunches at the Ritz with Noel Coward and, according to Coward's later statement, tells him he is taking instruction in the Catholic faith.
8. Visits Father D'Arcy at the Jesuit clergy-house in Mount Street, Mayfair. Later, goes to a cocktail party at which 'All the inevitable people' are present, and dines with John Betjeman and Gerald Heard.
9. Sees Father D'Arcy again, then lunches with Frank Pakenham, goes to a cocktail party given by the Beatons, and goes to the theatre with Audrey Lucas.
10. Attends a luncheon given by Lady Birkenhead; among the other guests are Cecil Beaton, Sacheverell Sitwell and the composer William Walton; later goes to see a performance of Wilde's *The Importance of Being Earnest*.
11. Visits Father D'Arcy for instruction, then lunches at the Ritz with Richard and Elizabeth Plunket Greene.
12. Sees Father D'Arcy again; later dines with Olivia.
14. Goes to a lunch given by Beatrice Guinness; among the other guests are Sophie Tucker, Lord David Cecil, Lady Birkenhead and Frank Pakenham.
15. Attends a luncheon given by Lord Bury; has tea with Victor Cazalet, MP on the terrace of the House of Commons and meets the Prime Minister (Ramsay MacDonald), the novelist John Buchan and others; dines with Harold Acton.
16. Lunches with his brother and sees Randolph Churchill.
17. Lunches with Frank Pakenham and Father D'Arcy at the Savile Club; dines with his brother and later goes to a party given by the Sutros and meets Douglas Woodruff and the Guinnesses.

18 Lunches with Father D'Arcy, Lord David Cecil and an Egyptian diplomat who is a Catholic convert; goes with Audrey Lucas to a cocktail party given by A.P. Herbert (humorous writer and MP), and meets the novelist Richard Hughes; later sees Pansy Lamb and Frank Pakenham.
21 Attends a dinner given by Lady Cunard for George Moore and Nancy Cunard; sees Harold Nicolson.
22 Lunches with Lord David Cecil.
23 Goes to a party and meets the novelist Rose Macaulay.
28 Goes to Coombe Bissett, the Lambs' house in Wiltshire, which he has taken for about three weeks and to which he brings his mother for a few days.

August

1 (Fri) Goes to Forthampton Court, the Yorkes' house near Gloucester, for the weekend; among his fellow-guests is Maurice Bowra.
5 Returns to Coombe Bissett and finds Audrey Lucas there.
9 Audrey leaves and Christopher Hollis and Douglas Woodruff arrive for the weekend; on the 10th they go to see the Cerne Abbas giant (phallic figure cut in chalk on a hillside).
12 Richard and Elizabeth Plunket Greene arrive (staying until the 18th).
15 Olivia arrives.
16 Frank Pakenham calls.
18 Visits Salisbury with Olivia.
22 Spends the night at his parents' home.
23 Goes to Renishaw Hall, the Sitwell family home in Derbyshire; among the other guests are Robert Byron, Harold Monro, Arthur Waley and William Walton; Osbert, Sacheverell and Edith Sitwell are all present. During his stay there, visits Hardwicke House.

September

Labels: A Mediterranean Journal is published during this month (the American edition is titled *A Bachelor Abroad*).

Early in the month, after leaving Renishaw Hall, goes to Eire with Alastair Graham and stays at Pakenham Hall, Westmeath, where John Betjeman is also a guest, for about ten days. During this time, they visit Lord Dunsany (Frank Pakenham's uncle) at his country house. It seems that on the basis of a conversation at Pakenham Hall, EW decides to go to Abyssinia to witness the coronation of the Emperor; on the 12th he asks A.D. Peters whether he can arrange for a newspaper to appoint him special correspondent.

29 Is received into the Roman Catholic Church by Father Martin D'Arcy; the only witness present is Tom Driberg, who reports the event in his *Daily Express* gossip column on 1 October. Soon after the 29th, goes to Stonyhurst to join Christopher Hollis in a Retreat. Douglas Woodruff, who is on the staff of *The Times*, is also there, and through him EW becomes an official correspondent for the coronation of the Abyssinian Emperor, Haile Selassie (Ras Tafari).

October

10 Leaves London for Marseilles.
11 Sails on the *Azay-le-Rideau* from Marseilles, reaching Djibouti on the 24th, and from there travels via Dirra-Dowa to Addis Ababa by train.
27 *The Times* publishes the first of EW's despatches from Abyssinia under the byline 'From Our Special Correspondent'; the series continues until 13 November.
30 The *Daily Express* publishes the first of EW's despatches from Abyssinia under the byline '"Daily Express" Special Correspondent'; the series of four pieces is concluded on 6 November.

November

2 (Sun) The Coronation takes place; EW attends the six-hour service. During the next few days, witnesses a procession (4th) and goes to a race meeting (5th), a review of troops (7th) and a museum (8th).
9 Goes to Mass at the French church.
10 Visits Debra Lebanos Monastery with an American scholar,

Professor Thomas Whittemore, returning to Addis Ababa the next day. (A full account of this excursion and other episodes in EW's African travels is given in *Remote People*.)

15 Goes by train to Dirre-Dowa, arriving the next day.
16 Tells his parents that Irene Ravensdale, who has been his companion during much of this tour, has left for Khartoum.
17 Tells Harold Acton he is setting off on a two-day ride to Harar, where Arthur Rimbaud and Sir Richard Burton formerly lived.
22 Leaves Harar by pony and the next day completes the journey back to Dirre-Dowa by mule; then (25th) proceeds to Djibouti by train, arriving there just in time to see the ship he had hoped to catch sail out of the harbour.
27 Leaves Djibouti by an Italian ship (the *Somalia*), arriving in Aden the next day.

December

10 (Wed) Sails to Mombasa and Zanzibar on the *Explorateur Grandidier*, reaching Zanzibar on the 16th.
29 Embarks on the *Mazzini* for Dar-es-Salaam, where he buys a *Pears' Encyclopaedia* and two novels by Edgar Wallace, and sees a Tarzan film.
30 Leaves Dar-es-Salaam and sails to Mombasa, arriving the next day and taking the train to Nairobi.

1931

January–February

Continues his African travels through Kenya and Uganda in the early weeks of the year, proceeding from Nairobi by cargo boat across Lake Tanganyika (an eight-day journey), then on the *Duc de Brabant* to Albertville. By train to Kabalo; by paddle-steamer up the Congo to Bukama; 17-hour train journey to Elizabethville, which is reached on 9 February. Spends two days at the Globe Hotel before beginning a train journey via Bulawayo, Mafeking and the Victoria Falls to Cape Town, arriving there on 17 February. From there, travelling third class, embarks for the three-week voyage home.

The diary breaks off after the entry for 19 February and is not resumed until 4 December 1932.

March

10 (Tue) Disembarks in Southampton.
27 Arnold Bennett dies.
Little is known of EW's movements during the next four months. At some stage he goes to France, but is back in England by 25 June.

August

During this month, stays at the Abingdon Arms, Beckley, in order to finish *Remote People*.
24 Ramsay MacDonald forms National Government.

September

10 Riots in London and Glasgow are provoked by the economic crisis.
15 Naval mutiny at Invergordon caused by pay cuts.
21 Britain abandons the gold standard; this is followed by a dramatic fall in the value of the pound.

October

27 In the General Election, the National Government wins an overwhelming victory.
28 EW's 28th birthday.

November

3 (Tue) *Remote People* is published (the American edition in the following year is titled *They Were Still Dancing*). In the later months of the year, is working on a novel provisionally titled *Accession* (later *Black Mischief*); from 7 November to the middle of December he stays at the Easton Court Hotel, Chagford, Devon, in order to work. (This hotel, referred to hereafter simply as 'Chagford', becomes a favourite place for EW when he wishes to devote himself to writing.)

1932

In the early part of the year, spends much time at Madresfield Court, near Great Malvern, Worcestershire, the home of Lord Beauchamp (he has been at Oxford with two of the latter's sons, Lord Elmley and Hugh Lygon, and is friendly with their sisters, Lady Mary and Lady Dorothy Lygon). There he continues work on *Black Mischief*.

January

21 Lytton Strachey dies.

April

15 (Fri) A dramatization of *Vile Bodies* opens at the Vaudeville Theatre, London, and runs for six weeks.
16 Goes to see Max Reinhardt's production of *The Miracle*, starring Lady Diana Cooper, probably meeting her for the first time after the performance. (A letter to Dorothy Lygon contains severe criticism of the play.) Goes to Chagford for about a month in order to finish *Black Mischief*.
After this time, sees Diana Cooper frequently. He also sees much of Teresa ('Baby') Jungman.

June

Finishes *Black Mischief* during this month.

August

Is in Venice during this month, returning home early in September after visiting Salzburg. Among those also in Venice at this time are Cecil Beaton, Diana Cooper, Randolph Churchill and Oliver Messel. On 29th, attends a party given on the island of Murano to celebrate Diana Cooper's fortieth birthday.

September

Early in the month, stays at Pakenham Hall, Co. Meath.

November

1 (Tue) *Black Mischief* is published.
8 Writing to Diana Cooper from Chagford, tells her he has written two short stories and a talk for radio since coming there. He has recently spent a weekend with Sacheverell and Georgia Sitwell at their Northamptonshire home and has also seen Hubert Duggan.
9 Visits Dartington Hall School in Devon.

Before leaving England at the beginning of the next month, sees Diana Cooper in Glasgow and Edinburgh, briefly visits Madresfield, sees Teresa Jungman several times as well as the Yorkes and other friends, visits his parents, and seeks advice from Peter Fleming on tropical equipment.

December

2 (Fri) Sets sail on SS *Ingoma* for the voyage from Tilbury to Georgetown, British Guiana, calling at Antigua, Barbados and Trinidad, and arriving at Georgetown on 23 December.

24 Dines at Government House as the guest of the Governor, Lord Denham.
25 Spends most of the day alone; attends an evening party at Government House.

Takes a three-day cruise up the Maszaruri River with Lord Denham; is back in Georgetown by the 29th.

1933

January

3 (Tue) Travels by train to New Amsterdam, then by paddle-steamer up the Berbice River to Takama and thence on horseback to Kurupukari, where he arrives on the 11th.
14 Still delayed in Kurupukari, reads Thomas Aquinas.
15 Sets out for Boa Vista, Brazil, but a recalcitrant packhorse forces a return to Kurupukari; sets out again the next day.
20 Arrives at the ranch owned by Mr Christie, the prototype of Mr Todd in *A Handful of Dust*, and stays overnight.
23 Arrives at the Bon Success Mission, and remains there until 1 February.
30 Hitler becomes Chancellor of Germany.
31 John Galsworthy dies.

February

4 (Sat) Arrives at Boa Vista, after a journey on horseback from the Bon Success Mission, and stays there, much of the time in a state of extreme boredom, as the guest of Brother Alcuin, a Benedictine monk.
13 Finishes a short story, 'The Man Who Liked Dickens' (the germ of *A Handful of Dust*); has 'thought of' the plot the previous day. It is published in *Hearst's International* (US) in September and in *Nash's Pall Mall Magazine* in November.
18 Sets off on an arduous four-day journey on horseback to the St Ignatius Mission.
27 Resting and reading *Dombey and Son*. Reichstag fire in Berlin.

March

5 (Sun) Sets off again: the journeyings of the next month, which involve many privations, are described in detail in the diary, which breaks off on 5 April (begins again 5 July 1934). Nazis win a large majority in the German elections.

April

Early this month, sails from Georgetown to Trinidad, where he spends Holy Week at a Benedictine monastery near Port of Spain.
1 (Mon) Persecution of Jews begins in Germany.

May

Is back in London early this month. Spends some time in Bath, enjoying the comfort of the Grand Pump Room Hotel after his ordeal in the jungle, and at this time is composing an open letter to the Cardinal Archbishop after *Black Mischief* has been described in the *Tablet* as 'obscene and blasphemous'. Probably goes to London on the 15th and spends much of the next few weeks there, staying at the Savile Club.

During this summer, EW's parents move to Highgate.

August

Goes on a Hellenic cruise with Alfred Duggan, who has become an alcoholic and an apostate. Also on the same cruise are Father Martin D'Arcy, Christopher Hollis and Gabriel Herbert (daughter of Mary Herbert).

September

At the conclusion of the cruise EW and Duggan visit Ravenna and Bologna and then go to Portofino, having been invited by Gabriel Herbert to the Villa Altachiara, one of the homes of the Herbert family. The house-party there includes Gabriel's brother Auberon and her sister Laura, EW's future wife.

October

12 From this date until 13 November, is at work on *Ninety-Two Days*, which is finished before the end of the year.
28 EW's 30th birthday.

1934

January

Early in the month, arrives in Tangier and proceeds by overnight train to spend a holiday in Fez.
4 (Thu) Writing from the Hotel Bellevue, Fez, tells Diana Cooper that all his cigars were seized by customs officials in Tangier and that he has slept with a young Arab prostitute the previous evening. Later in the month, tells the same correspondent that his novel (*A Handful of Dust*) is more than one-third completed, and that he has just reread *Vile Bodies* and *Decline and Fall* and considers his present work greatly superior. Later, but still from Fez, tells Diana Cooper that the new novel, of which almost 50,000 words have now been written, threatens to run to 150,000 words, and he is considering the possibility of finding a new ending in order to keep it substantially shorter. Also tells her that he is going to Marrakesh.

April

During this month, is correcting the proofs of *A Handful of Dust*.
15 (Thu) *Ninety-Two Days: The Account of a Tropical Journey through British Guiana and Part of Brazil*, dedicated to Diana Cooper, is published.
At the end of the month, joins a house-party at Pixton Park, near Dulverton, Somerset, and sees Laura Herbert, whom he has met for the first time in Italy (see entry for September 1933).

June

8 Oswald Mosley addresses mass meeting of British Union of Fascists in London.

July

5 (Thu) Diary is resumed. Attends a tea-party given by Lord Berners; among the other guests are 'Sitwells', Diana Cooper and Diana Guinness. Afterwards, drops in on Hugh Lygon, who mentions that he is about to leave for Spitzbergen with Sandy Glen; on an impulse, says he will accompany them.

6 Buys skis, ice axes, a sleeping bag, windproof clothing and balaclava helmets. Dines with his parents and later visits a prostitute named Winnie.

7 Goes to confession at Farm Street and orders a birthday cake for Teresa Jungman. With Lygon and Glen, travels by train to Newcastle and sails to Bergen. There they change ships for the journey up the Norwegian coast to Tromso en route to Spitzbergen, where their mission is to obtain information to assist the Oxford University Arctic Expedition planned for 1935–6. They reach Tromso on the 13th, on which date he writes to Diana Cooper that he does not like Norwegians and is growing a beard.

18 After a four-day voyage from Tromso, they arrive in Longyear City, whence they proceed by open boat to Bruce City, also known as Scottish Camp and consisting of 'four huts at the foot of a glacier'. From there they make their way, painfully, to the Mittag Leppler Glacier, return over the mountains, and return to Bergen by collier.

The surviving diary breaks off at this point and is not resumed until 7 July 1936.

August

19 Following the death of President Hindenburg, Hitler becomes Führer of Germany.

Is back in England before the end of this month.

September

4 (Tue) *A Handful of Dust* is published.
11 The *Daily Express* publishes a letter from EW responding to comments in the previous day's issue by its columnist 'William Hickey' (Tom Driberg); these have in turn been prompted by an adverse review of *A Handful of Dust* in the Catholic journal *The Tablet* (8 September), written by its editor, Ernest Oldmeadow.

October

28 EW's 31st birthday.

November

Early in the month, writing to Diana Cooper from Chagford, tells her that he has been established there for some time but has spent a weekend with Sir Robert and Lady Diana Abdy at Newton Ferrers, Cornwall, and another at Mells, where a fellow-guest has been Lady Violet Bonham-Carter.

At some point he writes another letter to Diana Cooper, also from Chagford, telling her that he has visited the Betjemans and has had lunch in Oxford with Maurice Bowra.

1935

May

3 (Sun) Writes to Laura Herbert from Belton House, Grantham, where he is the last remaining guest of a house-party. Tells Laura, with whom he is by this time in love, that he is working at his book on Edmund Campion.
19 T.E. Lawrence dies.
24 Writes to Katharine Asquith from Lytham Hall, Lancashire, where he is the guest of John and Violet Clinton.

June

23 Britain offers Italy concessions over Abyssinia which are rejected by Mussolini.

August

7 (Thu) Goes to Paris and thence to Marseilles, Port Said and Djibouti.
21 By this date is in Addis Ababa as correspondent for the *Daily Mail*. A few days later, undertakes an expedition to Harar and Jijiga.
27 The *Daily Mail* publishes the first of EW's despatches from Abyssinia; the series continues until 3 December.

October

2 Italy invades Abyssinia, bombs are dropped on Adowa the next day, and Adowa and Adigrat are occupied within the next few days.
19 The League of Nations imposes sanctions against Italy.
26 Tells Lady Mary Lygon that he is 'sick to death' of Abyssinia.
28 EW's 32nd birthday.

November

14 General Election, in which the government parties win a large majority.
19 Leaves Addis Ababa for Dessye, a four-day journey, and thence proceeds to Djibouti.

December

21 By about this date, is in Jerusalem and is spending four days (very uncomfortably) at a Franciscan monastery before moving to a hotel on Christmas Day. Is hoping to visit Petra the

following week, and has vague ideas of going to Baghdad.
23 Tells Katharine Asquith he plans to spend Christmas Eve in Bethlehem.
28 Tells Katharine Asquith he is leaving Jerusalem the next day.

1936

There are few surviving letters from this period, and the record for the first half of this year is in general scanty. But it seems clear that during the early months of 1936 EW was seeing Laura Herbert regularly and pursuing the proceedings for the annulment by Rome of his marriage to Evelyn Gardner (see 7 July), without which he would, of course, have been unable to remarry.

January

18 Rudyard Kipling dies.
20 Death of George V and accession of Edward VIII.
During this month, writes to Diana Cooper from the British Consulate at Damascus, telling her that after leaving Jerusalem he visited Petra, Amman and Baghdad; he has now been advised by the Vatican to visit Rome to discuss the annulment of his marriage.
    In Rome, sees Diana Cooper and interviews Mussolini.

March

7 Germany occupies the Rhineland.

April

At about this time, puts together the collection *Mr Loveday's Little Outing and Other Sad Stories*.
30 A.E. Housman dies.

May

At this time Laura Herbert begins a course at the Royal Academy of Dramatic Art, London.
9   Abyssinia is annexed by Italy.

June

7   Addresses a meeting of the Newman Society at Oxford.
14 G.K. Chesterton dies.

July

Early this month, goes to Ireland (perhaps to visit the Pakenhams).
7   (Tue)   Diary recommences. Returns to London after an overnight crossing from Ireland and learns that Rome has granted permission for the annulment of his marriage. Goes to Farm Street, where Laura Herbert is attending early Mass, and breaks the news of the annulment to her. Sees Diana Cooper; lunches with Laura, goes to see her perform at the Royal Academy of Dramatic Art, and sees her again in the evening.
9   Sees Laura, dines with Hubert Duggan and Lady Mary (Maimie) Lygon, and meets Laura again for supper.
10 Lunches with Hugh and Maimie Lygon and goes to see Laura in a play.
11 Spends the day with Laura, visiting Kew Gardens and going to a cinema.
12 Again spends the day with Laura; they go to Mass together and later go to hear the orators in Hyde Park.
13 Sees Laura again, lunches with Father D'Arcy, sees Christopher Sykes and dines with Patrick Balfour (the Yorkes and Maurice Bowra being among the other guests), calling on Laura again at the end of the evening.
14 Goes to early Mass and sees Laura; later sees Diana Cooper and goes to spend the night at his parents' home in Highgate, where he goes again for the weekend.
18 Spanish Civil War begins.
23 Dines with Lord Clonmore, Father D'Arcy and Christopher Hollis.

24 To Pixton Park with Laura for the weekend.
26 Goes to the Manor House, Mells, Somerset, the home of Katharine Asquith, to which he makes many subsequent visits. Sees Christopher Hollis, who lives in Mells village, and later returns to London.
28 Sees his literary agent, A.D. Peters, and is busy with preparations for the journey to Abyssinia. Sees Olivia Plunket Greene.
29 Leaves for Rome by the overland route, arriving the next day.

August

3 (Mon) Goes to Assisi, which he greatly likes, returning to Rome on the 6th and proceeding in the evening to Naples.
7 Sails from Naples on the *Leonardo da Vinci*, via Port Said (11th) and Masawa (15–16th), for Djibouti; reads *The Pickwick Papers* on the voyage. Arrives on the 18th, and the next day sets off by train for Dirre-Dowa, from where he makes an expedition to Harar.
22 Returns to Dirre Dowa and the next day goes on to Addis Ababa.
28 Leaves Addis Ababa without regret and returns to Dirre-Dowa.
29 Sets off to fly to Asmara, but lands at Assab; flies on to Massawa, from where he is driven in the evening to Gura.
30 Arrives in Asmara, Eritrea, and from this base visits Adowa, Aksum, Adigrat and Makale.

September

8 (Tue) Flies to Cairo (touching down at Khassala, Khartoum and Wadi Halfa), and the next day flies to Tripoli.
10 Flies to Ostia (stopping for lunch in Syracuse amd briefly in Naples); in the evening catches the train from Rome to Paris, and the next morning (12th) flies from Paris to Croydon, whence he reaches Highgate in time to have lunch with his parents, with whom he spends the weekend.
14 To Mells, where he calls on Christopher Hollis.

16 Returns to London and sees Laura, whose mother (Mary Herbert) is urging a further postponement of their wedding.
17 To Mells again, where he sees Katharine Asquith, Christopher Hollis and Conrad Russell.
18 Dines at Mells Manor, and the next day visits Prior Park, Bath. The next few days are occupied with house-hunting as well as various social engagements.
24 Mary Herbert arrives and now seems reconciled to the marriage. Returns to London with her the next day, and sees Laura.
26 Goes to Mells with Laura for the weekend; they look at houses, spend much time at the Manor, and see Harold Acton, Christopher Hollis and Conrad Russell.
28 Laura returns to London, leaving EW to continue house-hunting and to work on *Waugh in Abyssinia*, now nearly finished (see next entry).

October

2 Finishes *Waugh in Abyssinia* (his original title, *The Disappointing War*, has been rejected by his publisher). Visits Bristol and Bath and sees Christopher Hollis, Douglas Woodruff and other friends.
4 Returns to London and dines with Laura.
5 Sees Maimie Lygon (and again the next day).
6 Corrects the proofs of *Waugh in Abyssinia*.
7 Sees Diana Cooper, currently an intimate of the King and Mrs Simpson.
9 Reads P.G. Wodehouse, lunches with Laura, and goes to stay with the Woodruffs for the weekend.
12 Goes to Mells. Oswald Mosley leads an anti-Jewish demonstration in London's East End.
15 Begins *Scoop*.
16 Returns to London.
18 To early Mass, then to Cambridge, where he lunches with Father D'Arcy, tours the colleges, attends a tea-party for Catholic undergraduates, dines at Trinity College and addresses the Fisher Society.
19 Returns to London, quarrels with his publisher about the blurb for *Waugh in Abyssinia*, lunches with Laura and travels to Mells, where work on *Scoop* and negotiations for a house continue.

26 *Waugh in Abyssinia* is published.
28 EW's 33rd birthday. Lunches with his aunts at Midsomer Norton.
29 Sends the first two chapters of *Scoop* to the typist.
30 Returns to London and, with Douglas and Marie Woodruff and Lord and Lady Acton, crosses to Ostend.
31 They visit Bruges and Ghent.

November

1 (Sun) They return from Ostend to London, and EW sees Laura.
  The abdication crisis is at this time becoming intense. Rome–Berlin Axis declared.
8 Goes to Oxford with Christopher Hollis, who is speaking at the Newman Society. Lunches with Ronald Knox, dines at Campion Hall and sees Father D'Arcy, and attends Hollis's lecture.
9 Lunches at Campion Hall and then travels to Mells, where, over the next few days, he inspects more houses and works on *Scoop*.
13 Meets Laura and they go to Pixton Park.
20 Returns to London and goes to Sir Alexander Korda's film studio to discuss a project for a film to be scripted by EW; though the project eventually comes to nothing, EW spends much time working on it during the next few weeks (see also 14 January 1937).
23 Spends the day with Laura and in the evening goes to Mells, where over the next couple of days he tries to work, with little success.
27 To London for a charity ball, and the next day with Laura to Tetton House, near Taunton, Somerset, to stay for the weekend with one of Laura's aunts. Laura is unwell and the weekend is prolonged.

December

1 (Tue) Returns to Mells and remains there, spending much of the time working, until he returns to London on the 9th.

10 To Stroud with Laura to inspect houses. Abdication of Edward VIII, followed (12th) by the accession of George VI.
11 To Newton Ferrers, Collington, Cornwall, home of Sir Robert Abdy, with Laura, returning alone to London on the 14th.
18 With Laura to Mells, from where they are taken by Christopher Hollis to inspect yet more houses.
20 Dines with the Betjemans, Roger Fulford and John Sparrow.
21 Still looking at unsuitable houses, then sees and is delighted by Piers Court, Stinchcombe, Gloucestershire. Later in the day, goes to Pixton Park, where he and Laura are to spend Christmas. Father D'Arcy joins them on the 24th. Goes to Midnight Mass on Christmas Eve, goes fox-hunting, hunts with the stag hounds and beats for pheasants. Over the New Year period, works on *Scoop*.

1937

January

4 (Mon) Goes to Piers Court for discussions with an architect. (Before Christmas, has offered £3550 for the house; the offer is not formally accepted until late January.) Returns to Pixton on the 5th, hunts the next day, then on the 8th goes to Mells.
7 Tells Tom Driberg that his engagement will be announced the following week (see 13th below).
11 Returns to London and buys an engagement ring.
13 The engagement of EW and Laura Herbert is announced in *The Times*, after being mentioned the previous day in Tom Driberg's *Daily Express* gossip column.
14 Visits Alexander Korda, who has accepted EW's 'treatment' and contracted him to write the script for a film to be titled *Lovelies over London*.
During the next few days, sees Olivia Plunket Greene, Mia Woodruff, the Yorkes and other friends.
23 Goes with Laura to spend the weekend with the Betjemans.
25 With Laura to Piers Court for discussions with a builder and a lawyer, then to Pixton.

February–March

4 Feb (Thu) Moves to Chagford to work on the film script, *Scoop* and other projects, and spends most of his time there until early April. During this time, pays a few visits to London and becomes a director of Chapman & Hall's. Just before Easter, visits Ampleforth College (where Laura's brother Auberon is a pupil) and Castle Howard in Yorkshire.

April

Early in the month, is staying with Laura at Pixton.
5 (Mon) By this date five chapters of *Scoop* have been written.
12 Goes to London with Laura and stays at his parents' house until the 14th.
16 Dines with the Yorkes.
17 Marries Laura Herbert at the Church of the Assumption, Warwick Street, London; Henry Yorke is best man. The couple fly from Croydon to Paris, dine there, then take the Rome Express as far as Santa Margherita; they honeymoon in Portofino, where the Herberts have a house.
After a week in Portofino, they go to Rome for Holy Week.

May

1 (Sat) They attend a public audience given by the Pope, then travel to Assisi, from where they proceed on the 4th to Florence and on the 7th to Portofino, where EW resumes work on *Scoop*.
12 Coronation of George VI.
30 They take the train to Paris and the next day fly to London, where they go to live temporarily at 21 Mulberry Walk, Chelsea, while renovations are carried out at Piers Court.

June

In the first few days of the month, sees his parents, the Yorkes, Maurice Bowra and others.

After the entry for 4 June there is a gap in the diary until 12 November.

July

1 Begins to contribute weekly book reviews to *Night and Day*, of which Graham Greene is editor and film critic; the series continues to 23 December.

August

The Waughs move into Piers Court. Settling in holds up work on *Scoop*, which is not resumed until November.

November

12 (Fri) Resumes diary after realizing that his memory is unreliable. Makes a speech at the *Sunday Times* Book Fair in London.
13 To Oxford, where he visits Father D'Arcy at Campion Hall, later returning home.
16 To Bristol to record a radio broadcast for the BBC.
18 Graham Greene telephones to say that *Night and Day*, to which EW is still a regular contributor, is in serious financial difficulties.
20 The Woodruffs come to luncheon at Piers Court. At this time EW is spending much time and energy working on his garden.
26 To London for a directors' meeting at Chapman & Hall.

December

6 (Mon) To London, where he goes to Chapman & Hall's and also sees his agent, and, with Laura, visits her mother and dines with his parents.
7 Sees Duff and Diana Cooper and other friends. With Laura, returns to Piers Court in the evening.
8 Presents prizes and makes a speech at Dursley Secondary School.

9   Lunches with Christopher Hollis.

There are no diary entries between 10 December and 10 January. Christmas is spent at Pixton Park; after a week there, the Waughs go to Mells Manor before returning to Piers Court.

1938

January

10 (Mon)   Notes in his diary that during the previous month they have received visits from Father D'Arcy, Christopher Hollis and others; he has been twice to London for board meetings at Chapman & Hall's. Work on the house and garden at Piers Court continues; work on *Scoop* continues slowly and with frequent distractions.

After the summary-entry dated 10 January, there are no more diary entries until 28 June 1939.

March

25 (Fri)   Begins to contribute occasional book reviews to the *Spectator*.

The Waughs' first child, Maria Teresa, is born during this month.

May

7   (Sat)   *Scoop: A Novel About Journalists* is published.
25 Arrives in Budapest, where he is to attend celebrations of the ninth centenary of St Stephen as a special correspondent for the *Catholic Herald*.

June

From this time, writes regular weekly reviews for the *Spectator* (*Night and Day* has ceased publication).

29 (Wed) On behalf of Chapman & Hall, writes a letter of advice to Alex Comfort, who has submitted a novel.

August

Sets off with his wife on a three-month trip to Mexico, having been commissioned to write a book (*Robbery under Law*) about that country. They sail to New York on tthe *Aquitania*, then on the *Sibony* to Vera Cruz, from where they proceed to Mexico City, which becomes their base.

September

29 Munich Conference.

October

28 EW's 35th birthday.
By the end of this month the Waughs are back in England, and EW begins work on *Robbery under Law*.

December

The Waughs spend Christmas at Pixton Park.
　Towards the end of this year Chapman & Hall publish EW's collected works and Penguin Books (founded in 1935) publish a paperback reprint of *Decline and Fall*.

1939

January

20 (Fri) By this date 40,000 words of *Robbery under Law* have been written.

28 W.B. Yeats dies.

April

7 Italy invades Albania.
By the middle of the month, *Robbery under Law* is completed.

June

Robbery under Law: The Mexican Object-Lesson is published towards the end of this month (the American edition is titled *Mexico: An Object-Lesson*).

July

1 (Sat) Lectures on Mexico to a Catholic audience in Birmingham.
2 Goes to Malvern to meet Maimie Lygon, her new husband Prince Vsevolode Joannovitch, and other friends.
14 Goes to Pixton Park for two weeks, then to London.
28 Sees a lawyer concerning his allegations of libel against the *Daily Mail* (who have refused to publish an apology: see also 9 August below), then attends a board meeting at Chapman & Hall.
27 Spends two nights at his parents' home, then goes for the weekend to Carlton Towers, near Goole, Yorkshire, the home of Lord Howard of Glossop.

August

1 (Tue) Travels to Pixton Park, returning on the 4th to Piers Court, where he resumes work on the gardens. Is also occupied at this time with the writing of *Work Suspended*.
9 The *Daily Mail* has agreed to publish an apology and pay his legal expenses.
18 EW's parents come to stay, and the next day EW drives his father to Bath, where they lunch in the Pump Room, then to

Corsham, where they collect Alec Waugh, who spends the night at Piers Court.
23 Takes pride in the fact that his family are not listening to the radio during the current crisis (on this day, Parliament approves an Emergency Powers Bill).
25 Begins to look for war work, but is soon afterwards turned down by the Ministry of Information and the Foreign Office.
27 Lunches with Christopher Hollis at Mells. Feels that to join the army as a private would be a stimulus to his work as a novelist.
31 Evacuation of women and children from London begins.

September

1 (Fri) Germany invades Poland. Plants bulbs and helps with the arrangements for an orphanage tea; the installation of the panelling in his library is completed.
3 Britain and France declare war on Germany.
17 Is visited by a Dominican nun to discuss the evacuation of a school to Piers Court. The nuns begin moving in on the 26th and rent the house for the duration, the Waugh family establishing its wartime base at Pixton Park.
21 Visits Conrad Russell and sees Douglas Woodruff.
29 With Laura, leaves Piers Court and spends the weekend at Mells.

October

1 (Sun) To Pixton Park, where 54 people (including 26 evacuees) are now living.
16 Goes to London, hoping to find work in Naval Intelligence; the next day, visits the Admiralty and the War Office without results. Later sees Frank Pakenham, who is in uniform.
18 Visits the Welsh Guards and is accepted, with the possibility of a posting in six months' time. Returns to Pixton.
21 Is 'thrown into despair' by the news that the Welsh Guards do not want him after all.
23 Goes to Chagford to work on *Work Suspended*, and writes 4000 words in the next three days (a further 6000 have been completed by 17 November).

28 EW's 36th birthday, spent with Laura in Exeter; returns afterwards to Chagford, she to Pixton.

November

4 (Sat) In Exeter with Laura again, and by the 17th has visited her twice at Pixton.
17 Is discussing with Chapman & Hall, and also with Osbert Sitwell and Lord David Cecil, the founding of a new magazine, *Duration*.
18 Birth of Auberon Waugh, second child of EW and Laura; EW has hurried to Pixton Park on hearing that labour has started, and moves into a boarding-house in Pixton village.
24 Goes to London for a medical examination and interview for the Marines, and is accepted. Sees A.D. Peters, also the editor of *Life* magazine, who commissions two articles at $1000 each, after which he gets very drunk.
25 To confession in Farm Street; lunches with Henry Yorke, now serving with the Fire Brigade, then returns to Pixton.
27 Christening of Auberon Waugh; the godparents are Christopher Hollis, Frank Pakenham, Maimie Lygon and Katharine Asquith, but only the last of these is able to attend. Moves from the boarding-house to Pixton Park.
28 Receives a letter from the Admiralty instructing him to report for duty at divisional headquarters at Chatham, Kent, on 7 December.

December

6 (Wed) Goes to London and the next day to Chatham to report for training with the rank of second lieutenant. (The diaries contain much detail concerning the training courses attended by EW.) The next weekend is spent in London, visiting his parents, going to Mass at Farm Street, and seeing friends; the weekend of 16th–7th is again spent in London. An eight-day leave over Christmas is spent at Pixton Park. On the return journey to Chatham, he spends some time in London and sees the Yorkes and other friends.

1940

January

12 (Fri) Meets Laura in London, where they spend the weekend at a hotel, see a number of friends, and go to Mass in Farm Street: 'the happiest forty-eight hours of my life'.
14 Reports for a further training course at Kingsdown, near Deal, Kent.
28 Moves into a hotel near the camp, where he is joined by Laura.

February

During this month, with Laura, visits Piers Court. During a visit to London, they meet the Woodruffs at Farm Street.
16 (Fri) Moves to Bisley, near Aldershot, Hampshire, for further training.
Later in the month, spends a weekend in London with Laura; many subsequent weekends are spent similarly, staying at hotels with frequent lunches and dinners at the Ritz and elsewhere, and he soon finds himself overdrawn at the bank by some £500.

March

At the end of the month, spends the weekend in London with Laura: they have a suite at a Curzon Street hotel, he drinks at his club, and they go to see Walt Disney's *Pinocchio*.

May

10 Neville Chamberlain resigns and Winston Churchill forms a National Government.
20 Evacuation of British forces from Dunkirk begins.
At the end of the month, is inoculated against typhoid and attends the funeral of one of the men in his company who has committed suicide.

June

Early in the month there are numerous false alarms of impending action, including 'embarkation leave' on two successive weekends.

10 Embarkation orders arrive, and EW's Company proceed to Haverfordwest in Wales. (By this time he has been promoted to captain.) Italy declares war on Britain and France.
14 German troops enter Paris.
23 They march 6 miles to Milford Haven, embark on a decrepit and lice-infested boat, and wait two days before setting sail for Northern Ireland. Before they have got very far, their orders are cancelled, and they return to port and proceed by train to the Cornish coast. After ten days at Double Bois, they proceed to Whitesand Bay. According to Stannard (*Later Years*, p. 15), EW is shocked by this experience of military confusion and squalor.

July

17 Notes bitterly in his diary that their task is 'defending Liskeard', a small Cornish town. They are, however, being issued with tropical clothing.

At the end of the month, has a weekend leave, sees his wife and children at Pixton, and goes to London, where he dines with his parents, has lunch the next day with Diana Cooper, and dines with other friends. He also sees Brendan Bracken, Churchill's parliamentary private secretary, learns of plans to establish a new commando force, and asks Bracken to use his influence in securing him a transfer.

August

18 (Sun) After several moves, EW and his company are now in Birkenhead, where the troopship *Ettrick* awaits them. After various delays, they set sail on the 24th.
23 Beginning of the 'Blitz'.
26 They arrive in Scapa Flow, a naval base in the Orkneys, where exercises take place.

31   They set sail for Freetown, Sierra Leone. During the voyage EW is occupied with routine paperwork, including the censorship of letters. He also gives a lecture on Abyssinia and in a debate speaks for the motion 'Any man who marries under thirty is a fool'.

September

17   (Tue)   Arrival in Freetown. The previous day, EW has written to his wife instructing her to escape to Canada if the Germans should invade Britain.
23   A small fleet that includes the *Ettrick* arrives off Dakar at dawn with the purpose of lending support for its capture by the Free French under General de Gaulle. The mission is, however, cancelled.

October

 6   (Sun)   They leave Freetown for Gibraltar.
15   Arrival in Gibraltar after a tedious voyage alleviated only by the court-martial of two men who have been convicted of homosexual offences.
18   They sail from Gibraltar.
27   They reach Gourock in Scotland, and proceed to Kilmarnock, where they are given a week's leave.
28   EW's 37th birthday. He proceeds by train to Taunton, the journey involving long delays and taking 24 hours, and is reunited with his family at Pixton Park.

November

 7   (Thu)   At the end of his leave, EW returns to Kilmarnock, learns that he has been successful in his attempt to join the Commandos, and goes to London.
 8   In London he suffers much frustration in trying to obtain confirmation of his transfer. Sees a number of friends, including Duff Cooper, who is living at the Dorchester Hotel.
 9   Lunches with Mary Lygon on oysters and champagne, then

visits his parents, finding Highgate extensively damaged by bombing.
10 Goes to Mass at Highgate, and to a cinema with his brother Alec. Sees E.S.P. Haynes.
11 Lunches with John Betjeman. Dines with Diana Cooper and others.
12 Returns to Scotland, and stays overnight in Glasgow, where the shortage of hotel accommodation is so acute that he has to share a room with a stranger.
13 After attending early Mass, proceeds to Largs, where he remains for the rest of the month. He has now been seconded to No. 8 Commando for six months, serving as liaison officer with the rank of lieutenant (a demotion).
26 Lord Rothermere dies.

December

1 (Sun) Laura Waugh gives birth prematurely. The previous day EW has been summoned by telephone, but arrives shortly after the death of the baby, who has lived only 24 hours and has been christened Mary.
From this point until early in 1942, EW keeps no regular diary. On his return to Scotland, his unit leaves for a training exercise on Arran and Holy Island.
Christmas is spent on board the *Karanja*.

1941

January

During this month No. 8 Commando receives orders to sail to Egypt. Two weeks' leave is granted, then they board the *Glenroy* for the long journey via the Cape.
13 (Mon) James Joyce dies.

February

18 (Tue) Tells his wife that he is growing a beard, spending most of the day sleeping, and gambling very moderately (unlike Randolph Churchill, who has lost £400 playing *chemin de fer* the previous evening). He has read Michael Sadleir's *Fanny by Gaslight* and Prévost's *Manon Lescaut*.
23 Sends his wife a small sum he has won playing poker. He has had an enjoyable couple of days ashore at Cape Town. On arrival in Egypt, they are sent to a camp at Geneifa. EW's hopes of promotion are dashed, and he is appointed Intelligence Officer with the rank of captain. During five days' leave in Cairo, he sees a number of friends. On his return, his Company are sent, via the Suez Canal, to Sidi Bish, near Alexandria, where they spend a month awaiting further orders.

March

18 (Tue) Is elected to membership of White's club.
28 Virginia Woolf dies.

April

6 (Sun) Britain sends an army of 60,000 to Greece; Germany delivers an ultimatum to Greece and Yugoslavia.
19 The Commandos leave Alexandria and sail to Bardia, on the coast of Libya, where an enemy garrison is believed to be stationed. The town is attacked but is found to be deserted. EW later publishes a colourful and partly fictitious article on this episode in *Life* magazine (November 1941); there are numerous discrepancies between this account and that given in his diary. After this, he spends much of his time in B Company's camp at Mersa Matruh, near Alexandria; in order to save money, he makes only infrequent visits to the city. British evacuation of Greece begins.
25 Tells his wife that he has been reading E.M. Forster's *Guide to Alexandria*, also that he has been to Easter confession and has had the priest arrested for 'asking questions of military significance'.

May

20 (Tue) Crete is invaded by the Germans.
22 Boards the destroyer *Isis*, the Commandos now being dispatched to Crete; unable to land at Castelli, however, they return to Alexandria and are then ordered to proceed to Suda in order to mount a counter-attack. Now in the *Abdiel*, they sail the next night to Suda harbour, where they find such confusion that their mission changes from a counter-attack to assistance with the evacuation of Allied troops. EW, who is serving as liaison officer, spends five days in Crete, witnesses scenes of considerable chaos (12,000 British troops fall into enemy hands) and regards the military operation as a disaster and a disgrace.

June

2 (Mon) Tells his wife that he has visited Cairo and met a number of friends there. Has been reading Dickens's *The Old Curiosity Shop*.
22 Germany invades Russia.

July

Begins the long journey home, travelling on the *Duchess of Richmond* by a circuitous wartime route to Liverpool via Mombasa, Cape Town, Trinidad and Iceland. During this voyage *Put Out More Flags* is written.

September

3 (Wed) Disembarks in Liverpool. No. 8 Commando has been temporarily disbanded, and EW is now serving with 12 Royal Marines Defence Force and is stationed at Hayling Island.
26 Congratulates Randolph Churchill on his promotion to major, and tells him that owing to the paper shortage *Put Out More Flags* (dedicated to him) is not likely to be published until after its topicality has faded.

October

4 (Sat) EW, his brother Alec and their parents meet for the last time; Alec is about to depart for service in Syria as an intelligence officer, leaving EW with responsibility for his parents.
6–7 Writes an article on the Commandos, commissioned by *Life*; it is published by the London newspaper *Evening Standard* on 14–15 November and by *Life* on 17 November.

November

During this month EW is in a camp a few miles from Hawick, in south-east Scotland, on a training course with the Royal Marines, and tells his wife on the 16th that he is finding it 'very disagreeable'. The first section of *Work Suspended* (later retitled 'A Death') is published as 'My Father's House' in this month's issue of *Horizon*.

2 (Sun) Sends *The Children's Encyclopaedia*, to be kept for the later use of his son Auberon.
26 EW makes a will for the first time – very informally, though he later claims he has taken legal advice – and sends it to his wife a few days later. It is 'punitively "aristocratic"' (Stannard, *Later Years*, p. 51) in leaving Piers Court in trust for his son Auberon in disregard for the interests of his wife. Soon afterwards he sets off for a two-week sea exercise.

December

This month *Horizon* publishes a letter from EW responding to an article 'Why Not War Writers? A Manifesto' in the October number.
7 (Sun) Japanese attack on Pearl Harbor; the next day Britain and the United States declare war on Japan.
Spends his Christmas leave depressingly in London.

1942

January

5 (Mon) Is sent on a course in Edinburgh. His wife joins him there, and he also meets the writer Eric Linklater.

February

7 (Sat) The Edinburgh course ends; returns to Hawick and for the next month is in low spirits.

March

Put Out More Flags, published this month, is favourably reviewed and becomes a commercial success.

April

1 (Wed) On leave in London (to 11 April). Dines with Diana Cooper at the Carlton Grill.
2 Lunches with Frank Pakenham, then takes part in a broadcast of the BBC 'Brains Trust' programme; his fellow-guests are Sir William Beveridge and W.R. Matthews (Dean of St Paul's), and EW's diary is scathing about the regular panel members, Professor C.E.M. Joad and Commander Campbell. Afterwards, by train to Frome, Somerset, where he joins his wife at Mells.
3 (Good Friday) Attends Mass at Downside.
4 Attends Mass in Frome. Ronald Knox joins the house-party at Mells.
6 With his wife to Pixton, where he remains until 9th, when he returns to London.
9 Dines with Frank Pakenham and Mary Lygon.
10 Returns to Hawick by night train after 'the happiest leave of the war' (*Diaries*).
11 Is preparing to move to Pollock Camp on the outskirts of Glasgow, where 5 RM are now stationed.

May

11 (Mon) After a month in the Glasgow area, moves to Special Services Brigade headquarters at Ardrossan, on the west coast of Scotland.
31 Tells Nancy Mitford that he has read and admired Eric Gill's *Autobiography*.

June

10 (Wed) Birth of EW's daughter Margaret (his diary, perhaps revealingly, gives the date as 'about 11th or 12th'). Is granted ten days' leave and visits his wife at Pixton, arriving on 13th, but is recalled to attend a five-week course at Matlock, beginning on 16th.
20 Writes to his wife from Renishaw Hall, near Sheffield, home of the Sitwell family. He has arrived in a hired Daimler, been entertained by Osbert and Edith Sitwell, and has met the artist John Piper.

July

In the third week of the course, is joined by his wife; afterwards he goes on leave, and among other social activities visits Duff Cooper at Bognor Regis.

August

24 (Mon) Returns to Ardrossan.

September

14 (Mon) Travels by overnight train to London.
15 Stays with Laura in a suite at the Hyde Park Hotel.
16 Flies to the Isle of Wight, spends the day with the Marines, and sleeps at Portsmouth.

17 Visits 12 Commando and spends the night at Diana Cooper's home at Bognor Regis.
18 Returns to London.
19 Spends the day at White's and takes the night train to Glasgow.
24 Visits 1 Commando in Dundee and spends the night at William Stirling's country house, Keir, Dunblaine, Perthshire.
28 Tells Diana Cooper that there is a small painting by John Martin in the Kilmeny Hotel, Ardrossan.

October

5 (Mon) Goes to Sherborne, Dorset: Brigade HQ is being moved there, and he has been sent to assist in making arrangements. Passing through London, he sees Randolph Churchill. After a few days his wife joins him in Sherborne, but returns to Pixton on the 17th.
27 Writes to his wife from London; returns to Sherborne that evening.
28 EW's 39th birthday: his diary sums up the past year as a good one. At this point there is a gap of nearly five months in the diary.

Notes in his diary this month that he has been reading a biography of Walter Savage Landor (presumably that by Malcolm Elwin, published in 1941), has written a review of Graham Greene's *British Dramatists* for the *Spectator*, and is 'meditating' a new novel.

December

21 (Mon) Publication of *Work Suspended*, after prolonged negotiations, in a limited edition of 500 copies.
28 Tells his wife that he has spent a bibulous Christmas and has seen many friends.

1943

February

21 George VI announces that a 'sword of honour' is to be presented to Stalingrad (the presentation is made later in the year when Churchill meets Stalin in Teheran). EW later makes use of this symbol in naming his fictional trilogy.

March

25 (Thu) Visits London, goes to Heywood Hill's bookshop (where Nancy Mitford is working), lunches at White's, goes to Combined Operations HQ, has his hair cut, returns to White's, and stays overnight with Mary Lygon and her husband in Montpelier Place.

April

1 (Thu) Goes to London (until 6th). He has applied for the position of force commander but has been told he is too old for parachuting. Stays one night at the Hyde Park Hotel, then at Mary Lygon's. Visits his parents and finds his father very deaf.
12 In London again, for a three-day visit.

May

29 (Sat) On leave for Easter, and attends a dinner at Campion Hall, Oxford; among his fellow-guests are the architect Sir Edwin Lutyens and Lord David Cecil.
30 Hears a brilliant address by Ronald Knox, calls on Rachel Cecil (wife of Lord David), lunches with Maurice Bowra at Wadham College, goes for a walk with Ronald Knox, and dines at Campion Hall with John Rothenstein.
31 Joins his family at Pixton.

June

3 (Thu) Publishes in *Tablet* a review of *The Reader Over Your Shoulder: A Handbook for Writers of English Prose* by Robert Graves and Alan Hodges.
26 Death of Arthur Waugh. EW and his wife go to stay at Highgate in order to assist EW's mother. Brigade HQ leaves London for Sicily in order to take part in Operation Husky; EW, who has been told by Colonel Laycock in March that his unpopularity is a serious problem, is left behind.

August

During this month, pays two visits to the Coopers at Bognor Regis (the second on 16–17th). During the first visit they play gin rummy and read Anstey's *Vice Versa* aloud, and also go to Chichester, where they have tea with the Bishop at the Palace.
31 (Tue) Visits Windsor Castle and is shown over the library by the Librarian; he finds the Castle ugly, and buys books in Eton.

September

3 (Fri) The Allies invade Italy.
19 Tells his wife that he has had 'an uneventful week'. He has (13th) visited his mother and (14th) attended a dinner given by Osbert Lancaster in honour of Maurice Bowra; the other guests are John Betjeman and the Earl of Birkenhead. The next day he has entertained Bowra to lunch at White's and has dined and slept at Mary Lygon's. On the 16th he has attended a christening at Bray (Lord Louis Mountbatten and his wife and daughter being among the guests), and on the 17th has lunched with Christopher Sykes and his wife Camilla and dined with Cyril Connolly. On the 19th he lunches with the Woodruffs and dines with Nancy Mitford.
27 Spends the evening with his mother.
29 Visits Frank Pakenham and later dines with him.

October

- 4 (Mon) Receives a visit from his wife. They stay at Claridge's and go to Highgate to help order a gravestone for EW's father. Fitzroy Maclean undertakes a military mission to Marshal Tito of Jugoslavia.
- 5 They dine with Frank Pakenham and Father D'Arcy. Laura leaves London the next day, but EW spends the following weekend at Pixton.
- 12 Visits his friend Hubert Duggan, who is dying. (For a full account of EW's curious involvement in Duggan's last days, see Stannard, *Later Years*, pp. 192–4.)
- 13 Visits Duggan again: since he appears to be 'on the point of death' (letter to Laura Waugh, 14 October), EW sends for a priest, but Duggan is still alive the next day. (He dies, however, soon afterwards.) Lunches with Randolph Churchill; dines with Earl Fitzwilliam and his wife.
- 14 Lunches with Charles Scott and dines with Cyril Connolly and his wife.
- 25 Goes to Pixton Park and intends to stay there in order to get on with his writing.
- 28 EW's 40th birthday.

November

- 2 (Tue) Leaves Pixton and goes to Oxford as the guest of Father D'Arcy. They are joined by Frank Pakenham.
- 3 Goes to London and attends a Requiem Mass for Hubert Duggan at Farm Street.
- 4 Attends a lavish party at the Savoy, organized by Randolph Churchill, to welcome home Robin Campbell, who has been a prisoner of war. Leaves at 1.30 and goes on to a nightclub.
- 5 Apologizes to his wife for having been ill-tempered during his recent leave.
- 8 Receives a visit from his wife in London; they believe he is about to depart for North Africa, but the next day the orders are cancelled.

December

Early this month, breaks his fibula in a parachute jump (he has joined the Special Air Service and taken part in a parachuting course near Manchester). Is sent to an RAF sick bay. Tells his wife that he has enormously enjoyed his experience of parachuting, but is distressed (7 December) that she is unable to leave their children, who are suffering from mumps, and come to his assistance. He later goes to London and is nursed at the home of Mary Lygon.

1944

January

At this time, has requested three months' leave without pay in order to write a novel, which he expects to complete within that period; leave is conditionally granted.
25 (Tue) Tells his wife that he is in low spirits.
31 After a weekend at Pixton, moves to Chagford, intending to begin work on his novel the next day. Initially titled *The Household of the Faith*, this later becomes *Brideshead Revisited*.

February

1 (Tue) Begins writing and has completed 1300 words by dinner-time. By the end of the next day he has written over 3000 words, by the 8th over 10,000 words: on the latter date, expresses pleasure at his rate of progress, which is producing 1500–2000 words a day. By the 13th, is engaged in some rewriting, but after dinner that day writes 3000 words in three hours.
8 Asks A.D. Peters whether he would like to see the first two chapters (typed but not revised).
10 His wife joins him at Chagford for a short time (and again on the 18th). On the 23rd, urges her to visit him again soon.
19 Germany resumes heavy bombing of London.

26 Learns that his application for leave has been rejected and he is to become ADC to General Thomas.
27 Goes to London.
28 Meets General Thomas and the next day proceeds to his headquarters on a week's trial. The first evening, gets slightly drunk in the mess.

March

2 (Thu) Returns to London, having been told that he is not acceptable as General Thomas's ADC; fears that he will consequently have to return to Windsor, but it is now suggested that he might become General Graham's personal assistant. When this position is offered to him, he accepts it. Since he will not be required for his new duties for six weeks, is given leave for that period.
9 Writes affectionately to his daughter Teresa on her fifth birthday.
10 Returns to Chagford, having collected his wife from Pixton on the previous day. They spend a happy weekend together.
13 Learns that the arrangement with General Graham has been cancelled. Alone again, finds it difficult at first to resume work on *Brideshead* and is sleeping badly. On the 16th, however, writes 2700 words, and composition proceeds well for the rest of the month.

April

1 (Sat) Is ordered to report back for military duties on the 4th.
2 Tells A.D. Peters that he has written 62,000 words of *Brideshead*, and seeks advice on whether he should expand what he has already written and publish it as a volume of 70,000 words, with a sequel to appear the following year.
3 Goes to London and spends the next two weeks at the Hyde Park Hotel, waiting for further orders.
16 By this date, tired of waiting in London, has gone to Pixton.
28 By this date is back in London and learns from the military authorities that they have no employment for him. Social activities and drinking occupy the next few days.

May

2 (Tue) Attends a dinner at the Dorchester Hotel, London, in honour of Cardinal Griffin, recently appointed Archbishop of Westminster. Graham Greene is among the guests.
4 Resumes work on *Brideshead Revisited* (he has reached, and is having great difficulties with, the scene in which two characters make love on a liner). He wakes the next morning realizing that everything written on the 4th must be rewritten: on the 6th records progress as 'slow' and on the 7th as 'at a standstill'.
5 Receives a telegram from Windsor instructing him to report for duty in London on the 11th.
7 Is reading Jane Austen's *Pride and Prejudice*.
10 Goes to London.
11 Is interviewed and offered a choice of three jobs, none of which appeals to him. With the help of Laycock and Stirling he is posted again to No. 2 SAS and granted six weeks' leave.
12 Returns to Chagford to finish *Brideshead Revisited*.
13 Birth of Harriet Waugh. EW does not visit Pixton Park to see his wife and children until 22 May.
28 (Whit Sunday) Harriet Waugh is christened in London.
30 Returns to Chagford but in the evening receives a telegram ordering him to report to Windsor before assuming his new duties.
31 Travels to Windsor, is given the address of the No. 2 SAS Regiment, gets drunk and is sick in the hotel bedroom.

June

1 (Thu) Travels to Exeter and spends the night there.
2 Returns to Chagford and the next day resumes work on *Brideshead*.
4 The Fifth Army enters Rome.
5 Is now working on the final chapter of his novel. Hopes to finish the book by Corpus Christi day (and does so).
6 Is told by a waiter at breakfast of the Normandy ('D-Day') Landings. Describes the death of Lord Marchmain.
8 (Corpus Christi) After attending communion, finishes his novel and posts it to the typist.

- 9 Laura Waugh arrives and spends a week with her husband, during which he corrects the typescript of his novel.
- 16 Goes to London. Drinks heavily during the next few days, is seriously frightened by a flying-bomb raid (see 23 June below) on the night of the 19th, and resolves not to drink again.
- 20 Submits the manuscript of *Brideshead Revisited* to his publisher, Chapman & Hall.
- 21 Leaves by overnight train to Scotland to resume his military career; he stays at Archdullary Lodge, Strathyre, Bill Stirling's hunting-lodge in Perthshire, 25 miles from his unit's base.
- 23 Advises his wife not to go to London, where the flying-bomb attacks have begun on 15 June.
- 28 Learning that Randolph Churchill is in London and wishes to see him, he sets off for London at once.
- 29 (Feast of St Peter and St Paul) Arrives in London and attends Mass at Brompton Oratory, then goes to see Churchill at the Dorchester Hotel. Churchill invites EW to join him on a military mission to Croatia. EW accepts with enthusiasm and goes to Pixton for the weekend to say goodbye to his family.

July

- 3 (Mon) Returns to London. Visits his mother to say goodbye.
- 4 Lunches at the Beefsteak Club and meets Harold Nicolson. Setting off at midnight, flies with Churchill from Hendon to Swindon and thence to Gibraltar. Their ultimate destination is the island of Vis off the coast of Dalmatia, where they will join a military mission giving aid to Tito and his partisans, which is led by Brigadier Fitzroy Maclean.
- 5 Arrives in Gibraltar in time for breakfast. Flies to Algiers, where he finds Duff and Diana Cooper and other friends and stays at the British Embassy. During the next two days there are numerous social engagements.
- 8 Flies to Bari (the Rear Headquarters of Maclean's mission) via Catania and Naples. Dines alone and wakes up the next morning on Randolph Churchill's bathroom floor.
- 10 Flies to Vis and attends a lunch at which Tito and his staff are present.

12 Returns to Bari.
16 On the return journey to Croatia, the plane crashes on coming in to land and two of the nineteen aboard are killed. Suffers burns and loses all his kit.
17 At dawn EW and others are transferred by ambulance to Topusko. Later in the day they are taken to the airfield and spend the night there.
18 They are flown back to Bari and EW enters hospital there. Later he is visited by Dorothy Lygon, who is serving in the Women's Auxiliary Air Force. For the first six days Randolph Churchill is a fellow-patient.

August

2 (Wed) Leaves hospital and goes to Rome, where he stays at 5 Via Gregoriana in a flat belonging to John Rayner. Duff and Diana Cooper are also in Rome at this time. Before leaving Bari, has developed a carbuncle on the back of his neck; this becomes more serious and causes him great pain.
?4 Enters hospital for treatment of his carbuncle and suffers a period of pain and depression.
15 Leaves hospital and returns to Rayner's flat.
17 Tells his wife that he is in better spirits and enjoying looking at architecture. A number of friends appear in Rome, including (on the 22nd) Diana Cooper.
25 Paris is liberated.
29 Drives in a jeep with Randolph Churchill to Naples, where they spend two nights at Harold Macmillan's villa.
31 EW and Churchill fly to Corsica and, after many difficulties in finding accommodation, stay at Isle Russe.

September

1 (Fri) Tells his wife that he is missing her very badly.
By about the 11th he is back in Bari, whence they return to Croatia, EW serving as second-in-command to Churchill, who is responsible for liaison between the British army and the Jugoslav partisans. They are based at Topusko, a spa town much damaged by bombing. For the first three days they live in a log cabin in a

forest, then move to a farmhouse on the outskirts of the town.
17 Attends mass in Topusko.
29 The Russian army invades Jugoslavia.
30 Tells his agent that the American publishers of *Brideshead Revisited* must not change its title without his permission but may if they wish call it *A Household of the Faith*. Warns A.D. Peters that revisions at the proof stage may be 'extensive'.

October

14 (Sat) Tells his wife that he has recently read two of Erle Stanley Gardner's Perry Mason novels.
20 Russian and Jugoslav troops enter Belgrade.
28 EW's 41st birthday.

November

2 (Thu) Tells his wife that he has decided he dislikes Randolph Churchill.
20 Proofs of *Brideshead Revisited* are dropped by parachute and EW spends the next week correcting them, completing the task on the evening of the 26th.
30 Learns that he is being posted to Ragusa, but travel is at present impossible.

December

2 (Sat) Learns that the road to Split is now open again, and makes preparations to move.
3 Attends Mass and then sets off, travelling by jeep over snowcovered roads via Sluni and Plitvice to Korenica.
4 Resumes his journey and arrives in Split in the evening.
5 Leaves by boat for Brindisi, arriving early the next morning.
6 Travels to Bari.
8 Lunches with Constant Lambert and dines with Jonathan Blow.
10 Takes communion at 'a little church in the slums' (diary). Attends a dinner he has helped to organize for Dorothy Lygon.

18 Leaves Bari by boat for Dubrovnik, where he is to run a small military mission.
19 Arrives in Dubrovnik.
25 Spends Christmas Day alone in his quarters after attending mass and taking communion at a Franciscan church. Writes to Dorothy Lygon and Nancy Mitford, telling the latter that he has recently read and greatly enjoyed Howard Sturgis's *Belchamber*.
During this month he is also reading Wilkie Collins's *The Woman in White*.

1945

January

7 (Sun) Learns that the corrected proofs of *Brideshead Revisited* have reached his publisher. Tells A.D. Peters that the American magazine *Harpers* may only serialize the novel if they use the revised text. Thanks Nancy Mitford for the gift of a copy of Cyril Connolly's recently published *The Unquiet Grave*, which he is reading with strong disapproval, both of Connolly's views on Christianity and of his parading of his classical knowledge. (On the 16th he records that he is 'annotating' the book: on his annotations, see Stannard, *Later Years*, pp. 131–5.) Her letter praises his novel as a 'great English classic'.
12 Commissions a portrait bust from a sculptor named Paravicini, who is in desperate need of food.

February

3 (Sat) Attends celebrations for St Blaise's Day. Antoravic, described in EW's diary as a 'pubescent cretin' and hostile to the British in general and EW in particular, becomes town commander of Dubrovnik. Yalta Conference between Churchill, Roosevelt and Stalin.
7 Is instructed by the partisan corps command to go to Trebinje

and refuses to do so. The order is repeated, and again refused, on the 10th.
12 Writes to Maclean suggesting that he (EW) should devote himself to writing a report on the state of the Roman Catholic Church in Croatia. Maclean agrees.
13 Moves to a partisan corps stationed at Gacko and remains there for three nights, spending most of the time indoors reading Trollope.
16 Returns to Dubrovnik.
20 Sets sail for Bari, arriving the next day after a rough crossing. There, finds letters and cigars awaiting him and sees various friends.
23 Tells his wife that the Jugoslav partisans have expelled him from Dubrovnik for interference in local affairs. (His letter makes no reference to his incompetence or unpopularity.) Is ambitious to return to Dubrovnik as consul (his application to do so is unsuccessful). Has just read Dickens's *Dombey and Son*.
24 Flies to Rome, where he has a number of official appointments in order to report on the situation in Jugoslavia; also meets various friends, including Randolph Churchill.

March

1 (Thu) Visits the Vatican and is disappointed by the condition of the paintings in the Sistine Chapel.
2 Has a private audience with the Pope in order to report on the state of the Church in Jugoslavia. (The conversation is conducted largely in French.) Is given rosaries for his children and a blessing. Has gone into St Peter's beforehand in order to pray for guidance.
3 Flies to Naples but is unable to continue his journey to Bari.
4 Flies to Bari.
9 Is in despair after his bag, containing clothes, diaries, papers and notes for his official report (see next entry), appears to be lost. It turns up the next day.
11 Notes that he intends to start writing his report on 'Church and State in Liberated Croatia'. It is half-finished by the 13th, and by the end of the month has been submitted through Maclean to the Foreign Office.
14 Flies to Naples.

15 Flies to Lympne Airport and proceeds to London, where his wife joins him at the Hyde Park Hotel the next day.
25 The window of EW's sitting-room at the Hyde Park Hotel is shattered by the blast from a rocket-bomb.
29 A Foreign Office memorandum notes that EW has in an interview requested permission to circulate the findings of his report. The request is refused, the Official Secrets Act being invoked. (See also 30 May below.)
31 A summarizing diary entry records that he has spent two weeks in England, mainly at the Hyde Park Hotel except for two nights spent with his family at Pixton and a visit to his mother, who is temporarily living at Midsomer Norton with her sisters. Is living at considerable expense, but feels affluent. Has been reading, with disapproval, the novel *Loving* by Henry Green (pseudonym of his friend Henry Yorke).

April

1 (Easter Sunday) Attends Mass at church in Warwick Street.
2 Goes to a theatre in the afternoon. Henry Yorke and his wife come to dinner. Later in the week there are visits from his mother-in-law (4th) and his mother (5th).
10 Laura Waugh returns to Pixton for a short time, leaving EW in London.
11 Sees Clive Bell.
12 Spends the evening at Cyril Connolly's home, where the artist Augustus John, the Anglo-Irish novelist Elizabeth Bowen and the American novelist Edmund White are also present. Is rude to White and the next day fails to keep a promise to show him round London.
13 Laura Waugh rejoins her husband in London; during her absence he has been drinking heavily and has suffered from insomnia. Anthony Powell and his wife come to dinner.
17 Laura Waugh returns to Pixton Park. Attends a sale of Hugh Walpole's possessions (Walpole had died on 1 June 1941) and buys a small painting by William Mulready.
18 Goes by train to Oxford with Frank Pakenham and spends two nights at Campion Hall.
19 Lunches in Oxford with Pakenham and John Betjeman, and also visits Rachel Cecil and Maurice Bowra.
20 Travels by train to Windsor, reports for military duty, and

is given 28 days' leave. Returns to London and thence to Pixton.
23 Goes by an early train to London and spends £25 on a gold repeater watch, which he immediately breaks. Returns to Pixton in the afternoon.
30 Goes to Chagford to begin work on his new novel.

May

1 (Tue) Has learned, without regret, that his application to return to Jugoslavia has been turned down. Records in his diary that he will now settle down to work on his novel *Helena*.
6 Feels he has done sufficient research to begin the writing of *Helena* the next day. (It was not published until 1950.) Suffers from depression, however, and after a week abandons work on the novel (not to be resumed for another seven months) and returns to London, where he is offered and accepts a diplomatic position in Athens (never taken up) and negotiates for the purchase of a castle in Ireland (see 14 July below).
8 VE day.
14 Thanks Ronald Knox for a list of misprints in *Brideshead Revisited* and tells him he is writing an 'unhistorical' book about St Helena.
27 Tells John Betjeman that Helena will be based on his wife, Lady Penelope Betjeman.
28 Publication of *Brideshead Revisited* in England. The first printing sells out almost immediately, and the reviews are almost uniformly favourable. Though not yet published in America, it has been chosen by the Book of the Month Club and EW expects to make £20,000 out of US sales.
23 *The Times* publishes a letter from EW concerning the plight of the Roman Catholics under Tito; in order to avoid a breach of the Official Secrets Act, he has signed it 'A British Soldier Lately in Yugoslavia'. On the 26th another correspondent, also lately a British officer in Yugoslavia, dismisses EW's views as ill-informed, and EW responds with a further letter on 5 June. (He has assumed, incorrectly, that his critic was Maclean.)
30 At EW's instigation, John McEwan asks a question in the

House of Commons concerning the welfare of Catholics in Croatia.

June

12 (Tue)   Clive Bell writes to EW describing *Brideshead Revisited* as 'a masterpiece'.
23   Henry Reed, reviewing *Brideshead Revisited* in the *New Statesman*, describes it as 'a fine and brilliant book'.
28   Asks A.D. Peters to arrange for the earnings from *Brideshead Revisited* to be paid in the form of a salary of £5000 a year.

July

1 (Sun)   Is back at Pixton after spending most of June in London, where his life has been largely divided between the Hyde Park Hotel and his clubs, with daily visits to Nancy Mitford's bookshop and frequent meetings there with Osbert Sitwell and Lord Berners. Later in the month, returns to London.
14   Assures his wife that he will not pursue plans to live in Ireland unless she is willing.
21   Lunches with Diana Abdy and afterwards goes with her to the Wallace Collection.
22   Goes to Ickleford (see 28th) to inspect Randolph Churchill's house. Dines with Malcolm Bullock, MP.
26   General Election, in which the Labour Party secures a resounding victory. EW does not vote.
27   Randolph Churchill, who has lost his parliamentary seat, appears in EW's room at 7:30 a.m.
28   Goes with Churchill to the Old Rectory, Ickleford, Hitchin, Hertfordshire, where they are to share a home for a time until White's, one of EW's London clubs, reopens. (Churchill has separated from his wife, who has left the house and taken much of the furniture with her. Later (1 August) EW describes the house as 'comfortless'.)
30   Goes to London and spends the night there, returning to Ickleford with Churchill the next day.

August

1 (Fri) Tells his wife that the nuns who are occupying Piers Court are due to leave on 12 September.
6 Atomic bomb dropped on Hiroshima. EW hears the news on the radio at 6 p.m.
10 Goes to London and dines with Robert Boothby.
11 Congratulates Tom Driberg on retaining his parliamentary seat, tells him that he is gratified by Winston Churchill's downfall after his betrayal of Poland, and compares Clement Attlee, the new Prime Minister, to Hooper in *Brideshead Revisited*.
14 Japan surrenders.

Towards the end of the month EW's son Auberon spends a week with him at Ickleford, and the visit is in general a success. Less than successful, however, is a day (24th) on which he shows his son the sights of London, including the Zoo and St Paul's, as a result of which he feels absolved from showing further interest in the child (see diary entry for 31 August).

30 Thanks George Orwell for sending him a copy of *Animal Farm* (see next entry).
31 Dines with Claud Cockburn. Has read *Animal Farm* with enjoyment and has found E.M. Forster's *A Passage to India* very impressive on rereading. He is less admiring, however, of Nancy Mitford's *The Pursuit of Love*, which he has helped to revise and for which he suggested the title (see also 3 January 1946).

September

3 (Mon) Spends the day in Oxford with George Selwyg.
8 Has seen a performance of Wilde's *Lady Windermere's Fan*.
9 Visits his mother, who is lonely after Alec Waugh's departure for New York, and attends Mass in Highgate.
10 Returns to Piers Court, which is being vacated by the nuns who have been living there. (They do not finally move out until the morning of the 12th.) (Later, on 12 January 1947, tells Diana Cooper that when he returned to Piers Court in 1945 he found that his love for it was 'quite dead'.)
17 Goes to London and sees Randolph Churchill.

18   Goes to Windsor for his discharge from the army, then to Philip Dunne's wedding and to lunch afterwards with Randolph Churchill, where he meets many old friends, including Anthony Powell and Christopher Sykes. Returns to Piers Court in the evening.

October

2   (Tue)   Notes in his diary that the food shortage is severe: they eat meat only twice a week.
28   EW's 42nd birthday.

November

10   (Sat)   'A Pilot All at Sea', EW's review of Cyril Connolly's *The Unquiet Grave*, appears in the *Tablet*. (See also 27 July 1946 below.)

December

At about this time, begins a story based on his school diaries, set in 1919 and titled 'Charles Ryder's Schooldays'. It is never completed and the fragment is published only after his death. During this month *Brideshead Revisited* is published in America and (with the notable exception of Edmund Wilson in the *New Yorker*, 5 January 1946) is enthusiastically received by reviewers. (For EW's response to this reception, see 11 January 1946 below.)

14   (Fri)   Maurice Baring dies.
18   *The Times* publishes a letter from EW attacking the paintings of Picasso – a contribution to a controversy sparked off by an exhibition of the work of Picasso and Matisse at the Victoria & Albert Museum, which EW has visited. On the 27th, writes a long letter to Robin Campbell explaining and defending his views.
22   A version of the first three chapters of *Helena* is published in *The Tablet* as 'St Helena Meets Constantius: A Legend Retold'.

1946

January

3 (Thu) Tells Diana Cooper that since Maurice Baring's death (14 December 1945) he has been rereading, with disappointment, his novels. He also praises the first half of Nancy Mitford's *The Pursuit of Love*.
4 Goes with his family to a pantomime at Bristol.
5 Tells Nancy Mitford that he has just resumed work on *Helena*.
11 Refers in a letter to the 'disgusting popularity' of *Brideshead* in America.
15 Asks Penelope Betjeman for criticism of the published portion of *Helena* and seeks advice on the presentation of his heroine's physical and sexual response to horse-riding (she replies on the 23rd).
16 Tells A.D. Peters that *Helena* (at this stage referred to as *The Quest of the Empress Dowager*) is 'one third written & very good'.
24 Seeks advice from Robert Henriques on Jewish sources to provide background for the description of Helena's visit to Jerusalem. By this time the first three chapters are completed and EW is doing research for the next part of his novel.
28 Goes to spend two nights with the Asquiths. Asks Nancy Mitford for information about the Wandering Jew, for use in *Helena*.
29 Nancy Mitford facetiously reproaches EW with imposing on the innocence of the *Tablet's* editors, who have published part of *Helena* in good faith and have failed to spot what she regards (perhaps teasingly) as its obscenity. The same letter refers to Penelope Betjeman as 'St Helena Betjeman', recognizing her as the model for EW's heroine.
31 Writes a wittily threatening letter to *Life* magazine, who have expressed the intention of publishing an illustrated article dealing with the individuals on whom some of the characters in his novels are based.

February

2 (Sat) Thanks Robert Henriques for help with the Jewish background of *Helena*, and puts further questions to him.

4   Tells Mary Lygon that he has been in London for a day and has got drunk. The same letter states that *Helena* (referred to now as *The Life of the Empress Helena*) is based on the 'early sex life' of Penelope Betjeman.
7   Another letter to *Life* begins sarcastically, but then extends an invitation to their representative to visit Piers Court.
24 The *Life* representative calls on EW, who tells A.D. Peters the next day that he is willing to write an article on his characters for them if the fee is generous.

March

22 (Fri) Goes to London to make arrangements for visits to Germany and France. Dines with Mary Lygon and her husband Prince Vsevolode.
23 Has a meeting with a director of Saccone & Speed, wine merchants, where Prince Vsevolode is employed, to discuss writing a history of the firm (the payment will be one dozen bottles of champagne per thousand words).
30 Goes to London and runs into Maurice Bowra in the queue for visas at the French consulate. (EW has been invited to visit the Coopers in Paris.)
31 Rises at dawn and flies by troop-carrier to Nuremberg, where the war crimes trials are in progress (verdicts are not reached until 30 September). His diary describes the city as consisting of a luxury hotel, a luxury courthouse and 'a waste of corpse-scented rubble'; during the afternoon he tours the old town, Baedeker's guide in hand, trying to identify the ruins. Is officially and gratifyingly classified 'VIP' (Very Important Person) on this visit.

April

1   (Mon) Attends the trials, sitting in the front tow of the gallery, and witnesses the cross-examination of Ribbentrop.
2   Goes with Dame Laura Knight to see a picture she is working on showing the war crimes defendants in the dock. Later, attends the court again. (Plans to write about his Nuremberg experiences come to nothing.)

3   Flies to Paris in an American troop-carrier and is met by an Embassy car. Stays with the Coopers at the British Embassy; among his fellow-guests are Auberon Herbert, Peter Quennell, Maurice Bowra, Nancy Mitford and Julian Huxley. Each evening of his stay, gets ' a little drunk ' *(Diaries)* and on Saturday night (6th) 'quite drunk'.

6   Is driven in the evening with Diana and her son to their country house, the Château de Saint Firmin at Chantilly. *Tablet* publishes 'A New Humanism', EW's review of George Orwell's *Critical Essays*.

7   Attends mass at the village church, and is then driven to Senlis, Ermenonville and Mer de Sable. At a luncheon party Randolph Churchill is among the guests.

8   Has lunch with Bowra and later flies back to London, where he spends the night at the Hyde Park Hotel, returning home the next day. Publishes an article in *Life* magazine entitled 'Fan-Fare' (reprinted in *A Little Order*), for which he is paid $1000. Stannard *(Later Years,* p. 161) describes it as 'a rare and important statement of his artistic aims'.

13 Notes in his diary that the children have come home for the holidays and that his mother has paid them a two-day visit.

18 Writes to the Golden Cockerel Press to propose a limited edition with illustrations of *Helena:* it is a work over which he is taking a considerable amount of trouble, and he is more interested in seeing it well produced than in making money out of it. (See also 16 May below.)

25 Spends the day in London and meets Harold Nicolson at the Beefsteak Club. Both have received, and declined, an invitation to join a committee intended to promote the claim that Lord Alfred Douglas is 'the greatest sonneteer since Shakespeare'; Dr Marie Stopes, a *bête noire* of EW's, is another member of the committee. Later he attends a board meeting at Chapman & Hall's (he has resumed his position as literary adviser there in 1945).

26 Notes in his diary that he has fasted and has given up wine during Holy Week as well as attending church services.

30 Tells Diana Cooper that he has recently read Christopher Isherwood's *Prater Violet* and reread Norman Douglas's *South Wind*.

At about this time, writes 'What To Do with the Upper Classes: A Modest Proposal', an ironic vision of the aristocracy assigned to reservations and viewed there by tourists; he sends it to the left-wing *New Statesman* 'in the hope of annoying its editor, Kingsley Martin' (Stannard, *Later Years*, p. 165), but it is refused by Martin and a number of other British editors. For its eventual publication in America, see 1 September 1946.

May

6 (Mon) Goes to London for a haircut.
7 Notes in his diary that his children's company during the school holidays has become a burden to him.
12 Thanks Randolph Churchill for a gift of cheese, and tells him that Douglas Woodruff has been staying at Piers Court.
15 Is working on *Wine in Peace and War*, his monograph for Saccone & Speed (see 23 March above), and also thinking about the speech he is to make to the Oxford Union (see 23rd).
16 Is annoyed to learn that the Golden Cockerel Press (see 18 April above) have turned down his proposal for a limited edition of *Helena*.
23 Feeling unwell, goes to Oxford and speaks in a Union debate.
24 In Oxford, still feeling ill. Lunches with Bowra, dines with the Deakins and the Cecils, buys books.
25 Returns home. Accepts an invitation to visit Salamanca, where a conference is to be held to celebrate the quatercentenary of the birth of Francisco de Vittoria, the founder of International Law. (EW and Woodruff will attend as representatives of the *Tablet*.)

June

8 (Sat) Victory Day   EW remains at home after refusing an invitation from *Empire News* to go to London to report on the celebrations, which he describes in his diary as a 'masquerade'. The same word is used in a letter to Nancy Mitford, who has gone to live in France and is told that she will be wise not to return to England. The diary entry is sour on the subject of Attlee, the new Labour Prime Minister, but

gratified in noting that he has so far earned fourteen dozen bottles of champagne for his work on *Wine in Peace and War* (see 23 March above).

11 Tells Betjeman he has been reading D'Arcy's *The Mind and Heart of Love*, recently published.
14 Goes to London and buys books.
15 With Woodruff, flies from Croydon Airport to Madrid. (This visit to Spain later becomes the basis for *Scott-King's Modern Europe*.) On arrival, becomes convinced that he and Woodruff are receiving second-class treatment and begins a series of complaints.
16 They gatecrash a coach-tour for academic delegates from which they have initially been excluded, and proceed to Valladolid.
17 After a morning's sightseeing, a mayoral banquet and an excursion to Simancas to see the Royal Archives, they are driven to Burgos.
18 They visit two monasteries and Burgos cathedral and attend another mayoral banquet. In the evening they are driven to Vitoria, where they dine and go to the theatre, seeing the second half of Wilde's *Lady Windermere's Fan* performed in Spanish.
19 Feels ill, takes to his bed and misses a banquet, but soon recovers.
20 A long drive to Salamanca; arriving late, they are in time to see the Corpus Christi procession and fireworks.
21–25 They spend five nights in Salamanca, where, quickly growing weary of the conference proceedings, they embark on private sightseeing. Is particularly impressed by a visit to Ciudad Rodrigo.
26 Travels via Avila to Madrid, where they spend six days, during which EW attends a bullfight.
30 Birth of EW's son James (see also 2 July).

July

1 (Mon) On their last evening in Madrid, Randolph Churchill appears unexpectedly and they dine with him.
2 After much uncertainty about their homeward journey, they fly to London, where EW finds a telegram announcing the birth on 30 June, after a difficult labour, of his son James.

He attends a cocktail party and a dinner.
3 Orders new suits, lunches at the Beefsteak and dines with a friend.
4 Entertains Mary Lygon to lunch and they drink three bottles of champagne.
5 Further social engagements in London.
6 Travels to Pixton by taxi to rejoin his wife.
10 Returns to London, and at the weekend (13th) goes to Mereworth to stay with Peter Beatty.
13 Edmund Wilson attacks EW in a *New Yorker* review of the American edition of *Campion*.
16 Spends a 'drunken day' in London: sees Ben and Harold Nicolson, who take him to see a newly discovered painting by Raphael. At the Beefsteak, gets drunk and insults the well-known politician R.A. Butler, then on to the St James's club, where he has more champagne and insults Beverley Baxter.
17 Goes to confession. Lunches with Mary Lygon and another friend at the Hyde Park Hotel and attends a cocktail party. In the evening, reads the second volume of Osbert Sitwell's autobiography.
18 Goes to Communion. Meets Prince Vsevolode for a discussion of the book he is writing for Saccone & Speed.
The diaries break off at this point, but EW evidently remains in London for the next three weeks, seeing friends and drinking. As Stannard points out (*Later Years*, p. 171), it became his habit for some years to spend such a period in London, entertaining lavishly at his suite at the Hyde Park Hotel, seeing friends and working off those to whom he owed social obligations.
27 'Palinurus in Never-Never Land Or, The Horizon Blue-Print of Chaos', an attack on Cyril Connolly, appears in the *Tablet*.
At the end of this month Diana Cooper appears in London and they have lunch and dinner together. EW has tea with Frank Pakenham at the House of Lords and meets Lord Maugham, brother of the novelist W. Somerset Maugham.

August

7 (Wed) Tells Nancy Mitford that he is glad that this is his last day in London: he is bored with having spent six weeks 'sitting about' in hotels and clubs.

8   Returns to Piers Court.
13 Goes with his wife to inspect an early Victorian house near Taunton to which they are both anxious to move, EW fearing that property developers will turn the Stinchcombe neighbourhood into a suburb. (The property is withdrawn from the market and they remain at Piers Court.)
24 Goes to stay with Randolph Churchill at Lady Pamela Berry's house near Aylesbury, but finds that Churchill has gone away. Among the other guests is John Betjeman, who reads his 'erotic poetry' to the company. Calls on Peter Fleming, a neighbour of the Berrys.
29 After three 'tedious' days at home with his children, goes to London for a board meeting at Chapman & Hall's, where he protests in vain at the appointment of a new director (see 31st). Meets his mother and takes her back with him to Piers Court.
30 To Gloucester, where his wife spends £100 on a cow and he spends £242 on paintings and antiques.
31 Resigns from the board of Chapman & Hall.

September

1   (Sun) 'What To Do with the Upper Classes: A Modest Proposal' (see April entry above) appears in *Town and Country* (later reprinted in *Essays, Articles and Reviews*).
22 At about this time, tells A.D. Peters that he would like to sever his connection with Chapman & Hall, but that the matter is not urgent since he does not expect to produce another novel for several years.
23 Goes to London for three nights to conclude his business with Saccone & Speed.

October

3   (Thu) Tells A.D. Peters that he has no objection to films being made of any of his books, with the exception of *Brideshead Revisited*. The same letter states that he would like to take his wife on a visit to Hollywood next February if a

luxurious, expenses-paid trip with minimal duties could be arranged (see 14 November).
4   Goes to London for one night to attend a ball, and gets very drunk.
16 Tells Nancy Mitford he is at work on a short story (the reference is to *Scott-King's Modern Europe*).
24 Tells Nancy Mitford that he is going to the cinema four times a week.
28 EW's 43rd birthday: he resolves to be 'urbane and industrious' and to keep his diary assiduously. Is considering the purchase of a nineteenth-century castle and estate in Ireland. Is reading Henry James.
29 To Oxford, where he dines at Campion Hall, meets Cardinal Griffin, and sees Ronald Knox, Douglas Woodruff and others. During this tour he suffers from a heavy cold.
30 Attends High Mass at St Aloysius's Church, where Knox preaches a sermon. Dines at Wadham College with Bowra and Deakin.
31 Goes to Wantage to stay with the Betjemans.

November

1   (Fri) Goes to Eton College, where he gives a talk to the boys and stays overnight.
2   To London (Hyde Park Hotel).
3   Dines with Richard Stokes, a Labour MP.
4   Meets Rayner Heppenstall to discuss an offer from the BBC to send EW on a European tour. (Since he does not really want to go he asks high terms, which are later refused.) Lunches with his mother. Is reading Henry Green's *Back* and in the evening visits Henry Yorke (Henry Green) and his wife, Frank Pakenham and Pansy Lamb also being guests. Early this month, writes to Yorke praising *Back*; writes again about the novel, in response to Yorke's reply, on the 12th.
5   His mother-in-law being on a visit to Piers Court, remains in London. Consults a Harley Street specialist about his piles, and an operation is recommended. Spends much of the day with Mary Lygon.
6   Returns home exhausted.

9   At this time, is working on *Scott-King's Modern Europe*. Is very enthusiastic about the possible move to Ireland (see 28 October above), principally as an escape from England and what he sees as its unpromising future as a nation. The next day, however, he disclaims these views and reflects that he ought to feel more at ease in his present situation. Two or three days later he is still thinking about Ireland.
14 Receives a cable from A.D. Peters, who is in America, saying that Metro-Goldwyn-Mayer are offering EW and his wife an expenses-paid trip to Hollywood to discuss a screen version of *Brideshead*.
17 Is reading, for the first time, Henry James's *Portrait of a Lady*.
21 Receives a visit from some twenty boys from Bristol Grammar School and their headmaster, John Garrett. Afterwards, regrets the cantankerous tone of the talk he has given them.
24 The Pakenhams come to lunch.
27 Receives an offer from America to write 50 words for a payment of £50, and reflects that 20 years earlier he received the same sum for his book on Rossetti.
30 On the point of going to Ireland to look at the castle he is thinking of purchasing, learns that there is an airfield within a few miles of it.

December

2 (Mon) With his wife, travels by train to Liverpool, then crosses by boat to Dublin, arriving early the next morning.
3 Accompanied by an estate agent and an architect, they travel 20 miles by car to inspect Gormanston Castle and its grounds. Afterwards they return to Dublin and go to the Abbey Theatre after dinner – remaining, however, for only one act.
4 They visit the bank and the solicitor's office, and EW buys his wife an astrakhan coat. They lunch with the Earl of Longford (brother of Frank Pakenham) and his wife. Leaves instructions for a bid to be made for the castle when it comes up for auction.
5 They hear of another castle for sale, Strancally in Waterford, meet the owners and see photographs of it. As they are boarding the boat to cross back to England, EW buys a local evening newspaper and learns that a Butlin's Holiday Camp

is to be built at Gormanston, and plans to acquire the castle there are promptly abandoned.

6 In London, visits estate agents to put Piers Court up for sale, then lunches at White's with Robert Boothby.

7 To Belton, a seventeenth-century country house near Grantham, to spend the weekend as guest of Perry Brownlow. 'When Loyalty No Harm Meant', EW's review of Christopher Sykes's *Four Studies in Loyalty*, appears in the *Tablet*.

8 Attends Mass. Sacheverell Sitwell and his wife Georgia arrive at Belton.

9 Returns to London and spends the day at White's.

10 Attends a performance of T.S. Eliot's *The Family Reunion*.

11 Returns home. His enthusiasm for the move to Ireland is waning, and he decides to postpone a second visit there.

14 Borrows a wireless set in order to listen to a talk on himself given by Betjeman.

16 Receives a copy of *Horizon* that includes an article on himself by Rose Macaulay.

19 Goes to London, visits his tailor, sees Harold Nicolson and Clive Bell at the Beefsteak, visits Duckworth (his publisher) to sign presentation copies of *When the Going was Good*, attends a cocktail party given by the publisher John Murray, where he meets Rose Macaulay, and gets very drunk.

20 Is driven back to Piers Court on icy roads by an estate agent, who inspects the property.

22 Writes to Betjeman concerning their respective religious positions.

23 Finds the presence of his children in the house deeply uncongenial and is depressed at the prospect of Christmas.

25 Drives to Midnight Mass with two of his children. Does not enjoy the day and notes gloomily in his diary that, though he has given many presents, the only ones he has received are a pot of caviare (eaten a week before Christmas) from his wife and a copy of George and Weedon Grossmith's *Diary of a Nobody* from his mother; he spends part of the day comparing the latter with the original serial version in *Punch*.

1947

January

At the beginning of the year EW spends three weeks in a private hospital in London, where he undergoes an operation for piles; he finds the experience humiliating as well as agonizing, and afterwards regrets his decision to undergo surgery as an irrational act. His visitors in hospital include his wife and brother, Mary Lygon, Christopher Sykes, Elizabeth Pakenham and Douglas Woodruff.

From the hospital, he writes (9th and 14th) two long letters to Betjeman, urging him to take instruction in the Roman Catholic faith.

After two days at home, whither he is conveyed by ambulance, he and his wife return to London. With EW still weak and depressed, they embark on the 27th for New York. His diary for the 25th notes disapprovingly that among the passengers are a number of working-class 'GI brides' travelling first-class.

31 (Fri) They arrive in New York, EW still feeling ill, elude the press and proceed to the Waldorf-Astoria hotel, where they are the guests of MGM. They are taken to the theatre, but leave after the second act.

February

1 (Sat) Dictates to a secretary in his hotel room a preface to a book by Christie Lawrence, who has served with him in Crete. Laura Waugh spends $2000 on clothes. They dine with Carl and Carol Brandt, literary agents.

2 Attends Mass at St Patrick's Cathedral and lunches with Mrs Kermit Roosevelt.

3 Calls on the editor of *Good Housekeeping*, which is to publish one of his stories (see March entry below), and lunches with the editor of *Town and Country*. The former offers him $4000 as an advance for a future story, and EW suggests that half of this fee should be in the form of a car to be delivered to Ireland. Later they take the train for California.

6 Arriving in Pasadena in the morning, they are met by a car from MGM and driven to Los Angeles.

7 Attends meetings at the MGM studios. During the next week there are more meetings as well as visits to Loyola University, a tea-party (11th) with the film star Anna May Wong, lunch (14th) with the nuns at a convent school, and dinner (14th) with the novelist Helen Howe and her husband. As time passes, EW spends less and less time at the studios, MGM become progressively less enthusiastic about *Brideshead*, and the project is eventually abandoned, to the relief of both parties. MGM's hospitality continues, however, and – especially after the arrival of his friend Simon Elwes and his wife – EW devotes his time to social activities and attends many Hollywood parties. He sees a private showing of Chaplin's new film *Monsieur Verdoux* and goes to a supper party afterwards at Chaplin's home. He also visits the Disney studios (he regards Chaplin and Disney as the only two real artists in Hollywood). Randolph Churchill turns up for a couple of days, is constantly drunk and behaves very badly, but gives a well-received lecture, attended by EW, at Pasadena.

March

There is a gap in EW's diary between 15 February and 7 April, but the summary-entry for the latter date notes that he has discovered a fruitful subject for fiction in the course of a visit to the Forest Lawn cemetery and states his intention to begin work at once on a story (*The Loved One*). On 6 March he has already told A.D. Peters that he is 'entirely obsessed' by Forest Lawn, is visiting it two or three times a week, has formed a relationship with the chief embalmer, is to meet the manager and is planning to write about the establishment. The same letter notes that at Forest Lawn a corpse is referred to as 'the loved one'.

During this month the short story 'Tactical Exercise' appears in *Strand* and (under the title 'The Wish') in the American magazine *Good Housekeeping*. In *Strand* it is accompanied by a cartoon of EW (which offends its subject, but the original of which he subsequently hangs in his library) and a short essay by Betjeman ('The Angry Novelist') based on the radio talk he has given the previous December.

22 (Sat) With his wife, sails back from New York. On their return, spends five days in London.

April

2 (Wed) Goes into retreat at Downside (it is Holy Week); see also 19th.
3 Betjeman thanks EW for sending him a copy of the Forest Lawn catalogue of statuary and other funerary items.
6 (Easter Sunday) Returns to Piers Court and is reunited with his wife and children. Sends to Osbert Sitwell a completed application form for membership of the Society of Authors (see also December 1950), and in the accompanying letter commends the wine, cheese and cemeteries of California.
19 Is reading the autobiography of Thérèse of Lisieux at the suggestion of 'Tusky' Russell, the monk whom he has consulted during the Easter retreat at Downside.
17 Writes to the editor of *The Times* commenting facetiously on Somerset Maugham's awards to young writers for foreign travel.
22 Goes to London to arrange another trip to Ireland and drinks a good deal. Visits Randolph Churchill.
23 Feels ill but attends John Sutro's birthday party.
24 Feels ill again, but drinks champagne with Randolph Churchill before returning home.
28 Goes to London.
29 Flies to Dublin to look for a house; dines with Terence de Vere White.
30 Goes by taxi to Mullinger and inspects two houses, neither of which he finds attractive. 'Why Hollywood is a Term of Disparagement' appears in the *Daily Telegraph*.

May

1 (Thu) Goes by taxi to Tipperary, inspecting two more unsuitable properties en route. Spends the night at Cahir. 'What Hollywood Touches it Banalizes' appears in the *Daily Telegraph*.
2 Sees another property on the shores of Loch Derg, then returns to Dublin and spends the evening alone. A letter to Betjeman this month states, possibly with some exaggeration, that for a week he inspected three houses a day.
3–4 Spends the weekend with friends at Templeogue, driving 5 miles to Mass on the Sunday.

1947

5   Lunches with Lady Rathdonnell at Lisnavagh (see also 28 May and 13 June below).
6   Inspects, and dislikes, a house near Shelton.
7   Lunches with friends and later flies back to London.
8   Attends a birthday dinner for Douglas Woodruff.
9   Lunches with Mary Lygon and insults Malcolm Sargent, the conductor.
10   Tells Diana Cooper that on returning from Ireland he learned of the death on 27 April of their mutual friend Conrad Russell (see also 24 November 1950). Goes to Downside, and the next day gives the boys a talk about Hollywood.
12   Is back at Piers Court after collecting his son Auberon from Bristol, where he has undergone an operation.
15   (Ascension Day) Auberon Herbert arrives as a self-invited guest. Notes in his diary that every Ascension Day he recalls what he regards as the most unhappy day of his life, when, a schoolboy at Lancing 30 years earlier, he spent a day's holiday alone after the other boys had left. (For a similar reference, see 26 May 1960.)
16   Christopher Sykes arrives for a visit.
17   Camilla Sykes (wife of Christopher) and Coote Lygon come to lunch.
18   EW and his wife are taken by Sykes to tea with Sir Max Beerbohm, who is living near Stroud and for whom he feels great respect and admiration. On 1 June, tells Penelope Betjeman that he found Beerbohm 'enchanting'. (See also 28th below.)
20   Finishes an article on Forest Lawn for the *Tablet* (see 18 October below).
21   Begins *The Loved One*.
22   Max Beerbohm writes a flattering letter to EW, rejecting the homage that EW has paid him and recognizing him as the more gifted writer.
23   Reports progress on *The Loved One* as very slow. Receives an unenlivening visit from an American who wishes to interview him.
28   Tells Betjeman that he is seriously considering the purchase of Lisnavagh, but if it were not for his wife would prefer to settle in Africa.

June

2 (Mon) Is trying a new method of composition with *The Loved One*, writing a rough draft of the entire story and then going over it carefully.
11 Goes to London with his wife. In the evening they fly to Dublin and then drive to Shilton, spending two nights there.
12 They inspect an unsuitable house near Bagenalstown.
13 They inspect, and like, Lord Rathdonnell's early Victorian country-house at Lisnavagh, Co. Carlow. (For EW's previous visit there, see 5 May above; for the asking price, see 25 July below.) They return to Dublin and dine with the de Vere Whites.
14 They take an early flight to London, lunch with Randolph Churchill, then go with him to Mereworth to attend a party. Plays poker and loses £21.
16 They return home.
23 Max Beerbohm having recommended the Third Programme, Laura Waugh has purchased a wireless set on EW's instructions; he has listened to it carefully, but is not entertained.
28 'The Last Days of Hitler', an attack on the Oxford historian Professor Hugh Trevor-Roper, appears in the *Tablet*.
29 Cyril Connolly and his 'concubine' arrive on a visit to Piers Court.

July

1 (Tue) Resumes work on *The Loved One*.
5 Simon Elwes and his wife come for the weekend.
During the following week, completes the first draft of *The Loved One* and begins the rewriting.
9 Tells A.D. Peters that he will need advice on whether it can be published in America without giving serious offence (see also September entry below).
13 At about this time, writes to the editor of *The Bell*, an Irish magazine, responding to a review in which he has been accused of snobbery.
19 Ronald Knox comes for the weekend and they discuss the article EW will write about him for *Horizon*.

20 The Pakenhams come for lunch.
23 Goes to London, stays with Randolph Churchill, dines with Ann Rothermere (where Diana Cooper and Maurice Bowra are also present), and attends – and greatly enjoys – a ball given by the Marchioness of Bath.
24 To Mells, where EW and his wife attend the first communion of their son Auberon the following day.
25 Returns to Piers Court and learns that the price of Lord Rathdonnell's house is £20,000.
29 As usual after his visits to London, has been unwell for several days.
30 To London. Dines with Ann Rothermere, Diana Cooper being among the other guests. They see a private showing of the Marx Brothers' *A Night at the Opera*.

August

1 (Fri) Spends the day reading Knox's past contributions to the *Tablet*. Dines with the Woodruffs.
2 Goes for the weekend to Pamela Berry's; among the other guests are Maurice Bowra and Oliver Stanley. Sybil Colefax and Edward Marsh appear the next day.
4 Visits the Betjemans and tours Victorian churches with John Betjeman. Notes that Penelope Betjeman intends to become a Roman Catholic.
5 Returns to Piers Court.
15 To London, where he sees the editor of the *Daily Telegraph* and attends Mass at Farm Street. Dines with Douglas Woodruff; they are joined by Randolph Churchill. India gains independence.
16 Sees an Italian producer who wishes to make a film based on the life of Cardinal Newman, and spends much of the day with Douglas Woodruff.
17 Flies to Stockholm – the beginning of a tour of Scandinavia financed by the *Daily Telegraph* and lasting until 2 September.
18–20 Sightseeing in Stockholm. On the 20th, lunches with the head of the Swedish Foreign Office and writes to tell his wife that he has decided not to settle in Ireland.
21 More social engagements in Stockholm.
22 Visits Gripsholm Castle.

23 Travels by train to Uppsala, which (except for its cathedral) EW admires.
25 Flies from Stockholm to Oslo, where he meets his agent, publisher and members of the press. He spends four nights in Oslo and deplores its ugliness.
29 Flies to Copenhagen and dines with his publisher at Tivoli. He finds Copenhagen attractive, enjoys his four-day visit, and is fêted as a popular writer.

September

2 (Tue) Returns to England and spends two nights in London, returning to Piers Court on the 4th.
5 To London for an unenlivening ten-day visit, staying (as usual) at the Hyde Park Hotel and seeing the usual circle of friends, including Cyril Connolly, Mary Lygon, the Sykeses, the Woodruffs, and various club cronies.
14 Sends the final version of *The Loved One* to A.D. Peters, who has read an earlier version and disliked it and has advised against its publication in America. Earlier, however, EW has sent it to the American novelist Helen Howe, and in a letter dated 1 September (forwarded to A.D. Peters on the 14th) she has given him the opposite advice.
16 Offers *The Loved One* to Cyril Connolly for publication in *Horizon* before book publication, with the stipulation that it must appear entire in a single issue; the offer is eagerly accepted.
28 Dines with Connolly (one of two such dinners this week).
29 'Death in Hollywood' published in *Life* (see also 18 October below).

October

At about this time, gives Nancy Mitford advice on the writing of a novel that is to become *Love in a Cold Climate*, published in 1949.
8 (Wed) During the past week, has been alone and depressed at Piers Court. Goes to Mells with Julian Oxford and his wife (who have been overnight guests on the 7th), sleeps in a cold and damp room, and develops fibrositis. After re-

turning home, spends the next week as an invalid, never venturing out of doors.
9   Laura Waugh returns home after a visit to her sister. Robert Henriques comes to lunch.
18 'Half in Love with Easeful Death. An Examination of Californian Burial Customs' (a version of the *Life* article already published: see 29 September) appears in the *Tablet*.
21 Goes to London, sees Cyril Connolly, participates in a Catholic brains trust, and stays overnight with his mother at Highgate.
28 EW's 44th birthday. Describes himself in his diary as 'physically infirm and lethargic' and notes that he has kept none of the resolutions made a year earlier, noting also, however, that he has written two good stories during the past year (*Scott King's Modern Europe* and *The Loved One*), has added some fine books to his library and has given generously to church funds.

November

During this month a version of *Scott-King's Modern Europe* appears in *Hearst's International Combined with Cosmopolitan* under the title 'A Sojourn in Neutralia'. Earlier, an abridged version of the work has appeared in the summer number of the London magazine *Cornhill*.
9   (Sun) During this weekend has completed his article on Ronald Knox.
16 Carol Brandt comes to lunch, bringing presents of food, and is given a list of further items required from America.
19 Goes to Oxford, visits Maurice Bowra, dines at Christ Church, sees Lord David Cecil and addresses a writer's club.
20 Finds the Oxford bookshops closed for Princess Elizabeth's wedding. Lunches with Christie Lawrence and returns home.
23–24 With his wife, spends two days attending a sale at Tetbury.

December

At about this time, suggests to A.D. Peters that *Scott-King's Modern Europe* could be made into a good film: he would be prepared to undertake the adaptation.

1 (Mon) Stuart Boyle, an artist who is to illustrate *The Loved One*, arrives for an overnight stay and proves receptive to EW's suggestions.
8 Receives an enthusiastic letter from Desmond McCarthy, who has read an advance copy of *Scott-King's Modern Europe* (see also 21 December).
10 Publication of *Scott-King's Modern Europe*, which sells well (14,000 copies by Christmas) despite lukewarm reviews.
11 Tells Cyril Connolly that *The Loved One* is in the hands of Doyle, the illustrator.
15 Tells Nancy Mitford that he has accepted an honorary degree of Doctor of Laws from Loyola University, Baltimore.
19 Drives with his wife to Ascot and collects his daughter Teresa from school; they go to lunch with the Laycocks and then return home, where the family are now assembled for Christmas.
21 Instead of being reviewed in the *Sunday Times* by McCarthy (see 8 December above), as EW had hoped, *Scott-King's Modern Europe* receives an unfavourable review in that newspaper from John Russell, with whom EW subsequently engages in correspondence.
25 Christmas begins with Midnight Mass at Woodchester Priory. Listens to a Christmas Message broadcast by John Betjeman and later sends him a card criticizing it.
26 Notes that he finds his children 'particularly charmless'. Is giving tuition to Auberon. Press cuttings of the reviews of *Scott-King's Modern Europe* are arriving. Tells Nancy Mitford that he is hurt by the fact that reviewers attack his character rather than discussing the book.
30 His 'disgust' with his family having reached a climax the previous day, he goes to London by an early train, goes to his clubs, sees Mary Lygon and Maurice Bowra, and gets drunk. Dines at Mary Lygon's, where he is coolly received by his host and breaks a decanter.
31 Goes to confession, sees Diana Cooper and Sykes, dines with the Woodruffs.

1948

January

1 (Thu) Attends Mass in Farm Street, lunches with Diana Cooper, and returns home.
2 Tells Cyril Connolly that he remained drunk throughout his visit to London.
7 Pays another visit to London.
8 Goes to Brighton for the day with the Coopers to visit mutual friends.
9 At Chapman & Hall's office, admires the illustrations done by Boyle for *The Loved One*. Dines with Cyril Connolly.
10 Sees Diana Cooper, visits his mother, goes to the film of Graham Greene's *Brighton Rock* and dines with the Woodruffs.
11 Goes to Mass at Farm Street and meets Greene there, taking him to the Ritz for cocktails. Lunches with Diana Cooper. Gives a party at the Ritz, the guests including Christopher Sykes and the Pakenhams.
12 Lunches with Basil Bennett and attends a party in the evening.
13 Returns home.
20 Tells Rupert Croft-Cooke that he is willing to be included in his anthology *How to Enjoy Travelling Abroad*, and that the fee should be dropped in the poor-box of the nearest Roman Catholic church.
25 Drives to Oxford. At Campion Hall, sees Frank Pakenham, Maurice Bowra, Lord David Cecil, Mrs Graham Greene and others. Gives a talk on Hollywood to a large and appreciative audience.
27 Tells the Marchioness of Bath that he has attended a party given by Penelope Dudley Ward. He has acquired a set of Beerbohm's works and is rereading him.

At this time Laura Waugh is suffering from fibrositis and also from depression.

February

The Loved One appears in this month's issue of *Horizon* and creates a considerable sensation.

2 (Mon) In a letter to EW, Connolly expresses disquiet concerning a possible libel action following the publication of *The Loved One*.
3 Goes to London, has his photograph taken, visits his agent, goes to an exhibition, lunches and dines with friends.
5 Has lunch with his mother and his daughter Margaret and then returns home.
11 Lent begins.
12 Tells Randolph Churchill that *The Loved One* is bringing about a revival of his popularity among 'highbrow' readers.
15 Though both have given up wine for Lent (and EW also tobacco), the Waughs drink copiously and EW has a hangover the next day.
16 EW and his wife lunch with Hiram Winterbotham, a collector, at Woodchester (he has called on them the previous day and dines with them on the 29th).

Writes to John Betjeman at about this time suggesting, diffidently, that the Eglinton Tournament would make a suitable subject for a poem, and stating that he is reading Proust, in English, for the first time and is unimpressed.

March

7 (Sun) Writes a letter of fervent welcome to Penelope Betjeman, who is to be received into the Roman Catholic church on the 9th.
10 Goes to London for the day.
11 Goes to Bristol to record a talk for the BBC.
16 Is reading the third volume (*Great Morning*, recently published) of Osbert Sitwell's autobiography.
24 Goes to Downside to begin a Retreat (it is Holy Week). Much of his time in the next two days is occupied with church services.
26 Visits his old nurse, Lucy Hodges.
27 His fast now being over, he returns to smoking and drinking.
28 After Mass, returns home. Between now and mid-August, makes only one entry in his diary.

April

3 (Sat) Goes to spend the weekend with the Marquis and Marchioness of Bath at Longleat. During this visit, he calls on Olivia Plunket Greene. From Longleat, he goes to Mells for one night and then proceeds to London, where he spends four days.
27 Tells Harold Acton he has been reading his *Memoirs of an Aesthete* with very great pleasure.

May

During this month, joins the selection committee for a film award sponsored by the *Daily Express*, and during this summer goes frequently to the cinema.
3 (Mon) Congratulates Graham Greene, whose *The Heart of the Matter* is a Book Society Choice in the USA, and offers advice on how to deal with the financial and other results of his success.
4 Records with extreme relief that the school holidays have come to an end.

June

5 (Sat) 'Mea Culpa?', EW's review of Greene's *The Heart of the Matter*, appears in the *Tablet*; it is reprinted in the American magazine *Commonweal* on 16 July. (See also 17 July below.)
21 Tells George Orwell of a rare P.G. Wodehouse book dating from 1909 and relevant to the correspondence they have been having about Orwell's essay 'In Defence of P.G. Wodehouse', which appeared in *Tribune* (16 February 1945) and was reviewed by EW in the *Tablet*.

July

17 (Sat) The *Tablet* publishes a letter from EW retracting his comments on the character of Scobie in his review of *The*

Heart of the Matter published on 5 June. (He has received a letter from Greene correcting him on this point.)

August

16 (Mon) Notes that he has been unwell since 9 July (he has been suffering from nettle rash and depression).
19 Attends his aunt Lilian's funeral at Bristol.
20 Tells A.D. Peters that Laurence Olivier has suggested that *The Loved One* might be made into a film; EW considers the notion absurd. (It was filmed in 1965.)
23 Goes to London and goes to the cinema with Maurice Bridgman.
24 Lunches with Patrick Kinross and Christopher Sykes, sees a doctor about his nettle rash, and goes to the cinema again.
25 Dines with the Woodruffs.
26 Is entertained to lunch by members of the film industry and attends a 'film supper' with Woodruff at which they see an Italian film, *Paisa*.
27 Sees another film. Much of his time this week has been spent at the doctor's and the dentist's.
28 Has spent a week editing and abridging Thomas Merton's autobiography, already a best-seller in America (under the title *The Seven Storey Mountain*) and published in England (1949), with a foreword by EW, as *Elected Silence*. Gives a dinner for the Pakenhams and others.
29 Attends Mass at Farm Street. Father D'Arcy dines with him.
30 Sees the doctor again. Lunches at the Ritz with the Pakenhams. Goes to the cinema with Christopher Sykes.
31 Sykes takes EW to visit John Hayward, and EW behaves badly. Afterwards EW and Sykes go to the cinema.

September

1 (Wed) Sends flowers to Sykes as an apology for his behaviour the previous evening. Meets a publisher to discuss a limited edition of Ronald Knox's sermons selected by EW (published the following year).
2 Returns home and spends the next two days tackling his correspondence.

3 Tells *Life* magazine that he is keen to write an article for them on American Catholicism (see 5 October below).
4 The Donaldsons, neighbours of the Waughs, come to dinner.
28 Goes to London, where Graham Greene has invited him to lunch at his flat at 5 St James's Street, and meets Catherine Walston. Hayward is also present. Attends a dinner given at the Savoy by the editor of the *Daily Express* (see May entry above); among the other guests are C.A. Lejeune, film critic, and Kenneth Clark, art historian.
29 Attends press showing of Carol Reed's film *The Fallen Idol*, scripted by Greene. Lunches with Father Caraman, who is taking over the editorship of the Jesuit journal *Month*; they discuss the future policy of this publication, and EW offers him extracts from *Helena*. Is then driven in a car sent by Mrs Walston to Thriplow, near Cambridge, where she and Greene entertain him to a lavish dinner. Stays overnight.
30 Is driven to London and meets his wife and friends for lunch. Later, attends Ronald Knox's 60th birthday party and makes a speech.

October

1 (Fri) Lunches with his wife and later returns home.
2 The Donaldsons come to dinner.
3 Attends Communion. His valet gives notice and he resolves not to replace him and to adopt a simpler mode of life; the notice is, however, withdrawn the next day.
5 Receives a visit from a representative of *Life* magazine to discuss a visit to the USA, financed by *Life*, to enable him to gather material for an article to be published in that magazine. (*Life* agree to pay him $5000 and travel expenses.)
9 *Life* confirm their invitation to go to America. Dines with the Donaldsons. Greene, who has seen EW since his visit to Thriplow, thanks him for his understanding in relation to Mrs Walston.
14 Congratulates Randolph Churchill on his engagement to June Osborne. Soon afterwards he meets them both, and on the 23rd writes to Miss Osborne with considerable warmth of feeling.
24 Sends Nancy Mitford his criticisms of her *Love in a Cold Climate*, which he has read in manuscript.

28 EW's 45th birthday: his diary describes the past year as 'unproductive and unhealthy'.
The diary breaks off at this point and is not resumed for nearly four years (28 September 1952).
At the end of the month, embarks on the *Queen Elizabeth* for New York.

November

2   (Tue) Tells his wife that he is already missing her very much.
6   Arrives in New York. Dines with the *Life* publisher Henry Luce and his wife Clare Booth Luce.
During the next few days his business and social engagements, interspersed with medical treatment for a painful boil, are numerous.
7   Lunches with Anne Fremantle and later receives a visit from his brother Alec.
9   Attends a party at Fordham University.
10 Attends a party given by Anne Fremantle and meets W.H. Auden.
11 Makes an excuse for missing an engagement to see his brother again the previous evening. Visits Dorothy Day, publisher of the *Catholic Worker*, and entertains her and her staff to lunch at an Italian restaurant in the Bowery, to which he is driven in a Cadillac provided by the Luces. After a tea-party and a dinner-party, goes to the theatre, arriving in the middle of the second act.
Among many other engagements during his stay in New York, goes to the *Life* offices, calls on a literary agent and a lecture agent, sees Cecil Beaton and is guest of honour at a dinner-party given by *Life*. Edith and Osbert Sitwell and Maurice Bowra are also in New York at this time.
By the 14th, is in Boston, which reminds him of Highgate; there he meets Alfred McIntyre, President of the publishing firm of Little, Brown, also Bowra, who is lecturing at Harvard and with whom he visits Salem and other places. He has lunch at Loyola College, a Jesuit institution, and addresses the students.
19 Arrives in Baltimore, which he finds dull.
23 Attends a buffet supper given in his honour at Loyola College.
25 Leaves Baltimore and proceeds to Kentucky (where he vis-

its Thomas Merton at his monastery at Gethsemani) and then to New Orleans.

December

1 (Wed) Reproaches his wife with not having written, and tells her that on account of a dock strike he will be unable to return to England by sea in time for Christmas.
Finds a number of letters from his wife awaiting him when he returns to New York about a week later. In New York, lunches with Harold Acton, sees Tennessee Williams' play *A Streetcar Named Desire*, and is taken to Princeton by Anne Fremantle to meet Jacques Maritain.
At the end of the month, embarks for the return journey and is interviewed by a journalist whose subsequent article (*New York Herald Tribune*, 31 December) depicts him as critical of America and Americans. Irritated by what he judges to be misrepresentation, EW attempts to set the record straight in a contribution ('Kicking Against the Goad') to *Commonweal*, published on 11 March 1949.

1949

January

17 (Tue) Tells A.D. Peters that he does not wish his books to be published in the countries of the Communist bloc and fears that *The Loved One* might be used as anti-American propaganda.
18 Tells John Betjeman that he considers W.H. Auden a bad poet.
On or about the 20th, EW and his wife arrive in New York. His lecture-tour begins with engagements at the Waldorf-Astoria and the New York Town Hall.

February

Early this month, Robert Craft, the music critic, entertains the Waughs and the Stravinskys to dinner at Maria's, a New York Italian restaurant.

1 (Tue) Clothes rationing ends in Britain.
16 Lectures at the Walkerville Collegiate, Windsor, Ontario. From Windsor they proceed to Chicago, Milwaukee, New Orleans and St Louis. In Kentucky he again calls on Merton, and in St Paul meets the novelist J.F. Powers.
20 George Orwell reviews *Scott-King's Modern Europe* in the *New York Times Book Review*; his review opens with the statement that *The Loved One* is 'an attack... on American civilization' (see also 3 March below).

March

3 (Thu) *The New York Times Book Review* publishes Harvey Breit's account of an interview with EW in which he denies being excessively critical of America, declares that the best American writer is Erle Stanley Gardner, and admits that he wishes to write a novel dealing with the war that would examine the concept of chivalry (apparently the first reference to the *Sword of Honour* trilogy).

On his last night in New York, delivers a final lecture, preceded by a farewell dinner-party given by the Luces. The Waughs sail for England the next day.

During his absence, workmen have been constructing in the grounds of Piers Court, to EW's designs, 'a sort of Victorian Disneyland' (Stannard, *Later Years*, p. 242); after his return these plans are expanded to include, among other items, an artificial ruin, a grotto and two follies.

April

12 (Tue) Describes his mood to Nancy Mitford as deeply misanthrophic, and tells her of his dislike of Americans. Also states that he has given up cigars and 'secular reading' for

Holy Week, but has failed to abstain from wine as he had intended.
13 Goes into retreat at Downside.

May

During this month, accompanied by Christopher Sykes, makes a brief trip to Paris, where he sees Nancy Mitford and visits the Coopers at Chantilly as well as meeting Paul Claudel, the dramatist, and Père Couturier, the theologian.

10 (Wed) Tells William Gerhardie that he has been a significant influence on his own work.
27 Tells Merton that he is having difficulties writing the *Life* article (in the event it takes him nearly three months to complete; see also 19 September below).

June

6 (Mon) Cyril Connolly is on a weekend visit to Piers Court, and they drive to Wolverhampton and then have lunch with Viscount Monsell at Dumbleton Hall.

July

13 (Wed) Thanks Nancy Mitford for sending him a copy of her *Love in a Cold Climate*, which he is reading with pleasure.
17 Writes to George Orwell in praise and with criticism of *Nineteen Eighty-Four*.
20 Tells A.D. Peters that he is now concentrating on *Helena*, which has been taken up again, though progress is so far slow. (It is not to be completed until March 1950.)
23 Presents the prizes at the Oratory School and afterwards stays for the weekend with Lady Pamela Berry; during the weekend he visits the former Barbara Rothschild, recently married to the novelist Rex Warner, and sees the poet Cecil Day-Lewis and his wife (the actress Jill Balcon) and the novelist Rosamund Lehmann.

27 Thanks Lord David Cecil for sending a copy of his Oxford inaugural lecture, which he has read with great appreciation.
28 Tells Nancy Mitford that he has been reading Osbert Sitwell's *Laughter in the Next Room*, the recently published fourth volume of his autobiography.

August

18 (Thu) By this date, is staying with his son Auberon at La Baule, a French seaside resort, described in a jaundiced letter to Nancy Mitford. Lady Pamela Berry is also staying there.
29 Writes to Merton to express appreciation, and also tactful criticism, of his book *The Waters of Siloe* (see also 13 September).

September

13 (Tue) Writing to Katharine Asquith, is more severely critical of Merton's book, which he has offered to edit.
14 Tells Anne Fremantle that he has enjoyed reading the proofs of her biography of Charles de Foucauld (*Desert Calling*), invites her to send him New York gossip, and admits that progress on *Helena* is very slow.
18 Britain devalues the pound; this has the effect of significantly increasing EW's American earnings.
19 EW's article 'The American Epoch in the Catholic Church' appears at last in *Life*.

October

10 (Mon) Tells Nancy Mitford he has spent a week in London without enjoyment.

November

9 (Wed) Tells Nancy Mitford he has been on a lecture-tour of Scottish universities, including Edinburgh, Aberdeen, St Andrews and Dundee, has made nine appearances in nine

days, and has disliked the experience intensely. He is already regretting his resolution, made after the return from America, to comply with any request from a Catholic institution.
17 Gives a dinner at which the guests include the music critic Edward Sackville-West.

December

5 (Mon) Tells Nancy Mitford that he has been ill for a week after a visit to London during which he has been very drunk. During the same visit he has given a party for Clare Booth Luce. He has also recently chaired a meeting of the Catholic Guild of Arts and Crafts and conducted a 'Catholic Booklovers Weekend' at a Surrey convent. Has greatly enjoyed reading Robert Gathorne-Hardy's recently published *Recollections of Logan Pearsall Smith*.
8 A.D. Peters tells EW that Penguin Books wish to publish ten of his novels in paperback during 1951, and suggests that if the deal goes ahead the considerable profits that accrue should be put into a trust for EW's children.

By the end of the year, the second section of *Helena* has been completed and sent to A.D. Peters.

1950

January

3 (Tue) Tells Anne Fremantle that his wife is expecting another baby in the summer.
6 Britain recognizes Communist China.
7 Asks Penelope Betjeman if she will accept the dedication of *Helena*, and tells her that – in accordance with his vow (by now deeply regretted) to accept all Catholic invitations – he is to speak in Leicester and Middlesborough the following weekend.
11 Tells Nancy Mitford that his wife is seriously overdrawn at her bank and that he is in serious financial difficulties.

21   George Orwell dies.

February

23   (Thu)   General Election results in the Labour Government remaining in power with a reduced majority.

March

9   (Thu)   Tells Nancy Mitford that he has finished *Helena* and would now like to write a guide to Gloucester.
27   Thanks Graham Greene for presentation copies of his *The Ministry of Fear* and *Journey without Maps*, both of which he will reread at once. Having reread *Brideshead Revisited*, he intends to revise it during the coming summer.

April

Early this month, goes to Paris and visits Nancy Mitford, then continues by train to Rome, where he stays at the British Embassy, arriving there on the 12th.
13   (Thu)   A day of social engagements with English residents in Rome.
14   Visits various basilicas in the rain.
15   Tells Nancy Mitford that he hopes to succeed in obtaining permission from the Vatican to erect a private chapel at Piers Court (he did not). He is also pursuing a scheme (also unsuccessful) to have Knox made a cardinal.
19   Dock strike begins in London.
26   Is in Florence by this date after attending St George's Day celebrations at Portofino, where he has stayed with the Herberts. Among the other guests have been the actor Alec Clunes and the artist Osbert Lancaster. He has also seen Harold Acton and visited his parents' home, La Pietra, near Florence, and has visited Bernard Berenson at I Tatti, his villa in Settignano, and Sir Max Beerbohm and his wife at Rapallo.
27   Visits the Sitwells at Montegufoni, their castle near Florence.

?28 Goes to Verona with Harold Acton.

May

Returns to Piers Court during this month and corrects the proofs of *Helena*. Laura Waugh has gone to Pixton for her confinement. Cyril Connolly is a weekend visitor, as are Ronald Knox and Edward Sackville-West.

24 (Wed) A.D. Peters writes to MGM Pictures, who are negotiating to purchase the film rights of *A Handful of Dust* (the deal goes ahead, but the film is never made).
26 Goes to stay with Maud Russell (née Nelke) at Mottisfont.
28 Tells Nancy Mitford that he has been disappointed by Henry Green's new novel, *Nothing*.

June

During this month, visits Holland and takes part in a festival at The Hague, gives lectures, stays at various country houses and spends two days in Amsterdam.

25 Outbreak of Korean War.

July

4 (Tue) Writes a letter of sympathy to his wife, whose baby is overdue. He is glad to be back in London (where he is staying at the Hyde Park Hotel) after his visit to Holland.
8 Tells his wife that he looks in *The Times* each morning for the announcement of their child's birth. He has greatly enjoyed attending a ball and an aristocratic wedding. David Selznick, the Hollywood producer, is negotiating the purchase of the film rights of *Brideshead Revisited* (nothing comes of this project).
9 Birth of Michael Septimus Waugh. Visits his wife and child briefly after a week, but soon returns to London,
15 Expresses his deep gratitude to Greene, who has been reported as having agreed to write a script for the film of *Brideshead*.

21 Laura Waugh says she is missing him.
25 Lunches with Graham Greene, Catherine Walston and Edward Sackville-West.
26 From Piers Court, writes a long letter to his wife (who is still at Pixton), describing his social activities in London. He has been to a cocktail party at Graham Greene's and has also lunched with Greene at White's. At a dinner for Father D'Arcy, the other guests have included Randolph Churchill, Greene, Sackville-West, the Walstons, Woodruff and T.S. Eliot.
27 Thanks Greene for a presentation copy of *The Third Man*, though he does not expect to enjoy it as much as the film. Expresses his desire that the plan for the filming of *Brideshead* (see 15th above) will come to fruition.
29 Finds pleasure in rereading *Put Out More Flags*.
30 Tells his wife that he will come to visit her at Pixton as soon as her brother Auberon Herbert departs.

September

17 (Sun) Writes a letter bringing to an end a controversy with V.S. Pritchett in the columns of the *New Statesman*, sparked off by Pritchett's review of Merton's *Elected Silence*.
27 Tells Nancy Mitford that he has not enjoyed reading *Noble Essences*, the fifth and final volume of Osbert Sitwell's autobiography, and that he hopes to spend Christmas in Jerusalem.
28 Asks John Donaldson for advice on the technical language likely to be used by those discussing a chamber music recital.
Goes to London to sign presentation copies of *Helena*; goes to confession, visits an exhibition of art treasures from Woburn Abbey, and sees Cyril Connolly.
30 In a contribution to the *Tablet*, defends Hemingway's novel *Across the River and into the Trees* against the criticisms of British reviewers.

October

13 (Fri) Reviewing *Helena* in the *Spectator*, R.D. Charques describes it as 'not very substantial'; on the same day the *Times*

Literary Supplement also gives it a lukewarm review, as does John Raymond in the *New Statesman* on the 21st. According to Christopher Sykes, the reception of the novel that EW himself regarded as his best was 'the greatest disappointment of his whole literary life' (*Evelyn Waugh: A Biography*, 1975, p. 337). Graham Greene, however, describes it in a letter to EW as 'a magnificent book'. (Despite its critical reception, the book sells well: see 8 January 1951 below.)
During this month, EW and his wife visit New York (it is to be his last visit). There he leads a very active social life, meeting, among others, Anne Fremantle, Osbert and Edith Sitwell and Gladwyn Jebb (UK Permanent Representative to the United Nations). He attends a party at the Plaza given to celebrate his 47th birthday on the 28th, and goes with his brother Alec to see the musical *Kiss me Kate* (based on Shakesepare's *The Taming of the Shrew*), to which he becomes much addicted.

November

2 (Thu) G.B. Shaw dies.
8 Thanks Greene, who has sent a presentation copy of his children's story *The Little Fire Engine*.
9 Tells Nancy Mitford that he feels much better after his visit to New York. Thanks Betjeman for a letter in which he has praised *Helena*.
11 Tells Louis Auchincloss that he has read his book *The Injustice Collectors* during the voyage home from America and has greatly enjoyed it.
16 Thanks Greene for a letter of appreciation of *Helena*.
17 Writes to Maurice Bowra in praise of Knox's recent book *Enthusiasm* and urges that Knox should receive an honorary doctorate from Oxford University.
18 Tells Knox of his deep gratitude for the dedication of *Enthusiasm*. Lunches at Mells, where Conrad Russell (who died on 17 April 1947) is sadly missed.

1951

During this year EW's earnings amount to some £10,000 pounds, a very substantial sum at this time (Stannard, *The Later Years*, p. 291).

January

6 (Sat) Tells Nancy Mitford that he has felt unwell for some time and has seen a doctor. The same letter comments sardonically on Bowra's elevation to a knighthood in the New Year Honours.
8 By this date 15,626 copies of *Helena* have been sold.
20 With Sykes, sets off on a trip to the Middle East in order to write articles for *Life* (EW's is to be on the Holy Places); their itinerary includes Israel, Jordan, Syria and Turkey. Crossing to Paris, where they dine with Nancy Mitford, they then take the train for Rome, from where EW writes to Diana Cooper that they are proceeding to Jerusalem, Aleppo, Antioch and other places. From Rome they fly to Lydda (Israel), and thence travel to Tel Aviv.

February

2 (Fri) EW and Sykes cross into the Kingdom of Jordan.
7 Writes to his wife from Jerusalem, stating that he and Sykes will keep vigil in the Holy Sepulchre that night.

March

17 (Sat) Is back at Piers Court by this date. Thanks Greene for a presentation copy of his volume of essays, *The Lost Childhood*, and praises the discussion of Greene's *The Heart of the Matter* in Marcel More's *Dieu Vivant*. He will go to Downside for Holy Week.
25 Sends to Nancy Mitford praise and criticism of her novel *The Blessing*, a draft of which he has read, and thanks her warmly for the dedication.

31 Urges Nancy Mitford to work hard at revising *The Blessing*.

April

8 (Sun) Tells Nancy Mitford that he has spent a weekend with Frank Pakenham at his country home in Sussex.

May

4 (Fri) The Festival of Britain opens, marking the centenary of the Great Exhibition of 1851.
5 Under the title 'Two Unquiet Lives', the *Tablet* publishes a savage review by EW of Stephen Spender's autobiography, *World within World*.
17 The BBC Third Programme broadcasts EW's talk 'A Progressive Game', attacking the National Book League's choice of the hundred best books by contemporary authors for an exhibition that forms part of the Festival of Britain celebrations. (Their choice of a book by EW has been *Decline and Fall*.)
21 Congratulates Greene on his novel *The End of the Affair*, which he has read in proof. (Later in the year he reviews it in *Commonweal* (August) and in *The Month* (September).)
25 Tells A.D. Peters that he is willing to write a biography of Sir Thomas More (the project is never carried out).

June

During this month the 'missing diplomats', Guy Burgess and Donald Maclean, flee to Russia. EW goes to France with his wife: they visit Monte Carlo and frequent the Casino, then EW accompanies her to Calais and himself returns to Paris after she has gone home. Writing from a hotel in Chantilly, he tells her that he has spent the previous day rereading his war diaries and has just begun work on *Men at Arms*. On the 29th, writing from Vineuil, he tells her that progress on the novel is slow (it is not completed until December).

July

21 (Sat) Congratulates Tom Driberg on his marriage.

August

18 (Sat) Thanks Greene for a presentation copy of *The End of the Affair* and invites him to visit Piers Court and to bring Catherine Walston with him (his wife is about to take the children to Italy on holiday and he will be alone for nearly a month).

21 Warns Greene that domestic comforts during his visit may be limited; EW dresses for dinner but guests are under no obligation to do likewise. Greene replies the next day in enthusiastic terms. Constant Lambert dies.

24 Tells Nancy Mitford that his novel (subsequently titled *Men at Arms*) is 'unreadable and endless'.

25 Tells Nancy Mitford he is receiving visits from a number of male friends (Greene, Sykes, Pakenham) during his family's absence; also that he put on weight while in France and has been on a diet. (A subsequent letter, dated only 'September', describes the visit paid by Greene and Catherine Walston.)

October

By this time some 50,000 words of *Men at Arms* have been written; at this stage the title of the novel is *Honour*.

17 (Wed) Writes to Bruce Cooper agreeing to stand for election as Rector of Edinburgh University (he does so, but is unsuccessful) and mentioning that he has never voted at a general election.

25 In the General Election, Attlee's Labour government is defeated and Winston Churchill again becomes Prime Minister.

November

3 (Sat) The *Tablet* publishes an angry letter from EW, threatening legal action, a reviewer of Dorothy Sayers's *The Em-*

peror Constantine in the issue of 27 October having made disparaging remarks concerning *Helena*.
17 The *Tablet* publishes a second angry letter from EW; others, including Father D'Arcy and Ronald Knox, subsequently join in the correspondence. At some stage EW consults his solicitor and is advised that it would be unwise to take the matter to the courts.
23 Goes to the BBC's Bristol studio to record a talk introducing a radio dramatization of *Helena* (see 15 and 16 December below).
29 Tells Maurice Bowra of his admiration for the Victorian painter Daniel Maclise. Is suffering from rheumatism and reading P.G. Wodehouse.

December

15 (Sat) 'St Helena Empress', EW's talk introducing the radio version of *Helena*, is broadcast on the BBC Third Programme.
16 The dramatization of *Helena* is broadcast; EW listens to it on his servants' wireless set and considers it very bad.
18 Tells Professor Jacques Barzun, who has visited him the previous evening, that he is unwilling to write an article on Constantine for *Life*, but would be willing to do Sir Thomas More or Ignatius Loyola.
21 'The Plight of the Holy Places' appears in *Life*.

1952

January

8 (Tue) Writes to the editor of *The Sunday Times*, attacking the published views of its television critic, Maurice Wiggin, on the relationship of art and conduct. Tells Clarissa Churchill that 1951 was not a good year for him on account of tax bills, rheumatism, unpopularity and hard work (he has completed *Men at Arms* and at this stage conceives of it as the first of four or five projected volumes). Tells Nancy Mitford that he would like to go abroad at Easter.

14 Complains to Nancy Mitford about his financial situation.
19 A.D. Peters, who has visited Piers Court to discuss with him his taxation problems, advises him that he must limit his expenditure to £4000 a year. (He is substantially in debt to the Inland Revenue.)
23 Writes deprecatingly to Mary Lygon about *Men at Arms* and also tells her of his financial troubles.
28 Tells Diana Cooper that he has enjoyed reading Ford Madox Ford's *Parade's End*.

February

6   (Wed) Death of George VI and accession of Elizabeth II.
15 Tells Nancy Mitford that he has been suffering from rheumatism and a cold, and is depressed. He writes to her of the King's death, deplores the speech broadcast by Churchill, and points out that the King appears to have died at the moment Princess Elizabeth put on trousers in the course of her visit to Kenya.
26 Churchill announces that Britain has produced an atomic bomb.
27 Tells Graham Greene that although *Men at Arms* has a few good pages of farce it is for the most part tedious. He has been disappointed by a rereading of Norman Douglas's *South Wind* (Douglas had died on 9 February).

March

At the beginning of the month, goes to France and thence to Sicily, writing to his wife on the 17th from Taormina that his rheumatism is much better but that the island is cold and swarming with tourists and that the town does not live up to its reputation. He has visited Palermo, and on the return journey stops off in Rome and Siena, also in Cap Ferat on the French Riviera (where he stays for two nights with Somerset Maugham). Diana Cooper joins him in Nice and together they visit the convent chapel at Vence, decorated by Matisse, then drive to Paris. On returning home he has gone to Downside for an Easter retreat.

April

9 (Wed) Goes to Downside for a retreat (it is Holy Week).
21 On about this date, goes to London for an eleven-day visit during which he sees Pamela Berry, Ian Fleming and his new wife Ann (Viscountess Rothermere), and other friends, and runs into Edward Marsh in the Tate Gallery, but spends much of his time alone.
28 Tells his wife that he deplores the attempt by their son Auberon to become a member of White's (one of his own clubs).

May

1 (Thu) Dines with the South African poet Roy Campbell.
2 Returns home.
10 Tells Nancy Mitford that in London he has attended a party given by Pamela Berry at which the guests included Sir Laurence Olivier and his wife (Vivien Leigh) and Frederick Ashton. Is correcting the page-proofs of *Men at Arms*.

June

During this month a London dealer values EW's library at £3000. (The valuation is presumably made with a view to its possible sale, though no further action seems to have been taken.)
 1 (Whit Sunday) Tells Nancy Mitford that the film director Carol Reed seems willing to offer him work (see also 31 July).

July

21 (Mon) Tells Angus Wilson that he is reading his novel *Hemlock and After*.
27 Writes an entertaining letter to Nancy Mitford, describing how he deals with thirteen different varieties of fanmail.
31 Tells Nancy Mitford that he has ceased to work for Carol Reed, has dined with Cecil Beaton, and has seen Frank Pakenham in London.

August

13 (Wed) Writes a regretful (and implicitly reproachful) letter to Clarissa Churchill, a Roman Catholic, who is marrying Anthony Eden, a divorced man, the next day.
31 Frederick Lonsdale comes to lunch.
Towards the end of the month, visits Cambridge, where his new bootmaker is located, meets Catherine Walston by chance, is taken to her home for luncheon and meets her husband.

September

Men at Arms is published early this month. Announced as the first volume of a trilogy, it receives mixed reviews.
1 (Mon) Tells Ann Fleming that he is deeply upset by Clarissa Churchill's 'apostasy' (see 13 August above), also that he has written a profile of Sir Osbert Sitwell for an American paper.
2 Goes to London to sign presentation copies of *Men at Arms*. Writes to Clarissa Eden (and again on the 6th), expressing his deep regret at her marriage, but assuring her of his affection.
8 Writes to Cyril Connolly in response to the latter's somewhat unfavourable review of *Men at Arms* in the previous day's *Sunday Times*. Tells Connolly that he shares his admiration for Hemingway's *The Old Man and the Sea*. Congratulates Alfred Duggan on his engagement to Laura Hill.
17 Angus Wilson writes to EW, praising *Men at Arms*.
14 To tea with Alfred Duggan.
28 Resumes his diary after a gap of nearly four years: he has this day visited Hilaire Belloc at his home in Sussex (a letter to Diana Cooper, written the next day, gives a vivid account of the occasion), and has afterwards visited the Pakenhams. Has quarrelled with Frank Pakenham concerning the stylistic merits of his autobiography *Born to Believe*.
29 Is in Bath with his wife and staying at the Royal Crescent Hotel.

October

This month, publishes in the *Month* a very favourable review ('A Clean Sweep') of Angus Wilson's *Hemlock and After*, which

he has read three times with great admiration and has asked to review.
2 (Thu) Graham Greene writes to EW, praising *Men at Arms*.
7 Tells Greene that he would like to attend the first night of his play *The Living Room* (see 16 April 1953).

November

12 (Wed) Thanks Graham Greene for the gift of his children's book *The Little Horse Bus*.
19 Asks A.D. Peters whether he can place in a popular newspaper an article attacking the Foreign Secretary (Anthony Eden) for inviting Marshal Tito to Britain. (EW has written on this subject to *The Times*, which has not published his letter.) (See also 30 November below.)
28 EW's 49th birthday. Tells John Montgomery (assistant to A.D. Peters) that he would like to travel to Goa (a Portuguese possession until 1961), where a Catholic festival is to be held to celebrate the quatercentenary of the death of St Francis Xavier. As a result of Montgomery's efforts, *Picture Post* subsequently agrees to sponsor the trip (*Life* and *Everybody's* having declined to do so).
30 'Our Guest of Dishonour' appears in the *Sunday Express*.

December

5 (Fri) Thanks Alfred Duggan for the gift of his book *Thomas Becket of Canterbury* and tells him that he is going to Goa but will cut short his trip in order to act as Duggan's best man, as he has already agreed to do; later, he assures Duggan that he will be back in London on 13 January (see also next entry).
7 Duggan's mother, Lady Curzon, urges EW to discourage her son from marrying Laura Hill; EW does not comply with her wishes (see 8 and 13 January 1953).
16 Flies to Bombay, where he arrives the next day and stays overnight at the Taj Hotel.
18 Flies from Bombay to Belgaum, then takes a bus to the Goan border and another bus to Panjim, the Goanese capital, where

he stays at the Mandovi Hotel, which is still under construction but remains his base.

19 Takes a taxi across the border into Goa and finds it crowded with pilgrims. Inspects the remains of St Francis Xavier in the sanctuary of the Cathedral. Has tea with the Indian Consul-General and his wife.

20 Returns to Goa before breakfast and joins the pilgrims in the Cathedral and 'kisses' (probably no more than shows veneration for) the foot of the saint. Later in the morning, goes to Government House to meet the Governor-General and other officials. Attends a luncheon at the Palace of the Patriarch (five courses and champagne), where he meets various clergy.

21 Attends early Mass in Panjim Church, then travels by car to Calangute, and later attends a reception at the Governor's house, described in a letter of this date to his wife. The same letter tells her that he is very happy in his present situation.

22 Spends a tiring day with the Archbishop, visiting churches and convents.

23 Visits various temples.

24 Is fasting (Christmas Eve). Attends Midnight Mass in the hot and crowded Cathedral.

25 Spends a lonely Christmas Day.

26 Visits English and Goan cemeteries, then drives to Santanna and inspects churches there. Dines with the Indian consul. Tells his wife that he is lonely but not unhappy. By this date has changed his mind and will leave Goa in order to see other places in southern India.

27 Visits Margao.

28 Attends Mass and Communion held in a room over a café, then goes on an excursion to Sanguem, Valpoi and Ponda.

29 Visits Old Goa and the island of Divar.

1953

January

1 (Thu) At the beginning of the month, travels to Mysore, from where he makes various excursions.

4   In Bangalore.
5   To Somnathpu and Seringapatam, where Tipu Sultan's palace reminds him of the Royal Pavilion at Brighton.
6   To Sravanabelagola, where he sees the 50-foot statue of Gomateshwara, reached by being carried up 600 steps in a wicker chair; then via Hassan to Belur.
7   Returns to Bangalore by train.
8   To Madura, where he spends two nights and pays two visits to the temple. The *Daily Mail* reports that EW is planning to return from Goa to act as best man at the wedding of his friend Alfred Duggan (see also 13th below).
9   Lunches at the Bishop's house.
10 To Trivandrum.
11 Attends Mass, and later in the day flies back to Bangalore.
12 Flies to Bombay, and after half a day there takes the plane for home.
13 Spends one night in Rome, the onward flight having been cancelled on account of fog in London, and is thereby prevented from attending Duggan's wedding the next day. In Rome he attends a dinner-party at which a footman accidentally pours gravy on the head of Freya Stark, the explorer and author.
14 The flight being still grounded, takes the train.
15 Arrives in London, learns that his children are in quarantine for mumps, and sees Randolph Churchill.
16 Sees A.D. Peters, then travels to Piers Court and is reunited with his family. The next couple of days are spent catching up on accumulated mail.
17 Tells Diana Cooper that he has enjoyed India, but has found the erotic scuptures disappointing.
21 Is reading back numbers of the weekly journals to catch up on news missed during his absence.
22 Learns that his friend Clare Booth Luce has become American Ambassador to Rome. Tells Duggan of his great regret at missing his wedding. Thanks Eric Linklater for sending him a copy of his autobiography *A Year of Space*, which he has greatly enjoyed; he has also recently read, with less pleasure, Aldous Huxley's collection of travel essays, *Jesting Pilate* (1926).
27 Has been working pleasurably on the illustrations for his book *Love Among the Ruins*, but is otherwise lethargic and unproductive.

February

5 (Thu) Spends a long and exhausting day in London, where among other activities he has a meeting with Stanley Salmen (Managing Director of the American publishing house of Little, Brown), sees Cyril Connolly and visits his mother.
8 Tells A.D. Peters that he is willing to give his article on Goa as a broadcast talk (the idea comes to nothing, but is evidence of his need for additional income).
13 In London again and drinks a great deal. Sees Robert Harling at the Queen Anne Press, which is to publish EW's book *The Holy Places*, attends a cocktail party given by *Life* (where he seems to have behaved badly despite his intention of repairing his relationship with the Luces) and dines with Diana Cooper, but has little recollection of any of these events. (Soon after returning home he writes a letter of apology to Lady Diana for being drunk.)
14 Visits his mother, goes to confession in Farm Street, then takes the train to Robertsbridge, Sussex, to visit Lady Curzon (her house is in the grounds of Bodiam Castle); Alfred Duggan and his wife are also present.
15 Attends Mass and in the afternoon visits Harold Nicolson at his home in Sissinghurst, Kent.
16 Takes the train to London and later in the day returns to Piers Court.
18 Tells Nancy Mitford that he has gone deaf in one ear.
19 Tells his daughter Margaret that he has given up sleeping draughts for Lent.
22 Starts work on the second volume of his *Sword of Honour* trilogy, at this stage known as *Happy Warriors* but later to be titled *Officers and Gentlemen*.

March

4 (Wed) Goes to Downside and, unenthusiastically, addresses the boys on Tito. Spends the night at Mells.
5 Takes his son Auberon to the cinema and then returns home.
6 Travels to London with his wife, spends the day at his club, and in the evening goes with her to a performance of Wilde's *A Woman of No Importance*.

7 Travels to Glasgow by train.
8 Attends Mass and in the afternoon gives a lecture in St Andrew's Hall to an audience which he estimates in his diary at 'well over 3,000', later returning to London by overnight train.
9 Has a meeting at Chapman & Hall concerning the layout of *Love Among the Ruins,* spends the afternoon at his clubs, then meets his wife at the station and they travel home together. While in London he has written to Malcolm Muggeridge, editor of *Punch,* offering to write an article revealing that Tito was a woman: nothing comes of this project. The *Daily Express* publishes an article ('Waugh on Tito') attacking his references to the Tito visit in his Glasgow lecture.
15 *Sunday Chronicle* publishes an interview with EW in which he again attacks the idea of Tito's visit to Britain.
18 Tells Diana Cooper that he has begun the second volume of his trilogy (i.e. *Officers and Gentlemen*) and is pleased by what he has written (the same news is communicated to A.D. Peters on the 22nd).
24 Queen Mary dies.
31 Thanks Graham Greene for sending him a copy of his novel *The Confidential Agent,* originally published in 1939, and tells him he will reread it when he resumes reading after Lent.

April

1 (Wed) EW's children are arriving home for the Easter holidays. Goes to a Holy Week retreat at Downside.
4 Dines with Christopher Hollis.
5 Returns home.
8 To London for the day to get his hair cut, taking with him two of his children.
9 Pays his last visit to the house at Midsomer Norton, Arthur Waugh's old home and well known to EW in his early years. (It is to be sold following the death of his Aunt Elsie, and the legal formalities involved in the winding up of her estate, which fall on EW in the absence of his brother, cause him much annoyance.)
10 Tells Christopher Sykes that he has been elected an honorary Gregorian (member of the old boys' society of Downside).

16 To London with his wife. They attend the first night of Graham Greene's play *The Living Room*, preceded by a champagne reception at Claridge's. Afterwards they dine with Edward Sackville-West, Christopher Hollis and Raymond Mortimer.
17 Goes to Paris, where he is met by Diana Cooper and driven to Chantilly. Duff Cooper and his nephew Rupert Hart-Davis are there. They go to the circus.
18 A heatwave having apparently rendered both EW and his host exhausted and irritable, Cooper delivers a tirade against EW. (Stannard suggests that this was 'probably the occasion on which Cooper described Waugh as "a common little man"': *Later Years*, p. 329.) See also 17 September below.
19 Luncheon guests include Isaiah Berlin and Ian and Ann Fleming. Is exhausted and depressed during this weekend.
21 Lady Diana leaves for a three-day visit to London, where her first grandchild (the writer Artemis Cooper) is about to be born. EW returns to Paris, sees friends and spends a bad night in a hotel. Congratulates Graham Greene on his play.
22 Spends the day in Versailles with Nancy Mitford.
24 Returns to Chantilly, where Douglas Fairbanks and his wife are among the guests.
27 Back in London, having crossed by the night ferry: the trip has not been a success.
28 Signs copies of *Love Among the Ruins* at Chapman & Hall, but finds that the book is full of misprints. Later in the day returns to Piers Court. Learns, to his dismay, that the taxation authorities have taken legal action to secure payment of his tax debts relating to Hollywood earnings in 1945.

May

20 (Wed) Visits a convent school in Lechlade with a view to moving his daughter Margaret, who is unhappy at her present school.
24 Tells Diana Cooper that he does not intend to be in London for the Coronation.
30 His daughters return home from school for the Coronation holiday. Tells Nancy Mitford that, while in London at the end of April, he toured the principal streets by taxi in order

to inspect the Coronation decorations and found them 'abominable'.

31 Learns that there is criticism in the village of the absence of decorations for the Coronation at Piers Court; the next day he has a triumphal arch erected and gives a party for the Dursley Dramatic Society (of which he is President), entertainment being provided by the Stinchcombe Silver Band.

Towards the end of the month, *Love Among the Ruins* is published, and soon afterwards EW complains (with considerable exaggeration) that it is receiving very bad reviews: see 3 July below.

During this month, abandons a projected lecture-tour of South America after disagreements with his sponsor, the magazine *Criterio*.

June

2 (Tue) Coronation of Queen Elizabeth II. Attends Mass and then throws himself into the day's celebratory activities.
3 Susan Mary Patten (wife of an official at the American Embassy in Paris) arrives, and the Waughs give a 'gala dinner', EW wearing white tie and decorations.
4 Takes Mrs Patten to Gloucester Cathedral, then to Stratford, where they see Michael Redgrave in *Antony and Cleopatra*.
5 Goes to London to dine with Frank Pakenham. Visits the Victoria & Albert Museum to look at Victorian paintings and meets Graham Reynolds, an expert on that subject. Thanks Graham Greene for sending him a copy of *The Living Room*.
10 In London.
11 Thanks Christopher Sykes for his favourable review of *Love Among the Ruins*, published (anonymously) on the 5th in the *Times Literary Supplement*, and says that he has been distressed by the abuse his book has received from the Beaverbrook Press.
12 Graham Greene arrives at Piers Court for a visit (to 15th); he tells EW the plot of his new play and also discusses his problems of faith.

At this point the diary breaks off until the beginning of 1954.

July

3 (Fri) *Time and Tide* publishes 'Mr. Waugh Replies', a protest by EW against the reception of *Love Among the Ruins*.
5 Tom Driberg visits Piers Court and gives EW a copy of his autobiography *The Best of Both Worlds*.
8 Tells Nancy Mitford that he is 'obsessed' by Ruskin (see entry for 17th).
16 Is invited by the BBC to be interviewed (see 18 August below).
17 'Ruskin and Kathleen Olander', EW's review of a volume of Ruskin's love letters, appears in the *Spectator*.
21 Asks Randolph Churchill to excuse him for the 26th: he has already accepted Churchill's invitation, but has now learned that Duff Cooper is to be one of the other guests.
24 Diana Cooper tells EW that she will not attend the Requiem Mass to be held for Hilaire Belloc, who has died on the 17th. He replies with anger and bitterness, to which she responds with tact and dignity on the 29th.
27 Complains to Randolph Churchill of Duff Cooper's behaviour towards him during his April visit and tells him that he has never cared for Cooper. Churchill shows this letter to Cooper, thereby generating much anger and gossip.

August

5 (Wed) Goes to London, where he attends the Requiem Mass for Belloc.
18 Is interviewed at Piers Court by Stephen Black for the BBC Overseas Service programme 'Personal Call': according to Stannard (*Later Years*, p. 334) the experience 'changed his life'; according to Auberon Waugh (quoted by Stannard), it 'eventually drove my Father mad'. Subsequently refuses to allow the interview to be published in *The Listener*. See also 1 September below.

September

1 (Tue) Is invited by the BBC to be interviewed for the programme 'Frankly Speaking'.

2   Replies that he is willing to give the interview provided that the fee is adequate and that he is not required to display any feigned intimacy with his interviewers.
9   Is reassured by the BBC's reply, but tells them that a more generous allowance for expenses is necessary and that he would prefer the interview to be given in his own home rather than at Broadcasting House in London. (The increased expenses are agreed, but not the change of venue.) See also 28 September.
17 Though the quarrel with Duff Cooper has been made up by this date, EW's assurance to Nancy Mitford that they are on terms of 'tender intimacy' perhaps need not be taken literally. (After a very cool exchange of letters between the two men, Cooper has written on the 14th in friendly terms, accepting EW's apology.)
28 Goes to Broadcasting House to be interviewed for 'Frankly Speaking'. See also 16 November.

October

At the beginning of the month the Waughs, accompanied by their neighbours the Donaldsons, take a short holiday in Belgium. They spend the first night at Ostend and are at the casino until 1 a.m.; then they proceed to Bruges.

2 (Fri) 'Apotheosis of an Unhappy Hypocrite', EW's review of Edgar Johnson's biography of Dickens, appears in the *Spectator*. This review involves him in an exchange of letters with Lady Pansy Lamb, who takes exception to his disparagement of Dickens.
8 By this date the Waughs are in Brussels, the Donaldsons having returned home. They also visit Antwerp, where they enjoy the restaurants and art galleries.
17 Tells the BBC that he is, on reflection, dissatisfied with his performance in the interview (see 28 September above) and would value the opportunity to repeat it. This is agreed to, and towards the end of the month he visits London for a further interview.
28 EW's 50th birthday.

November

6 (Fri) The BBC send for EW's approval transcripts of the second interview and of a 'composite' interview using material from both recordings.
16 The 'Frankly Speaking' interview is broadcast on the BBC Home Service.
24 The *Daily Mail* publishes a letter from EW defending the reputation of P.G. Wodehouse.

December

EW's article 'Goa: The Home of a Saint' appears in this month's issues of *Month* and *Esquire*.

9 (Wed) Thanks Cyril Connolly for *The Golden Horizon*, sent as a birthday present, and tells him that he wishes they met more often.
11 Tells Nancy Mitford that work on *Officers and Gentlemen*, some 25,000 words of which have been written in the past few weeks, has come to a halt. (It has originally been promised to Chapman Hall for 1 November.) See also 11 January 1954.
20 Thanks Cyril Connolly for the gift of a rare edition of Prudentius.

1954

January

1 (Fri) Duff Cooper dies suddenly while on a sea-voyage to Jamaica, accompanied by Lady Diana. EW attends early Mass. Reads Max Beerbohm aloud.
2 Learns of Duff Cooper's death and at once writes to Lady Diana, who has disembarked at Vigo and accompanied her husband's body back to England.
3 Goes to church. Diary entries at this time reflect his depression.
4 Visits London with his family. Meets Frederick J. Stopp, a

Cambridge don who is to write a book about him, and sees Carol Reed and his wife.
5 Lunches with Alfred Duggan and Anthony Powell.
6 Attends Mass at Brompton Oratory. Visits Diana Cooper and later attends Duff Cooper's memorial service at St Margaret's, Westminster.
7 Back at Piers Court, bringing Ronald Knox to stay there; the Donaldsons come to dinner. On this and the next few days it is intensely cold, and EW reports himself on the 10th as 'comatose'.
11 Christopher Hollis and his wife come to luncheon. Tells John Montgomery that *Officers and Gentlemen* is still unfinished (the revised deadline of 1 January having come and gone), and he cannot tell when it will be finished. A little later he promises Stanley Salmen that he will write an introduction to an American edition of his short stories, and mentions that he is thinking of going abroad in order to finish his novel.

At this point the diary breaks off and is not resumed until June of the next year. Mark Amory suggests that EW probably kept a diary during the traumatic journey to Ceylon but subsequently destroyed it.

Around the middle of the month, learns from his brother Alec that their mother is seriously ill, and pays a brief visit to her.

Towards the end of the month, tells his daughter Margaret that he is going to Ceylon and hopes to finish his novel on the journey out. He has had a cold and has been in pain from rheumatism. (This understates his sickness of mind and body at this time.)

February

At the beginning of the month boards the *Staffordshire*, bound for Colombo via Gibraltar, Port Said and Aden.
3 (Wed) Writes to his wife from Cape St Vincent. He has concluded, no doubt correctly, that the chloral he has been regularly taking for insomnia has poisoned his system. Complains that his cabin is very noisy: among the noises are voices that mention his name – the first hint of the experiences later to be shared by the protagonist in *The Ordeal of Gilbert Pinfold*.

8   Writes to his wife from a hotel in Cairo. He has been in a seriously abnormal mental condition on the ship and feared he was going mad; the 'voices' have, however, ceased now that he has left the ship. (He has in fact been tormented by severe auditory hallucinations and persecution mania.) As a result of this experience, he has left the ship at Port Said, and now plans to fly from Cairo to Colombo.
9   Tells John Lehmann that he has enjoyed the first number of the *London Magazine*.
12 Writes to his wife from Colombo, the letter indicating the continuance of serious mental disturbance. In Colombo he runs into Monroe Wheeler, an art historian whom he has previously met in New York, and together they spend two or three days in sightseeing and visit the home of George Keyt, an artist.
15 In Kandy.
16 Writes to his wife about the activities of the last few days, cheerfully and coherently until the final paragraph, which refers to the 'voices' reaching him from Aden (which the *Staffordshire* has now presumably reached).
17 Goes to the cinema and sees an Indian film.
18 Writes to his wife from the hill-station of Nuwara (the Colombo hotels all being full), telling her that he has received her cable urging him to return home; he plans to return to Colombo on the 20th and to make arrangements for a flight home within the next few days. Again, the letter reads normally until the final paragraph, which refers to his mental disturbance. On the same day he writes to Diana Cooper a letter showing signs of mental imbalance.

Soon afterwards he flies home and is met in London by Laura Waugh: his condition at this time is seriously disturbed. At the Hyde Park Hotel he is seen by Father Caraman and by a Catholic psychologist (Dr E.B. Strauss), who is able to dispel his fears that he is possessed by the Devil. He is also seen by a doctor, who concludes that his hallucinations have been the result of poisoning by the bromide taken for insomnia. Afterwards the Waughs return to Piers Court, where EW spends the next three months largely as a convalescent.

March

5 (Fri) Thanks Nancy Mitford for sending him a copy of her *Madame de Pompadour*, which he is reading with great pleasure (this reaction is confirmed in a letter to Diana Cooper the next day). Tells her that he has been suffering from a short period of insanity caused by drugs, and that the trip to Ceylon was 'disastrous'.

7 Tells his daughter Margaret that he has now fully recovered but will never again travel alone.

May

2 (Sun) Offers his public support to Graham Greene, whose *The Power and the Glory* has been condemned by the Holy Office fourteen years after its publication.

5 Tells Nancy Mitford that he has been in London and seen Cyril Connolly.

June

6 (Sun) Randolph Churchill and his wife turn up at Piers Court, and they and the Waughs go to Bath to see a house that the Churchills are buying.

7 Tells Ann Fleming that he has read Ian Fleming's *Live and Let Die*, recently published.

8 Tells Nancy Mitford that Cecil Beaton's recently published *The Glass of Fashion*, which contains references to EW and his friends, is full of errors: EW has been asked to review it, but has declined.

24 Tells his brother that it is his (Alec's) responsibility to arrange for their mother's welfare, and also reproaches him with his handling of their aunt's estate.

28 Tells Lady Mary Lygon that he has read Christopher Isherwood's *The World in the Evening*.

August

14 (Sat) A garden fête in aid of the local church is held at Piers Court and attracts widespread attention. EW has thrown himself into the preparations with great energy and enthusiasm.

September

15 (Wed) Tells Nancy Mitford that he has just returned from a week in London, mostly spent drinking in his club. He has seen Randolph Churchill and other friends, and dined at Ann Fleming's house. He expresses disapproval of Graham Greene's action in writing an open letter to the Archbishop of Paris (published in the newspaper *Le Figaro*), protesting at the refusal to allow prayers to be said at the funeral of the novelist Colette.

October

6 (Wed) Writes to his daughters from the Royal Crescent Hotel, Brighton, describing his visit to Rheims, where he has been a guest at celebrations to mark the restoration of the cathedral.
23 Asks Joan Saunders, who undertakes research on his behalf, for medical information for use in his novel, and also for the words of Cole Porter's song 'Night and Day'.
28 EW's 51st birthday. Thanks Graham Greene for the gift of his *Twenty One*, a volume of short stories. (He has also written to Greene earlier this month, congratulating him on his election to membership of White's, one of EW's own London clubs.)

November

1 (Mon) Tells Diana Cooper that he has been disappointed by Lord David Cecil's *Lord M*, the second and concluding volume of his life of Lord Melbourne. The same letter in-

cludes a disparaging reference to the novelist Charles Morgan, who has been a fellow-guest at the Brighton hotel where EW has stayed early in the previous month.

4 *Officers and Gentlemen* is completed by this date. Tells A.D. Peters that it is 'rather better' than *Men at Arms*. On 16th he tells Nancy Mitford that it represents a completion of the narrative begun in *Men at Arms*.
13 Spends an enjoyable day at Mells and sees Katharine Asquith, Christopher Hollis and Anthony Powell.
16 Tells Diana Cooper that he has read the autobiographical volume *Mercury Presides* by their mutual friend Daphne Fielding and has enjoyed the sections dealing with her childhood.
28 Those Happy Homes', EW's review of Ralph Dutton's *The Victorian Home*, appears in the *Sunday Times*.

December

6 (Mon) Death of Catherine Waugh, mother of EW, aged 84.
7 With his wife, attends the first communion of their son James, and afterwards goes to London.
8 Attends his mother's funeral.
9 Returns home.
11 Writes a touching letter to his daughter Margaret, saying he wishes she had known his mother when she was young.
18 Tells Nancy Mitford that he has been to Oxford and has visited his 'first homosexual love', Richard Pares of All Souls, who is now paralysed and helpless.
29 Tells P.G. Wodehouse that he has been reading his *Jeeves and the Feudal Spirit*.

1955

January

9 (Sun) Tells Cyril Connolly he has read his article 'One of My Londons', published in *Encounter*.

Later in the month, writes to his daughters from a Cunard liner bound for Bermuda, whence he will fly to Jamaica. It is a rough crossing, and he has been playing Scrabble with the popular journalist Beverley Nichols and drinking with friends from White's who happen to be fellow-passengers.

25 Writes to his wife from Roaring River, St Anne's Bay, Jamaica, where he is a guest of Lord and Lady Brownlow. He will soon start work on a book based on his recent mental illness.
27 Writes to his son Auberon, offering paternal counsel and describing the agreeable nature of his surroundings.

After two weeks with the Brownlows, he moves to the Flemings' house at Goldeneye.

March

11 (Fri) By now back in England, thanks Graham Greene for a presentation copy of his *Loser Takes All*.

April

24 (Sun) Tells Diana Cooper that he has enjoyed P.H. Newby's novel *Picnic at Sakkara* (it is also recommended to Christopher Sykes on 15 July).
25 Congratulates Anthony Powell on his novel *The Acceptance World*, of which he thinks very highly.

May

3 (Tue) Urges John Betjeman to come for a visit.
13 Tells Betjeman that he has, on his recommendation, bought William Plomer's volume of verse *A Shot in the Park* and has a poor opinion of it.
15 The *Sunday Express* publishes an attack on EW's pretensions to gentility and describes him as 'a self-made man'.
26 The Conservatives are successful in the General Election.

June

14 (Tue) Congratulates his son Auberon, whose short story 'Caligula' has been published by the magazine *Lilliput*. Tells him that his uncle Alec has had a great success with his novel *Islands in the Sun*, but that another uncle, Auberon Herbert, has failed to win the parliamentary seat for which he was a Conservativee candidate.

20 Thomas Pakenham (Frank Pakenham's eldest son) and Mark Girouard (later well known as an art historian) spend the night at Piers Court; EW is impressed when the young Girouard recognizes the provenance of a Victorian washhandstand that John Betjeman has given to EW as a 50th birthday present.

21 Nancy Spain and Lord Noel-Buxton of the *Daily Express*, who have been refused an interview by EW, arrive at Piers Court and are angrily sent away by EW.

23 To London: there has been a rail strike, and this is the first visit for many weeks. Has his hair cut and then goes to Chapman & Hall to sign presentation copies of *Officers and Gentlemen*. The *Daily Express* publishes Nancy Spain's article 'My Pilgrimage to See Mr. Waugh', and EW sees it at lunchtime. He contacts Malcolm Muggeridge, the editor of *Punch*, to ask whether he will publish a reply, and Muggeridge agrees to do so: for the outcome, see 8 July below. Has received an invitation to meet Cardinal Gracias at the Indian Embassy, but instead of going he remains at his club talking to Randolph Churchill. Dines with Ann Fleming.

24 Spends most of the day drinking and then travels home, the drinking continuing on the train.

25 Tom Driberg and a photographer visit Piers Court.

26 Goes to Mass. Is reading Peter Quennell's *Hogarth's Progress* (his review of it for *Time and Tide*, written on 2 July, appears on the 9th).

30 An American television company spend the day at Piers Court, recording an interview with EW, who finds the experience 'excruciating'.

July

2 (Sat) Spends the weekend with Antony Head (then Secretary of State for War) and his wife at Winkfield.
3 Goes to Mass at Eton, lunches at the Heads', and returns home later in the day. Cyril Connolly reviews *Officers and Gentlemen* unfavourably in the *Sunday Times*, as Kingsley Amis does in the *Spectator* on the 8th.
4 Tells a London estate agent that he wishes to put Piers Court up for sale.
7 Sees, for the second time, the film of Greene's novel *The End of the Affair*, but leaves before it is over. Rereads the novel and notes the divergence between book and film.
8 EW's 'Awake my Soul! It is a Lord!' (his riposte to the attempted invasion of his house by Nancy Spain and Lord Noel-Buxton and the former's article in the *Daily Express*) appears in the *Spectator*. (On 29 June Muggeridge has declined to publish an earlier version, written on the 26th, in *Punch*, as being libellous, but on the same day Ian Gilmour, editor of the *Spectator*, has asked to have it, and it has been rewritten on 1 July and further polished at the proof stage on the 5th. EW has thoroughly enjoyed its composition and revision, and is still pleased when he sees it in print the next day.)
9 Goes to confession.
10 Takes Holy Communion.
11 Notes that *Officers and Gentleman* has been unfavourably reviewed in England, favourably in America; he himself is 'complacent' concerning its merits.
12 Complains in his diary of the uneventfulness of his life, and notes again the next day that he is suffering from boredom. Is unable to sleep without drugs.
14 Thanks Maurice Bowra for his praise of *Officers and Gentlemen*, adding that this opinion is not shared by the reviewers. (Though the reviews have been mixed, the book is selling well, with 26,000 copies sold within a month of publication.) Tells Bowra that he has much more to say about the subsequent experiences of his characters. Expresses his delight at the news contained in a letter from Edith Sitwell that she is about to be received into the Roman Catholic Church.

15 Thanks Christopher Sykes for his review of *Officers and Gentlemen* (published in *Time and Tide* on 2 July), and tells him that he has complained to the Director General of the BBC about the behaviour of participants in the radio programme 'The Critics', who have referred to him as 'Waugh' rather than 'Mr Waugh'.
16 Anthony Powell comes to luncheon. The Waughs go with the Donaldsons to see a performance of T.S. Eliot's *Murder in the Cathedral* in Gloucester Cathedral.
17 Takes Holy Communion.
18 Comments to Nancy Mitford on the reconstructed Palace of Minos at Knossos in Crete. Begins to read a new novel by Agatha Christie.
19 Tells Father Caraman that he fears Edith Sitwell's decision to be received into the Roman Catholic Church in London rather than some quieter spot may attract some unwelcome publicity. (In the event his fears prove unjustified.)
21 Goes to London for the day, calls on Graham Greene and sees Randolph Churchill and other friends.
22 The *Spectator* publishes a delightfully barbed letter from EW concerning his controversy with Lord Noel-Buxton and Nancy Spain. Diana Cooper is a guest at Piers Court (until the 23rd), and the Waugh children return home for the holidays: they enjoy a lively dinner, with charades afterwards.
23 Is gratified to see letters in the *Spectator* attacking Lord Noel-Buxton. He and his wife dine with friends and after dinner they read aloud Kipling's story 'The End of the Passage'.
24 *The Times* publishes a letter in which EW suggests, not without irony, that an appropriate place for a proposed statue of Lloyd George would be the House of Lords.
25 Is depressed in the evening by an escapade that day on the part of his son Auberon, who has been collected from Stroud police station. The next day, accompanies Auberon to the Juvenile Court, where he is fined.
28 To Bath, where he meets Graham Greene, who returns to spend the night at Piers Court.
29 Travels with Greene to London, where they separate. Meets Diana Cooper and they drive to St Margaret's Bay, Kent, where Ann Fleming's house-party includes the dancer and choreographer Frederick Ashton.

31 Is driven to early Mass by Diana Cooper. They dine at Noel Coward's home in Aldington. The *Observer* publishes a 'profile' of EW.

August

1 (Mon)   Reads Aldous Huxley's recently published novel *The Genius and the Goddess*.
2 Diana Cooper drives him to the Grand Hotel, Folkestone, where he instals himself in order to work on *The Ordeal of Gilbert Pinfold*. Three days later he reports to Nancy Mitford that he is not getting any work done.
4 Goes to London for the day in order to attend Edith Sitwell's reception into the Roman Catholic Church, held in Farm Street, at which he stands godfather. Sees Father D'Arcy there and meets the actor Alec Guinness. A banquet is held in Edith Sitwell's club, the Sesame, nearby. Returns to Folkestone and receives a visit in the evening from Ann Fleming.
5 Tells Nancy Mitford that he considers the *Observer* 'profile' (see 31 July above) 'grossly impertinent'.
6 Dines with friends in Sandwich.
7 Attends Mass.
8 Visits Ann Fleming in the evening. Has decided to leave Folkestone on the 10th.
9 Goes to luncheon with Ann Fleming and afterwards with her and her children to the funfair at Folkestone. Tells Edith Sitwell that he enjoyed meeting Alec Guinness and hopes to see him again.
10 Leaves Folkestone (to some extent driven away by a garrulous fellow-guest) and travels home via London.
14 To Mass and Communion; prays to be kinder to his eldest son Auberon, who is at present at home.
15 Attends early Mass.
17 Learns that *Officers and Gentlemen* is selling well (800 copies weekly) and that sales of *Men at Arms* have picked up again (100 a week).
18 Goes to Birmingham with his wife and daughters, stopping at Evesham for tea on the way. They stay at the Queen's Hotel and go to the theatre in the evening.
19 In the morning to Birmingham Art Gallery, where they visit

an exhibition of Pre-Raphaelite paintings, then to Stratford-on-Avon, where they dine at the theatre and see Laurence Olivier and Vivien Leigh in *Titus Andronicus*, which EW has not expected to enjoy but finds enthralling (see also 2 September below). Afterwards he takes his daughters to meet Vivien Leigh and they return home.

21 Attends Communion.
28 Has read a biography of Alfred Austin. Is dieting and losing weight. Visits a Jacobean house with Catholic chapel near Winchcombe which is for sale.

September

1 (Thu) Thanks Nancy Mitford for sending him her essay 'The English Aristocracy', published in *Encounter* (later reprinted in her volume *Noblesse Oblige*).
2 The *Spectator* publishes EW's laudatory review of the Laurence Olivier–Vivien Leigh *Titus Andronicus* (see 19 August above).
3 Receives a visit from an estate agent, but is undecided whether or not to sell Piers Court.
7 Spends the day in London and visits an exhibition of Victorian paintings in Peckham.
14 Takes his son Auberon to Downside, where the new term is beginning.
15 Sees Maimie Vsevolode, whose husband has left her. The Waughs' Italian gardener, Mario, who has for some time been showing signs of mental instability, is taken to a mental hospital.
19 By this time several people have shown an interest in buying Piers Court.
20 To London with his family to attend a wedding at St Paul's, Knightsbridge, followed by a reception at the Hyde Park Hotel.
21 To Ascot with his wife, to take their daughters back to school, then on to Brighton, where they stay at the Royal Crescent Hotel.
22 A rainy day, spent mostly indoors; later they go to the theatre but leave after the first act and go to a cinema.
23 They walk on the pier and visit antique shops, where EW buys a clock; to the theatre again in the evening.
24 They visit Petworth House, which EW finds disappointing,

and go again to the theatre, seeing an enjoyable adaptation of Isherwood's 'Sally Bowles'.
25 To Mass. At some stage during the Brighton visit they also visit Arundel Castle.
26 They return home, stopping en route to see the Stanley Spencer paintings in the Sandham Memorial Chapel near Whitchurch, Hampshire, and to inspect a house for sale at Calne, Wiltshire.

October

1 (Sat) Begins to write an account of his first meeting with Max Beerbohm. Goes to the cinema and to confession.
2 To Communion.
6 To London, where he visits his club, sees Ann Fleming, and lunches with Nancy Mitford, whose recent *Encounter* article on upper-class speech habits has attracted wide attention. She is concerned at having heard of EW's intention to respond to this.
15 During this weekend the Waughs, though temporarily without servants, have a number of guests, including the Pakenhams and the Sykeses.
19 Tells Nancy Mitford that he will send her a proof of an open letter he has written to her in response to her article; it is to be published in *Encounter* (and duly appeared in the December issue).
28 EW's 52nd birthday. Is reading R.H. Benson in preparation for writing an introduction to an American edition of his writings. (He is much occupied at this time with writing reviews and other minor literary tasks.)
29 To Ascot with his wife, who is unwell, in order to collect their daughters for the half-term holiday.
30 To London, where they attend Mass at Farm Street, returning home later in the day.

November

14 (Mon) Goes to London and attends a luncheon given by Burns & Oates, the Roman Catholic publishers, at the Hyde

Park Hotel to launch Ronald Knox's translation of the Bible. Sits next to Sir Kenneth Clark. Goes to an exhibition of Portuguese paintings at the Royal Academy, which he does not enjoy, and later dines at the Ritz with Ann Fleming.

15 Lunches with Clare Booth Luce; Randolph Churchill and Patrick Kinross are also present. Goes with Diana Cooper to an exhibition of Stanley Spencer's paintings at the Tate Gallery, and later returns home.
17 Goes with his wife to the Disney film of *Twenty Thousand Leagues under the Sea* and is deeply disappointed by it.
19 Receives an offer from *Life* of $5000 for an article on St Francis of Assisi. Has been suffering from a cold all this week.
28 Is reading Graham Greene's *The Quiet American* and finds it 'masterly but base' (see also 5 December below). Invites Diana Cooper to accompany him to Italy, where he will collect material for his article on St Francis.

December

1 (Thu) Goes to London and thence to Oxford, where he stays at Campion Hall and attends a dinner at which Lord David Cecil and Nevill Coghill are among the other guests.
2 Visits the Ashmolean Museum, lunches with Sir Maurice Bowra, then returns to London, where he goes to the theatre, and has supper at Boulestin's afterwards with Richard Stokes.
3 Goes by train to Frome, Somerset, where he is met by his wife and their son Auberon; they inspect a house that is for sale, but find it unsuitable. They spend the night at Mells and see Anthony Powell and his wife.
4 Goes to Mass, then pays a visit to the Hollises, returning afterwards to Piers Court.
5 Thanks Graham Greene for sending a presentation copy of *The Quiet American*: he praises the novel and has already written a review of it.
10 To Oxford with his daughter Teresa, who is interviewed by Somerville College and learns on the 13th that she has been awarded a history scholarship. On the way home, visits the church at Swinbrook and sees the grave of Unity Mitford, sister of Nancy.
14 To London with Laura and Teresa; they lunch at the Ritz.

15 Attends a four-hour lunch and then goes to a dinner at the Ritz, but is unwell and can eat and drink nothing.
16 Dines with Graham Greene and Cyril Connolly.
17 Sees Connolly again, and later returns home.
18 Attends Mass and then goes back to bed, where he spends most of the next two days.
22 Thanks Graham Greene for a Christmas present and tells him he is 'deeply fond' of him.

Both EW and his wife are unwell at this time, but he recovers by Christmas, which is spent quietly at home. Apart from a day excursion with his daughter Harriet to Bristol, where they have been to a pantomime and have visited the art gallery, he has been out rarely; has done no writing and only light reading.

1956

January

3 (Tue) Notes that he has agreed to contribute £500 to the cost of a coming-out ball (shared with two other girls) next summer for his daughter Teresa.
6 Goes to Mass (it is Epiphany).
7 To Mells, where Diana Cooper is also a guest.
8 Calls on the Hollises. Plays Scrabble, reluctantly, with Ronald Knox (and beats him).
9 Returns home and finds that *Life* no longer wishes him to write an article (see 19 November 1955).
20 The children's return to school does not prevent EW from feeling depressed.
23 On a sudden impulse, goes with his wife to Brighton, where they stay as usual at the Royal Crescent Hotel. To a theatre in the evening to see Bernard Shaw's *Misalliance*. They remain in Brighton until the 31st, spending their time in shopping and going to the cinema and the theatre.
31 Laura Waugh returns home, EW goes to London, where he has an engagement to speak at the Staff College, Greenwich.

February

1 (Wed) Lunches with Ann Fleming, dines with the former Daphne Vivian and her new husband, Xan Fielding. During the next two days, there are many social engagements and much drinking. By the 4th he has reached what he characterizes in *Diaries* as the 'depressive' as distinct from the 'manic' phase of the visit, and has lost his appetite.

6 Returns home.

8 EW's brother Alec has sent a copy of his best-selling novel *Island in the Sun*, which EW reads with high enjoyment and thanks him warmly for on the 11th. His daughter Teresa leaves for Germany, a visit she has planned herself in order to learn the language. Wishes he had taken his degree at Oxford so that he could vote against the election of either W.H. Auden or Harold Nicolson as Professor of Poetry (the third candidate is G. Wilson Knight).

9 Flies from Bristol to Dublin and attends a dinner at which Father D'Arcy, the Earl of Wicklow and others are present. The weather is so bad that he decides to return home the next day rather than attempting any sightseeing.

12 The *Observer* publishes a letter from EW defending P.G. Wodehouse against the criticisms of his book *French Leave*, and his work generally, in a review by John Wain. A rejoinder by Wain is also printed, and EW now writes to the literary editor of the newspaper with some observations on professional critics and offering to develop the topic in a further letter or in an article (for a fee in either case). The offer is not taken up: see also 24 February below.

13 Is concerned at this time about his son Auberon, who is unhappy at school and wishes to leave. Rereads the diaries he kept at Auberon's age and is distressed by their 'vulgarity and priggishness'.

15 (Ash Wednesday) Resolves to make daily visits to the church and to give up gin and paraldehyde (the latter taken for insomnia) for Lent, but resorts to the drug on the night of the 16th.

23 Thanks Tom Driberg for the gift of his biography of Beaverbrook, but expresses considerable surprise that it lets its subject off so lightly.

24 Goes to see Moira Shearer in *King Lear* at a Bristol theatre.

The *Spectator* publishes 'Dr. Wodehouse and Mr. Wain' (see 12 February above).

March

3   (Sat) Goes to stay for the weekend with the Marquess of Lothian at Melbourne Hall, Derbyshire, birthplace of Lord Melbourne. In the afternoon they visit the church at Staunton Harold.
4   Attends Mass and Communion at the village church. The Bishop of Derby comes to lunch and turns out to be EW's former divinity master from Lancing College. They visit Kedleston and are shown round the house by Lord Scarsdale.
5   To London, where he lunches with Ann Fleming at the Ritz, then back to Piers Court.
10 To the theatre in Bristol.
13 The *Daily Telegraph* publishes an article titled 'One Brother and Another', comparing EW with Alec (see also 17th below).
15 To London with Laura and Teresa, in order that the latter may attend a debutantes' party. Meets Randolph Churchill at his club and finds his company very irksome. Lunches at Ann Fleming's house and does not care for his fellow-guests. Patrick Kinross joins them for dinner.
17 In the *Daily Express*, Nancy Spain makes an unfavourable comparison between EW's sales and those of his brother Alec, whose novel *Island in the Sun* is enjoying a considerable success (she has evidently been nettled by EW's dismissal in his *Spectator* article of 24 February of the literary influence of her newspaper). Writes at once to A.D. Peters, asking him to seek legal opinion whether a libel suit may be brought against her and the newspaper.
22 Thanks Nancy Mitford for sending him a copy of Sybille Bedford's novel *A Legacy*, which he has greatly enjoyed.
28 To Downside for the Easter retreat, returning home on 1 April (Easter Sunday).

April

At this time EW is engaged in discussions with his solicitor concerning a libel suit against the *Daily Express*.

8   (Sun)   Ludovic Kennedy and his wife Moira Shearer come to lunch.
10 To Paris for an eight-day holiday with his daughter Margaret. They fly from London and are met by Diana Cooper and taken to Chantilly. The next few days are spent in sightseeing and in various social engagements. On the 16th they move into a hotel (Lady Diana having gone to Monte Carlo) and run into Graham Greene and John Sutro. On the 17th, they visit Versailles, and the next day go to see Napoleon's tomb in the Invalides and then fly back to London.
19 Sees the headmaster of Downside to discuss the admission to the school of his son James. A reduced fee is agreed on the understanding that James will be a candidate for the priesthood. (Eventually, however, the boy goes to Stonyhurst College instead.)
24 David and Tamara Talbot Rice come to luncheon. Tells his brother Alec that he is confident of winning his libel action against the *Daily Express* and is counting on the damages to pay for his daughter Teresa's coming-out ball. Sends Alec a copy of *Noblesse Oblige*, edited by Nancy Mitford and with a contribution by EW.
27 To London for a discussion with lawyers concerning his libel action. Teresa's social season begins.
28 Returns home. Prospective buyers visit Piers Court (and again the next day).

May

7   (Mon)   By this date, the children having returned to school, EW is aware that he should be settling down to work and resolves to do so 'soon'.
18 Sets off on an excursion with his wife. They have a tedious drive to their overnight stop at Harrogate (Majestic Hotel).
19 They continue their journey to Marchmont, home of Jock and Bridget McEwen, who have been fellow-guests at Melbourne House on 3 March; the house-party includes the Austrian Ambassador and his wife.
20 Mass is celebrated in the house. EW finishes the house's supply of gin. They visit East Gordon, where an eighteenth-century ancestor of EW lived, and find Waugh graves in the churchyard. Max Beerbohm dies (see also 29 June below).

21 R.A. Butler (then Leader of the House of Commons) joins the house-party. A visit is paid to Abbotsford, home of Sir Walter Scott (EW was last there in 1941).
22 They leave after early Mass and Communion, and drive to Cambridge, where they stay with the Walstons.
23 They drive to London, where EW spends the rest of the day at his club and returns to Piers Court by train in the evening.
31 Congratulates Anthony Powell on receiving a CBE in the Birthday Honours; it is evident that EW is desirous of some honour, preferably a knighthood (see also 7 June 1956 and 7 May 1959 below).

June

3 (Sun) Inspects a house that is for sale near Stroud, but finds it impossible.
4 Father D'Arcy is an overnight guest; the Donaldsons come to dinner.
7 Writing to Nancy Mitford, describes the CBE as 'degrading' to a writer. (She accepts this award in 1972, after EW's death.)
13 Accepts an offer of £9500 for Piers Court.
14 To London for a three-night stay, most of his time there on this and the next day being divided between social engagements and his club.
15 To the theatre with his wife; EW sleeps during the performance.
16 To Ascot to visit his daughters.
17 Takes Communion at Brompton Oratory, then meets his daughters off the train, gives them lunch and takes them to the National Gallery; later they all drive home to Piers Court.
19 Engaged in house-hunting in Devon and Cornwall, without success; the next two days are spent similarly.
26 To London for another three-night stay, most of the time being spent in social engagements and heavy drinking.
29 Goes to Mass, then to Max Beerbohm's memorial service at St Paul's Cathedral. Lunches at the Ritz with Osbert Lancaster.
30 Drives to Radnorshire to inspect a house that is for sale.

July

5 (Thu) To London for his daughter Teresa's coming-out ball. The Waughs give a dinner-party at the Hyde Park Hotel. The ball is a success but EW becomes increasingly bored as the evening progresses. They return home exhausted the next day, but a small house-party descends on them the following day.
9 Drives with Laura and Teresa to inspect a house at Combe Florey; they like it and see it again the next day.
11 To London, where they attend a ball at St James's Palace.
12 Returns home.
18 Still house-hunting.
26 President Nasser of Egypt seizes the Suez Canal.
27 On this and the next two days Piers Court is full of Teresa's friends.
30 Diana Cooper pays a visit. She and EW visit Katharine Asquith and Ronald Knox.

August

1 (Wed) They take another look at the Combe Florey house.
8 They inspect a house near Exeter.
11 Goes with his daughter Margaret to stay with Pamela Berry at her home near Aylesbury.
12 With his daughter Margaret, attends Mass in Aylesbury.
16 Goes to London for the day with his wife.

September

11 (Tue) Learns, after much uncertainty, that his offer of £7500 for Combe Florey House, near Taunton, Somerset, has been accepted.
(A substantial sum needs to be spent on repairs and renovations.) Work on *The Ordeal of Gilbert Pinfold* has been resumed.
26 Writes to Ann Fleming about Rose Macaulay's *The Towers of Trebizond*.
28 Notes that, though he has had many idle days, his novel is progressing. Diary entries are very fitful at this time.

During this month, finds that he must pay an additional £257 towards the expenses of the coming-out ball, making a total of £757 – a blow to his straitened finances.

October

10 (Wed) Work on the novel is now going well, with a daily output of at least 1000 words.
11 Spends the day in London.
16 The *Daily Express* publishes a review of Rebecca West's *The Meaning of Treason*, a revised edition of which has just appeared in paperback: the reviewer appears to endorse the author's view of Waugh, Greene and others as creating through the 'intellectual climate' of their work conditions in which treason can flourish. (The Burgess and Maclean and Philby cases of recent years have made the matter intensely topical.) EW consults his solicitors and the result is two actions for libel (against, respectively, Pan Books and the *Daily Express*).
17 Jack McDougall of Chapman & Hall has read the first two-thirds of *The Ordeal of Gilbert Pinfold* and finds it 'terrific stuff'.
28 EW's 53rd birthday. The furniture is being removed from Piers Court. *Pinfold* is still not finished.
29 Tells Gabriel Fielding that he has been greatly impressed by Muriel Spark's first novel, *The Comforters*, especially the first half; he sends a warm commendation for the blurb and mentions that he is writing on a similar theme (see also 22 February 1957). Praises the novel again on 7 November in a letter to Ann Fleming, pointing out that the similarity of Muriel Spark's story to his own experiences is 'rather disconcerting'.
31 The Waugh family's last night at Piers Court. They are homeless for the next five weeks while workmen make Combe Florey House ready for them.

At this point there is a gap of just over four years in the *Diaries*.

November

At this time, asks Chapman & Hall whether a Francis Bacon painting can be used on the jacket of *Pinfold* (this is not done).

December

6 (Thu) The Waughs' furniture is moved into Combe Florey House.
13 Is successful in the case of *Waugh* vs. *Pan Books and Another*, heard in the Queen's Bench Division of the High Court: receives costs (but does not ask for damages), and unsold copies of the West book are withdrawn. (See 19 February 1957 for the next stage of his libel litigation.)

1957

January

10 (Thu) Harold Macmillan becomes Prime Minister after the resignation of Anthony Eden.
28 Tells Ann Fleming that he is spending a lot of money on furnishings for Combe Florey. Also tells her that John Minton, the artist, is dead, that Anthony Eden is dying and that he has visited Ronald Knox, who has had an operation for cancer, at a London hospital. Tells Diana Cooper that he is very pleased with his new ear-trumpet.

Pinfold is completed by the end of this month.

February

19 (Tue) The case of *Waugh* vs. *Beaverbrook Newspapers and Another*, arising from Nancy Spain's article on 17 March 1955, begins in the Queen's Bench Division of the High Court. EW and his wife and brother are called as witnesses. He has refused the defendants' offer to settle out of court, but is discouraged by the first day's proceedings.
20 After the jury have taken two hours to reach a verdict, EW is awarded £2000 damages as well as costs.

Later EW's complaint against Beaverbrook Newspapers in respect of the article published on 16 October is settled out of court, EW receiving £3000 and costs.

22 The *Spectator* publishes EW's enthusiastic review ('Something Fresh') of Muriel Spark's first novel, *The Comforters*; the review mentions that he has just completed 'a story on a similar theme'.
24 Instructs A.D. Peters to destroy earlier versions of the manuscript of *Pinfold*, which he has subjected to revision.

March

Early this month EW, who has been planning to go to Monte Carlo, agrees to spend three weeks looking after Ronald Knox, who is suffering from liver cancer (but does not know it). This is undertaken at the request of Katharine Asquith, who is herself undergoing treatment for arthritis. At Knox's request they go to the Imperial Hotel, Torquay. There EW makes final revisions to the galley proofs of *Pinfold*. It rains a great deal, and Knox is in low spirits. Laura Waugh spends a week with them, then EW and Knox move to another hotel at Sidmouth, after which (on the 20th) EW takes his dying friend for two weeks to Combe Florey, where Knox works on a lecture he is due to give in Oxford on 11 June (the lecture is duly given).

5 (Tue) Sends Nancy Mitford a highly entertaining account of his recent courtroom experiences.
22 The *Spectator* publishes EW's review of Randolph Churchill's *What I Said About the Press* under the title 'Randolph's Finest Hour'.

May

20 (Mon) To Monte Carlo with his wife for a week's holiday. Before leaving England, tells Knox that he is willing to act as his literary executor.
26 Tells Nancy Mitford that he is thoroughly enjoying Monte Carlo, where they are staying at the Hôtel de Paris; Laura plays roulette while he walks in the gardens, and they occasionally glimpse Sir Winston Churchill.

While in Monte Carlo, EW lunches with his brother Alec, who is staying in Nice. On the way home, the Waughs spend two nights at Chantilly with Diana Cooper.

June

6 (Thu) Tells Diana Cooper that he has read and enjoyed Douglas Woodruff's *The Tichborne Claimant*.

17 Declines Ann Fleming's invitation to attend the première of the film *Around the World in Eighty Days*, to be followed by a party in the Festival Gardens. Tells her that he has agreed to attend a Foyle's Literary Luncheon on 19 July to launch *Pinfold*: he dislikes the idea but has been persuaded to do so by Jack McDougall of Chapman & Hall. He is reading Stendhal's *La Chartreuse de Parme* in translation and cannot understand why it is regarded as the first psychological novel. Knox, who now knows that he is dying, asks EW and Laura to visit him.

22–3 To London, where he takes out his daughters.

27 Visits Knox at Mells. It is perhaps at this time that EW offers to write his biography.

At this time, is working on a film treatment of *Scoop* (the film is never made). His daughter Margaret, who is unhappy at school, is causing much anxiety, and is withdrawn from the school at the end of term.

During this month, tells Chapman & Hall that he refuses to appear on television.

July

19 (Fri) *The Ordeal of Gilbert Pinfold* is published. (The opening section has appeared in the *Observer* five days earlier under the title 'Portrait of the Artist in Middle Age'.) Is guest of honour at a Foyle's Literary Luncheon, at which his health is proposed by Malcolm Muggeridge (concerning whom EW is unflattering in a letter to Diana Cooper) and other guests include Father D'Arcy, Alec Guinness, Vivien Leigh, Rose Macaulay, Frank Pakenham and Douglas Woodruff. EW, who makes demonstrative use of his newly acquired ear-trumpet, refers in his speech to the three-week period of insanity he suffered three years earlier.

The reviews of *Pinfold*, on both sides of the Atlantic, are generally unfavourable.

August

Thomas C. Ryan's 'A Talk with Evelyn Waugh', based on an interview given earlier in the summer, appears in *The Sign*.

15 (Thu) Tells Robert Henriques that Pinfold's experiences are very closely based on his own, and that he has received letters from others who have had similar experiences. The same letter recommends Muriel Spark's *The Comforters*.

20 Tells Ann Fleming, who is about to pay a visit to Combe Florey, that he has recently stayed with the Duke and Duchess of Devonshire at Chatsworth and with Sir Osbert Sitwell at Renishaw Hall.

24 Ronald Knox dies at Mells.

31 The *New Statesman* publishes J.B. Priestley's article 'What was Wrong with Pinfold?': see also 13 September below.

September

1 (Sun) The *Sunday Times* publishes EW's 'A Tribute to Ronald Knox'. At about this time he begins the research for his biography.

13 The *Spectator* publishes 'Anything Wrong with Priestley?', EW's riposte to Priestley's article (see 31 August above); EW's piece is described by Stannard as his 'last journalistic *jeu d'esprit*'.

25 Tells Father Hubert van Zeller that he has begun to go through Knox's papers at Mells, and that he has no qualifications for writing his biography 'except love'.

28 Tells A.D. Peters that the biography will occupy him for at least a year, perhaps two years: he is at present working on it seven hours a day.

30 Tells Ann Fleming that he will have to go to Edinburgh soon to interview Knox's sister. (The visit takes place early in the following month.)

October

19 (Sat) Tells Chapman & Hall that another publisher is willing to pay an advance of £3000 for the Knox biography, but

that he would prefer to remain with his old publishers. (He is offered the same amount by Chapman & Hall.)
20 Thanks Anthony Powell for sending his new novel *At Lady Molly's*, which he has greatly enjoyed.
24 Thanks Nancy Mitford for sending her *Voltaire in Love*, which he is reading with great pleasure (see also 19 May 1959).
28 EW's 54th birthday.
29 Thanks Jack McDougall of Chapman & Hall for letting him see the manuscript of Frederick J. Stopp's *Evelyn Waugh: Portrait of an Artist*, published the following year. Has made various corrections and suggests that the book is over-long and repetitious (15,000 words are subsequently cut).

December

11 (Wed) Thanks Brian Franks of the Hyde Park Hotel for a dinner that he has attended there.
29 Receives a visit from Father Hubert van Zeller, who is helping him with biographical research, and another priest.

1958

January

4 (Sat) Publication of Ronald Knox's will, which leaves his manuscripts and copyrights (but not royalties) to EW.
10 Suggests to Graham Greene that they meet before EW goes to Rhodesia early in February.

February

5 (Wed) Attends the first night of Graham Greene's play *The Potting Shed*, and congratulates him warmly the next day. (He is less enthusiastic about the play in a letter to his wife written at the same time.)
7 Snow delays the flight to Rhodesia, but the plane finally leaves

in the evening, stops at midnight in Rome and in Khartoum for breakfast. At Salisbury EW is met by his nephew Andrew Waugh, and is driven in the dark to the home of his hosts, Lord and Lady Acton. He spends about three weeks there and meets the Governor-General (the Earl of Dalhousie) and others. It rains a great deal and he is not impressed with the country, but he collects much useful Knox material from Lady Acton, who had a close relationship with Knox in the 1930s and for whom EW comes to have a very high regard.

March

14 (Sun) Gives his impressions of Brian Howard to Lord Baldwin.

April

By this time some 40,000 words of the Knox biography have been written.
   Early in the month, lunches with Anthony Powell.
18 (Sat) Thanks John McDougall (of Chapman & Hall) for a recent lunch and tells him that he believes he has only one or two years left in which he will be capable of original work.
20 Tells Diana Cooper that a presentation copy of her autobiographical volume *The Rainbow Comes and Goes* arrived the previous day and that he has been reading it with enormous pleasure.

May

21 (Thu) Tells Ann Fleming that he is depressed over his financial affairs, and praises Diana Cooper's autobiography *The Rainbow Comes and Goes*.

June

9 (Tue) Auberon Waugh is seriously injured in an accident with a machine-gun in Cyprus, where he is doing his military service. His mother flies out alone to be with him.
13 Tells Diana Cooper that he will fly out to accompany his wife home if Auberon dies.
23 Tells Lady Acton that he has recently been to Ampleforth (Roman Catholic public school in Yorkshire) and to St Edmund's Hall, Oxford, in connection with his Knox researches.
25 Laura Waugh, still in Cyprus (where she is staying at Government House), asks EW to write to Auberon and to ask other members of the family to do so.

Auberon is flown home in early July and is transferred to a London hospital, where EW visits him three weeks later.

July

8 (Wed) Writes to his son Auberon, telling him that he is unable to visit him because he has an engagement to visit Munich to participate in the city's 800th birthday celebrations.

Leaves for Germany a day or two later, his first visit to that country, travelling overland via Ostend and Stuttgart. In Munich he gives a one-hour reading to a large audience.

16 Back at Combe Florey by this date and writes to Christopher Sykes asking him to visit Auberon, who has now been moved to another London nursing home, and suggesting suitable gifts.

August

6 (Thu) Tries to placate Edith Sitwell, who has taken offence at his sending her an appeal for a contribution to the Ronald Knox Memorial Fund.
28 Writes a very amusing letter to Ann Fleming about his experiences in Munich. The Woodruffs have been to stay at Combe Florey for the weekend.

October

9 (Fri) Pope Pius XII dies.
13 Has been reading Muriel Spark's *Memento Mori*.
28 EW's 55th birthday. Cardinal Roncalli elected Pope John XXIII.

November

18 (Wed) Writes to John Donaldson about Vladimir Nabokov's *Lolita* (see also 19 May 1959).

December

The biography of Knox is completed by this time.
31 (Thu) Tells Lord Kinross that he is going to East Africa again very shortly. The same letter contains some observations on Dame Rose Macaulay, who had died on 30 October.

1959

January

24 (Sat) Auberon Waugh enters the Westminster Hospital for further surgery.
28 Sets off for Genoa, the first stage of his journey to Rhodesia. There he spends two days with Diana Cooper and visits, with great interest, the Campo Santo cemetery.
31 Embarks on the *Rhodesia Castle*, which carries him via Port Said, Aden, Mombasa and Zanzibar to Dar-es-Salaam. During the voyage, reads a great deal and writes frequently to his wife, urging her to fly out to South Africa and join him on the return voyage (she declines).

March

4 (Wed) Writes to his wife from Tanga, Tanganyika: he has been in Dar es Salaam, has dined with the Paramount Chief of the Chagga tribe, and is now touring the hilly country inland; will soon go to Rhodesia to visit the Actons. Is well and in better spirits than usual.

April

11 (Sat) Returns home.
18 Goes to Oxford for the unveiling of a bust of Ronald Knox at Trinity College and delivers a speech (published in the next issue of the *Tablet* as 'The Quintessence of Oxford'). Katharine Asquith and the Woodruffs are among those present. Dines at Trinity College.
22 Tells Lady Acton that he has sent the proofs of his biography to Knox's sister, Lady Peck.

During this month Mark Gerson visits Combe Florey and takes photographs of Waugh and his family and of the house.

May

4 (Mon) Tells Mary Lygon that he has recently read Lady Curzon's *Reminiscences*, published in 1955, where it is implied that he had a homosexual relationship with Alfred Duggan.
7 Is offered a CBE: he receives the news with anger and declines the honour, having hoped for a knighthood. For his later regrets, see 7 May 1964.
19 Tells Nancy Mitford how much he has enjoyed rereading her *Voltaire in Love*, and expresses disapproval of Cyril Connolly's recent unfavourable review (in the *Sunday Times*) of the second volume of Diana Cooper's autobiography, *The Light of Common Day*. (He has recently been present at Hatchard's bookshop in Piccadilly when she has been signing copies of her book.) He thinks highly of Nabokov's *Lolita* as pornography but not as literature.

June

20 (Sat) Beginning of a six-week printing strike in Britain.
29 Congratulates Graham Greene on the success of his play *The Complaisant Lover*, which is receiving good reviews and which EW hopes to see. Has read a biography (by Priscilla Johnston) of the calligrapher Edward Johnston.

July

8 (Wed) Expresses his doubts to Jack McDougall of Chapman & Hall whether it would be worthwhile his signing copies of his books at Hatchard's bookshop (he does not do so).
29 Comments to John Montgomery on an American proposal to make a film based on *Men at Arms* and *Officers and Gentlemen*.
31 Tells Anne Fremantle that he is working, totally without enthusiasm, on a travel book about Africa in order to cover the expenses of his recent visit to Rhodesia.

At about this time, expresses an interest in writing a biography of Holman Hunt (the project is never carried out).

August

26 (Wed) Writes to his son Auberon concerning the novel the latter has written. (Auberon has spent some time in Italy and is about to go up to Christ Church, Oxford.)

September

17 (Thu) *The Times* publishes a letter from EW expressing disapproval of a reviewer's use of the term 'upper-middle-class' in connection with some of the characters in Ivy Compton-Burnett's novel *A House and its Head*.
27 To Dunster, to a lunch at which he meets the Oxford historian A.L. Rowse.

October

The Life of the Right Reverend Ronald Knox appears early this month, having already been serialized in the *Tablet*.

2 (Fri) The *Spectator* publishes EW's 'Aspirations of a Mugwump', in which he states that, though he hopes the Conservatives are successful in the forthcoming general election, he has never voted and never will.
6 To London, where he lunches with Ann Fleming and dines with Mary Lygon.
7 Lunches with Jack McDougall of Chapman & Hall.
8 General Election, in which the Conservatives under Harold Macmillan remain in power with an increased majority.
12 Admits to Douglas Woodruff that the Knox biography contains many printing errors and errors of fact.
13 Thanks Graham Greene for his review of the Knox biography in the *Observer* two days earlier.
20 Tells Lady Acton that the reviews of the Knox biography have been generally kind.
22 Thanks Maurice Bowra for his hospitality in Oxford the previous week.
24 The *Spectator* publishes a letter from EW in which he complains about the behaviour of Malcolm Muggeridge, who has revealed in the *New Statesman* that the figure identified only as 'C' in the Knox biography was the Prime Minister, Harold Macmillan, and has suggested that EW concealed his identity in the interests of the Conservative Party. (Muggeridge has extracted the information from EW's mother-in-law.)
28 EW's 56th birthday.
30 The Archbishop of Westminster tells EW that both the factual errors in the Knox biography and the tone of the book convey a misleading impression of its subject.

Towards the end of the month EW's son Auberon receives a fractured skull in a car accident.

December

14 (Mon) Tells A.D. Peters not to decline on his behalf an invitation to be interviewed on television, since he may be in need of the money. Stanley Spencer dies.

28 The *Daily Mail* publishes EW's article 'I See Nothing But Boredom . . .' – a pessimistic contribution to a series in which various contributors contemplate the prospect of the new decade. Towards the end of the month, asks Joan Saunders to undertake some research in the back files of newspapers to provide material for the novel that becomes *Unconditional Surrender*.

1960

February

2 (Tue) Verve Records of Beverly Hills offer EW $1000 for recording a one-hour reading from his work (see also 28 April below).
17 By this date, has undertaken with his wife a trip to Venice and Monte Carlo (where Randolph Churchill has turned up); they have spent one night in Homburg (not enjoyed), then she has gone home and he has continued to Rome, where he has had lunch with the French Ambassador and has attended a public audience of the Pope. (This trip has been financed by the *Daily Mail*, which is paying £2000 and providing free travel for four articles.) He is now going to Athens with his daughter Margaret.

March

11 (Fri) The *Daily Telegraph* reports the forthcoming publication of Auberon Waugh's first novel (*The Foxglove Saga*).
25 Tells Lady Acton that the Woodruffs visited Combe Florey the previous week and that he will as usual make his Easter retreat at Downside.

April

5 (Tue) Tells A.D. Peters that he is prepared to accept any journalistic commissions, however trivial, as he badly needs the money.

21 Writes an interesting letter to David Wright, co-editor of the literary magazine X, declining an invitation to contribute, explaining that he cannot afford to write for publications that do not pay well, confessing his ignorance of the work of the younger generation of writers, and describing at some length his views on the role of the older, established writer.
26 Kenneth Allsop's account of an interview with EW ('Waugh Looks Forward to Poverty') appears in the *Daily Mail*. (Allsop's further recollections of the interview are contained in his article 'War and Peace', published in the *Sunday Times* on 8 April 1973.)
28 Tells Ann Fleming that he is about to begin work on *Unconditional Surrender* (at this stage tentatively titled *Sword of Honour*); he has read, with some disappointment, Anthony Powell's *Casanova's Chinese Restaurant* (he reviews it in the *Spectator* on 24 June). Has spent a day in London the previous week and recorded readings from *Vile Bodies* and *Helena*, with interlinking commentary (see 2 February above). Declines an invitation for 6 May, when the marriage of Princess Margaret to Antony Armstrong-Jones (later Lord Snowdon) takes place – a match of which he strongly disapproves.

May

17 (Tue) Tells Father Philip Caraman that he has been to see Terence Rattigan's play *Ross* and thought very badly of it and, with the notable exception of Alec Guinness (whom he visits afterwards in his dressing-room), the actors. During this visit to his daughter Margaret, who is now working in London, they have also been to the Soane Museum, St Paul's Cathedral and the Stanley Spencer exhibition at the Royal Academy, and have dined with Mary Lygon.
18 Tells Nancy Mitford he has been much disturbed by reading *Hons and Rebels*, by her sister Jessica Mitford; he has also read Lampedusa's *The Leopard*. Has resolved (perhaps not entirely seriously) never to visit London again, his recent visit having been so exhausting.
26 Tells Ann Fleming that towards the end of his London visit he suffered a temporary recurrence of the symptoms described

in *The Ordeal of Gilbert Pinfold* and that he is losing his memory. He adds that this day in 1917 (it is Ascension Day) was the unhappiest of his life.

June

- 6 (Mon) Tells Tom Driberg that he has read his article 'MRA, The New Offensive' (on the Moral Re-armament movement) in the *New Statesman*.
- 7 The BBC broadcasts a radio adaptation of *The Ordeal of Gilbert Pinfold*.
- 11 Thanks Driberg for writing appreciatively about the Knox biography. Tells him that he did not hear the radio adaptation of *The Ordeal of Gilbert Pinfold*, but has agreed to be interviewed on television in John Freeman's 'Face to Face' series (see 26th below).
- 18 Thanks Anthony Powell for a presentation copy of *Casanova's Chinese Restaurant* (see 28 April above); *At Lady Molly's* is his favourite in the 'Dance to the Music of Time' sequence.
- 21 Tells Nancy Mitford he has seen, and disliked, Eugene Ionesco's play *Rhinoceros*.
- 26 The television interview with John Freeman, recorded about two weeks earlier, is broadcast.

July

A revised version of *Brideshead Revisited* (the revisions mainly taking the form of deletions) appears during this month.
- 21 (Thu) Tells Erle Stanley Gardner that he is a great admirer of his novels and corrects him in his use of the term 'davenport'.

At about this time his daughter Teresa tells him that she intends to marry an American, John D'Arms.

August

By the end of this month, has completed 30,000 words of *Unconditional Surrender* (now provisionally titled *Conventional Weapons*).

September

A Tourist in Africa is published during this month.
5 (Mon) Tells Ann Fleming that he has read Ian Fleming's *The Thrilling Cities* also *Picnic at Porokorro* (published in 1958) by her brother Hugo Charteris (the latter book he judges worthless).
22 Tells Ann Fleming that he is not sending presentation copies of *A Tourist in Africa*: it is a 'pot boiler' and he has a poor opinion of it.

October

5 (Wed) Tells Ann Fleming that work on his novel is going well and that he hopes to finish it by Christmas (but see 14 February 1961).
11 Thanks Muriel Spark for sending him a copy of her novel *The Bachelors*, which he praises very highly.
28 EW's 57th birthday.

November

At this time, declines an invitation to attend his son Auberon's 21st birthday party: he fears unwelcome attention from the press.
10 (Thu) Tells Ann Fleming that he has seen Peregrine Worsthorne of the *Sunday Telegraph* in London and, having drunk a good deal, has promised to go to Algeria to report on the war there (he subsequently withdraws from this promise). Deplores the outcome of the *Lady Chatterley* trial, being unable to agree that Lawrence is a great writer. Nancy Mitford arrives at Combe Florey for a visit.
18 The *Spectator* publishes a letter from EW declaring that D. H. Lawrence's paintings are worthless.

December

Resumes his diary at this time, but from now on there are many gaps and it is sometimes a collection of notes and reflections rather than a diary.

This month's *London Magazine* contains EW's review of Nancy Mitford's *Don't Tell Alfred*, and this month's *Encounter* contains a reply by EW to an article by Frank Kermode ('Mr. Waugh's Cities') in the previous month's issue.

9 The *Spectator* publishes a letter from EW on the death penalty as a blessing that enables the condemned to prepare for a known hour of death.

11 Thanks Graham Greene for sending him his story 'A Visit to Morin', published in the *London Magazine*.

14 Goes to London to attend the annual dinner given by the Hyde Park Hotel to its regular guests (an occasion referred to by EW as the 'vomit' or 'vomitorium').

24 Tells Diana Cooper that he has spent the summer indoors working on his novel and looks forward to going abroad as soon as it is finished. (He has been exploring with his literary agent, A.D. Peters, the possibility of a trip paid for by some newspaper or magazine, and on 25 November has expressed regret that no publication seems prepared to pay for him to go to India.)

28 With his wife, lunches at the home of Christopher Sykes and his wife.

1961

January

3 (Tue) Apologizes to Graham Greene, whose novel *A Burnt-Out Case* he has just read, for helping to promulgate the notion of Greene as a Catholic writer, which he sees as one of the issues of the book. (Three days earlier, has recorded in his diary that he feels unable to review it, as the *Daily Mail* has asked him to do; he tells Greene this on the 5th, in response to an understanding and affectionate reply from Greene.)

4 Tells Elizabeth Pakenham that he considers that Oxford has 'gone wrong' in recent years (the Pakenhams have decided to send one of their sons to Cambridge).

30 Notes in his diary that he has done nothing on this day but read American detective fiction.

February

4 (Sat) Goes to Mells, where Christopher Hollis is also a guest. Frank Pakenham telephones to announce the death of his elder brother, the Earl of Longford, and to ask EW to write an appreciation of him for the *Observer* (EW is unenthusiastic, but writes the piece three days later after a formal invitation from the newspaper).
5 Dines with Anthony Powell and his wife.
14 Tells Ann Fleming that he hopes to finish his novel by the end of the month (see 4 April below).

March

24 (Fri) In the course of reading the transcripts of the *Lady Chatterley* trial (published by Penguin Books), realizes that one of the sources of the hallucinations he had suffered (and fictionalized in *Pinfold*) is a scene in Lawrence's novel which he read long ago but had forgotten.
27 Tells Ann Fleming that he is going to Downside for the Easter retreat.
At about this time Auberon Waugh tells his father that he intends to marry Lady Teresa Onslow, a Protestant, whose parents (the Earl and Countess of Onslow) are divorced.

April

4 (Tue) Tells A.D. Peters that *Unconditional Surrender* is finished (that title is now decided on); suggests that the trilogy might be made into a film starring Alec Guinness; does not expect to write another novel for five or six years.
19 Sends A.D. Peters a selection of titles for the American edition of *Unconditional Surrender*.
27 A.D. Peters tells EW that his projected three volumes of autobiography could bring in an income of about £5000 a year for six years.

May

10 (Wed) P.G. Wodehouse expresses his concern that EW's broadcast on 15 July (see below) will include an attack on 'Cassandra' (the *Daily Mirror* columnist, William Connor), who is one of Wodehouse's friends.
22 Thanks Daphne Fielding for sending him a copy of her novel *The Adonis Garden*, which he has enjoyed and discusses at some length.
31 Goes to London and attends a dinner at the Mansion House.

June

1 (Thu) Gives a party at Quaglino's restaurant in London to celebrate Teresa Waugh's impending marriage to John D'Arms; among the guests are Diana Cooper, Ann Fleming and Alec Waugh. The wedding takes place in Taunton, Somerset on the 3rd.
19 Goes to London for two nights, and on the 20th records a talk for the BBC (see 15 July below), dining afterwards with the Director-General (Sir Hugh Carleton Greene, brother of Graham) and Christopher Sykes. Has told Sykes on the 9th to make arrangements for his entertainment on the evening of the 19th, and has expressed an interest in seeing the satirical revue *Beyond the Fringe*.

July

1 (Sat) Auberon Waugh marries Lady Teresa Onslow.
2 Ernest Hemingway dies.
15 The BBC broadcasts a radio talk by EW, 'An Act of Homage and Reparation to P.G. Wodehouse'. Notes in his diary that he has just reread Hemingway's *Fiesta*, having been prompted to do so by the writer's recent suicide.
18 Has been making preparations to begin the writing of his autobiography.

September

6 (Wed) Tells Nina Bourne of the New York publishing house Simon & Schuster, who has sent him a copy of Joseph Heller's *Catch 22*, that it is improper and excessively long, though amusing in places.
At about this time, goes to London and (with Diana Cooper) sees Peter Schaffer's *The Private Ear and the Public Eye*, in which he is greatly impressed by Maggie Smith's performance. Afterwards he has paid visits to Pamela Berry and Penelope Betjeman.

23 Tells Ann Fleming that he and Margaret will be unable to visit the Flemings at their home in Jamaica during their forthcoming visit to the Caribbean. Has read, with admiration, Angus Wilson's *The Old Men at the Zoo*. On 13 October the *Spectator* publishes a long letter from EW defending Wilson's novel against the unfavourable reviews it has received, specifically one by John Mortimer.

October

Unconditional Surrender is published. (The American edition is titled *The End of the Battle*.)

5 (Thu) Attends a dinner at the Garrick Club to celebrate the publication of Harold Acton's *The Last Bourbons of Naples*; he sits next to Arthur Waley and recalls meeting him nearly 40 years earlier at the Sitwells' home, Renishaw Hall.

26 Thanks Graham Greene for sending him his *In Search of a Character: Two African Journals*, and urges Greene to accompany him on his forthcoming journey to British Guiana.

28 EW's 58th birthday. Thanks Tom Driberg for remembering it, and assures him that he has not taken umbrage at an article ('Stout Party') concerning him, and partly written by Driberg, that has appeared in the *New Statesman*.

29 Thanks Cyril Connolly for his review of *Unconditional Surrender*, and denies that the magazine *Survival* in the novel is based on *Horizon*, to which he pays tribute; he also denies that Spruce in the novel is based on Connolly. (Subsequent letters make it clear that Ann Fleming has mischievously made these suggestions to Connolly.)

31 Tells Anthony Powell that he has not intended the trilogy to be interpreted as having a happy ending.

November

During this month, at a lunch given by Pamela Berry, meets Stephen Spender for the first time.

24 (Fri) Learns that his daughter Teresa is pregnant, and is pleased by the news.

26 Accompanied by his daughter Margaret, and at the expense of the *Daily Mail*, sets sail on the *Stella Polaris* for British Guiana. On arrival they spend about two weeks in Trinidad as guests of Lord and Lady Hailes.

1962

January

12 (Fri) Writes to his wife from Georgetown, telling her that he and Margaret have been travelling extensively in British Guiana, visiting (among much else) a bauxite mine and sugar and rice plantations. He has met Dr Jagan, the Marxist Prime Minister.

February

In the middle of the month, EW and Margaret return to England, sailing from Trinidad (where they again stay with Lord and Lady Hailes) on the *Antilles*; among their fellow-passengers are Harold Nicolson and his wife Victoria Sackville-West. During a stop at Lisbon, EW sees Daphne Fielding.

March

7 (Wed) Tells Nancy Mitford he has enjoyed Christopher

Isherwood's *Down There on a Visit* and has read John Sparrow's article on D.H. Lawrence's *Lady Chatterley's Lover* published in *Encounter*. Has asked for references to himself in Rose Macaulay's forthcoming (and posthumous) *Letters to a Friend* to be deleted.

20 The *Daily Mail* publishes 'Here They Are, the English Lotus-Eaters', the first of the articles based on EW's visit to British Guiana. ('Manners and Morals' appears in two parts on 12 and 13 April. The newspaper never publishes the fourth article, which it judges insufficiently light-hearted; this is eventually published, as 'Return to Eldorado', by the *Sunday Times* on 12 August.)

27 Tells Nancy Mitford that he is reading George Eliot's *Middlemarch* for the first time, and with pleasure.

April

1 (Sun) Pope John XXIII insists that Latin be retained as the language of the Roman Catholic liturgy.

June

16 (Sat) Tells Ann Fleming he has been reading Vladimir Nabokov's *Pale Fire*, Anthony Powell's *The Kindly Ones* and John Sparrow's replies to the critics of his article on *Lady Chatterley's Lover*.

July

At about this time, discusses with Peter Greenham, artist and royal portraitist, the possibility of a portrait of himself and his daughter Margaret (the plan is never carried out).

4 (Wed) Tells Nancy Mitford he has been reading Rupert Hart-Davis's edition of the letters of Oscar Wilde. Is at work on his autobiography. Declines an invitation to review Ronald Firbank's *The New Rhythm and Other Pieces*: once an admirer of Firbank, he now dislikes his work.

August

During this month Margaret Waugh tells her father that she intends to marry Giles FitzHerbert, an Irish Catholic (the first inkling EW has received of an attachment she has formed some time ago).
His distress at this news is evident in letters to his close friends at this time, especially in a letter to Diana Cooper on the 28th. The marriage takes place in October.

October

5 (Fri) Goes to London and attends a party given by the Flemings to celebrate the opening night of *Dr No*, the film based on one of Ian Fleming's James Bond stories, but judges the film to be rubbish. Afterwards they dine at a restaurant, the other guests including Cyril Connolly and Diana Cooper.
11 Tells Ann Fleming of his delight that he has made an appearance in *The Times* crossword: the solution to one of the previous day's clues was 'Brideshead'. Vatican Council opens in Rome.
27 Tells Nancy Mitford that the Second Vatican Council is an event of great importance. (He is proved right, since it approves the use of vernacular liturgies.)
In the last week of the month the Cuban missile crisis occurs.

November

8 (Thu) Father Caraman, who is to visit Combe Florey, says he is prepared to say Mass in the house.
23 The *Spectator* publishes EW's article 'The Same Again, Please'.
25 Archbishop Heenan congratulates EW on his article.

December

2 (Sun) The *Sunday Telegraph* publishes 'My Father', a version of part of EW's autobiography, on which he is now at work.

1963

February

At the beginning of the month, is on holiday in Mentone, France, but tells Nancy Mitford on the 2nd that he is bored and lonely. (His wife has accompanied him to Mentone, but is at this time on a ten-day visit to Naples.)

Later in the month, tells Nancy Mitford that things improved after Laura's return to Mentone. The Pope is said to be dying, and EW has written 'An Appreciation of Pope John' for the *Saturday Evening Post* (it is published on 27 July). Is seeking ecclesiastical permission to build a vault for twelve occupants at Combe Florey.

20 (Wed) Tells Ann Fleming that he went to Mentone to work but accomplished nothing. He and Laura visited Vence and Monte Carlo.

March

13 (Wed) Tells Ann Fleming he is reading, with great enjoyment, Robert Rhodes James's biography of Lord Rosebery. Has been revising *Basil Seal Rides Again*, which he wishes to dedicate to her. Is lame and overweight.
16 The *Tablet* publishes a letter from EW on the Eastern Uniate Churches.
18 Commends Robert Rhodes James's biography of Lord Rosebery to Diana Cooper.
28 Tells Ann Fleming that he has been rereading the diaries he kept at the ages of 16 and 17, for use in his autobiography.

April

2 (Tue) Thanks Randolph Churchill for the gift of Francis Crease's *Thirty-four Decorative Designs*, but is suspicious of Churchill's motives in requesting various (and sometimes multiple) presentation copies of EW's works.
22 Attends a luncheon given by the Prime Minister (Harold Macmillan) in honour of the Italian Ambassador; among the

other guests are Archbishop Heenan, Harold Nicolson, John Sparrow and the newspaper proprietor Roy Thomson.
25 Describes to Diana Cooper a recent visit to La Pietra, Harold Acton's house near Florence.

May

7 (Tue) Describes to Ann Fleming a recent visit to Rome with Diana Cooper.
24 Tells Nancy Mitford that he has been made a Companion of Literature (see 25 June below).

June

3 (Mon) Death of Pope John XXIII; his successor, Pope Paul VI, is enthroned at the end of the month.
4 John Profumo resigns his parliamentary seat.
19 Asks Alfred Duggan whether he objects to being mentioned by name in EW's autobiography.
25 Receives the Companionship of the Royal Society of Literature in a ceremony at the Skinners' Hall. His co-recipients, Aldous Huxley and Edith Sitwell, are unable to attend and are represented by, respectively, Stephen Spender and Sacheverell Sitwell. Laura and Margaret Waugh, Father Caraman and Ann Fleming are present, and EW's speech is a success.

August

At this time Father Caraman, who has been ejected from the editorship of the *Month* in painful circumstances that have caused both EW and his daughter Margaret great concern, is a frequent visitor to Combe Florey, often saying Mass in the house.
7 (Wed) Tells Ann Fleming that he is writing, unenthusiastically, a preface for an American edition of John Galsworthy's *A Man of Property*. At this time, is still fitfully at work on *A Little Learning*.
13 Alec Waugh tells EW that he intends to marry Virginia Sorensen, an American writer of the Mormon faith, with whom

he has been living for nine years, and asks for his brother's understanding. EW does not respond. (In the event, the marriage does not take place until 1969, when both Alec's former wife and EW are dead.)

September

7 (Sat) The *Tablet* publishes a letter from EW in response to an article by the Abbot of Downside on the Vatican Council.

October

18 (Fri) Harold Macmillan resigns as Prime Minister and is succeeded by Alec Douglas-Home.
25 With his wife, pays a two-day visit to Ian and Ann Fleming, the former of whom is seriously ill (he dies on 12 August 1964). Maurice Bowra is also a guest.
28 Publication of *Basil Seal Rides Again or The Rake's Regress*, EW's last work of fiction, on his 60th birthday. Dedicated to Ann Fleming, it appears in a limited edition of 750 signed and numbered copies. EW has earned $250 for publication in *Esquire* and £3000 for British serial rights. The reviews are generally favourable.

November

2 (Sat) Thanks Maurice Bowra for his birthday gift of a Maurice Baring manuscript.
14 Attends a reunion of the Oxford University Railway Club, held on the Brighton Belle (historic train running between London and Brighton) and organized by John Sutro, with whom EW has been corresponding frequently on this subject for the past three months. The other guests include Harold Acton, Robert Boothby, Cyril Connolly, Roy Harrod, Christopher Sykes and EW's son Auberon and son-in-law Giles FitzHerbert.
18 Thanks Alfred Duggan for sending a copy of his *The Story of the Crusades*.

22   Assassination of President John F. Kennedy in Dallas. Aldous Huxley dies.

December

3   (Tue)   Tells John McDougall that *A Little Learning* is finished, and that Richard Young, the prototype of Captain Grimes in *Decline and Fall*, has given written permission for references to him to be made.

1964

January

7   (Tue)   Recommends Mary McCarthy's *The Group* to Lady Acton.

February

16   (Sun)   Appears on television in the BBC 'Monitor' programme. During this month the Waughs pay another visit to Mentone; later in the year (6 August) he tells Nancy Mitford that the trip was spoilt by his illness.

March

3   (Tue)   Tells Ann Fleming that he intends to spend Easter in Rome in order to avoid the 'horrors' of the services conducted in English. This visit to Rome is marred by Diana Cooper's illness.

April

4   (Sat)   Death of Alfred Duggan. EW and his wife later attend the Requiem Mass (see also 2 July below).

At this time, tells Diana Cooper that he has made up his longstanding quarrel with Randolph Churchill, who is seriously ill.

May

7 (Thu) Seeks to persuade Graham Greene to accept a Companionship of the Royal Society of Literature (EW has been asked to undertake this task by Lord Birkenhead, Chairman of the Society); tells him that he is now 'ashamed' of having refused the CBE. Greene declines the honour.

July

10 (Fri) The *Spectator* publishes EW's 'Alfred Duggan: An Appreciation'. (This obituary had previously been given as a broadcast talk.)
19 Tells Randolph Churchill that he is enjoying Winston S. Churchill's *Marlborough: His Life and Times* (1933), a copy of which Randolph has sent him a few days earlier.
23 Alec Waugh visits his brother for the last time.

August

6 (Thu) Describes himself to Nancy Mitford as an old man, rarely leaving the house, physically weak, and hearing frequently of the deaths of his contemporaries.
12 Ian Fleming dies.
20 Sends his condolences to Ann Fleming, and urges her not to remarry.
23 The *Sunday Telegraph* publishes 'Words with Evelyn Waugh', based on an interview given at Combe Florey at EW's suggestion (he has been anxious to correct some statements concerning him in the issue of 16 August).

September

A Little Learning (subtitled *The First Volume of an Autobiography*) is published at the beginning of the month: with this event, according to Stannard, EW's life 'effectively ended' (*Later Years*, p. 480). The book is in general well received; its promised successors are never written.

4   (Fri) Dudley Carew reproaches EW with misrepresenting him and their relationship as schoolboys in *A Little Learning*.
9   Katharine Asquith complains that she has been shocked by an anecdote in *A Little Learning* referring to W.R.B. Young, the original of Captain Grimes in *Decline and Fall*. EW replies on the 14th, defending himself against the charge of obscenity. He also tells her that he has dined in London with Cardinal Heenan (Archbishop of Westminster) and has visited Anthony and Violet Powell.

October

This month, EW and his wife spend three weeks in Spain. On 10 November, tells Ann Fleming that he has found the trip very tiring and does not wish to undertake any more travels.

15   In the General Election the Conservatives are defeated by a narrow majority and Harold Wilson forms a Labour government.

November

1   (Sun) Tells Diana Cooper that he is depressed by the outcome of the Vatican Council.
14   Declines an invitation from Brian Franks to attend the annual dinner at the Hyde Park Hotel, which he has been accustomed to attend for many years; he is eventually persuaded to go, but does not enjoy the occasion (see 14 December below).

December

At about this time Diana Cooper tells him that she is seriously worried about his physical state and his dependence on alcohol and drugs.

9 (Wed) Edith Sitwell dies.
14 In London for the banquet at the Hyde Park Hotel. Two days later, tells his daughter Margaret that he was scarcely able to touch the food and wine and, having felt unwell beforehand, now feels worse. While in London, has attended part of the Requiem Mass for Edith Sitwell.
24 In response to an enquiry from Constantine FitzGibbon, who is writing a biography of Dylan Thomas, describes his recollections of a dinner party given by Cyril Connolly at which Thomas was present.

1965

January

4 (Mon) T.S. Eliot dies.
8 Ann Fleming tells EW that she is deeply concerned about his physical state, and asks whether he is seeing a doctor and a dentist.
12 Learns from A.D. Peters that he is heavily in debt to the Inland Revenue.
24 Sir Winston Churchill dies.
27 Tells Ann Fleming that he has had all his teeth pulled out and is thinking of acquiring false teeth (he does so, probably in March). Has refused numerous invitations to report the funeral of Sir Winston Churchill: his opinion of Churchill is a very poor one.
29 In response to his father's criticisms, Auberon Waugh defends his decision to join the staff of the *Daily Sketch*.

During this month, angrily declines an invitation to attend a Foyle's Literary Luncheon to launch *Objections to Roman Catholicism*, edited by Michael de la Bedoyere.

April

Shortly before Easter, notes in his diary that during the past year the process of vernacularizing the Roman Catholic liturgy has continued despite protests. On 15 April (Maundy Thursday), enquires of Monsignor McReavy whether attendance at Mass is required of the faithful: he finds the new liturgy so deeply uncongenial that he is tempted to transgress what he believes to be a strict requirement.

On the same day, makes the last entry in his diary: it records the death of Philip Dunne, who was one year younger than himself.

July

17 (Sun) John Betjeman sends thanks for a visit to EW (his last) at Combe Florey.
30 Tells his daughter Margaret that he has seen the film *The Knack* without much understanding or enjoyment.

September

Sword of Honour, the single-volume version of the trilogy of novels, produced by EW during the summer, is published.
5 (Mon) Tells Nancy Mitford that changes in the Roman Catholic Church have caused him great grief. He has enjoyed Hemingway's *A Movable Feast*, but he rarely goes out now and is very bored.
18 The *Tablet* publishes a letter from EW (his last to that journal), attacking an article that has appeared in the American Catholic journal *Commonweal*.
23 Tells Diana Cooper he has read Nigel Dennis's biography of Swift and finds temperamental resemblances between the latter and himself.

October

28 (Fri) EW's 62nd birthday.

December

19 (Mon) Margaret Waugh, who has recently spent a day with her father, expresses her concern that he is not eating and is

losing his strength, reminds him that it is only four years
since they set off together for British Guiana, and urges him
to seek medical help.

1966

January

During this month, congratulates Graham Greene on the award
of the Companionship of Honour and thanks him for a presentation copy of *The Comedians*, which he praises highly. For himself, he adds, 1965 was 'a bad year'. At about the same time he
tells Ann Fleming that it was a year of poor health and physical
weakness, inability to work and the loss of friends through death.

February

28 (Mon) Tells Nancy Mitford that his health is a little improved and that he intends to continue with his autobiography. He has evidently seen a draft of Maurice Bowra's autobiography (published later in the year as *Memories 1898–1939*): as a result of EW's denial, Bowra has removed a passage stating that EW and Nancy Mitford have had a sexual relationship.

March

6 (Sun) Tells Alec Waugh that, although he has been depressed, he has not suffered from hallucinations, as some press reports have claimed. He has been unable to work, being overwhelmed by having contracted to write four books – on the Crusades, the Popes and American history in addition to a second volume of autobiography.

9 Tells Lady Mosley that he has aged greatly in the past two years and has lost interest in life: the results of the Vatican Council have had a profound effect upon him.

30 Assures Lady Mosley that Lucy in *Work Suspended* was not

based on her, and repeats his conviction that recent reforms have irretrievably damaged the liturgy.

April

At Easter, his daughters Margaret and Harriet visit Combe Florey, the former with her husband and daughter. On Easter Sunday (10 April) morning, EW attends Mass celebrated by Father Caraman at Wiveliscombe, a nearby village. (Father Caraman, now living in Norway, is visiting England and staying with the Herberts at Pixton.) After Mass, the Waughs, Father Caraman and various friends return to Combe Florey, and there EW is found dead in a lavatory later in the morning, the cause being cerebral thrombosis. An autopsy is held, but no inquest is deemed necessary. The funeral is private, and a memorial service is held at Westminster Cathedral on 21 April; the address is given by Father Caraman and among those present (apart from family members) are John Betjeman, Diana Cooper, Ann Fleming, Anthony Powell, A.D. Peters and Christopher Sykes. By special dispensation the Latin Mass is said. The obituary in *The Times* on 11 April is notably hostile; in the same newspaper on 15 April Graham Greene describes EW as 'the greatest novelist of my generation'. EW left £11,744.

Laura Waugh died in 1973. EW's much-loved daughter Margaret was killed in a road accident in 1986.

The Evelyn Waugh Circle

Acton, Sir Harold (1904–94), of Anglo-American parentage, was at Eton and Christ Church, Oxford and spent most of his life at the family home, La Pietra, near Florence. As well as poems, novels and historical works, he published *Memoirs of an Aesthete* (1948), *More Memoirs* (1970) and a memoir of Nancy Mitford (1975).

Asquith, Katharine (1885–1977), née Horner, married (1907) Raymond Asquith (killed in action 1916), eldest son of H.H. Asquith, Prime Minister. A Roman Catholic convert, she lived at the Manor House, Mells, Somerset, inherited from her father, Sir John Horner; from 1949 Ronald Knox also lived there, and EW was a frequent visitor to the house.

Balfour, Patrick (1904–77), author and journalist, was educated at Winchester and Balliol College, Oxford, and succeeded to the title of 3rd Baron Kinross in 1939. As an *Evening Standard* correspondent, he covered the war in Abyssinia. The character of Lord Kilbannock in the *Sword of Honour* trilogy is based on Balfour.

Baxter, Beverley (1891–1964), born and educated in Canada, became a journalist in England and served for many years on the staff of the *Daily Express*. Later he served as a Member of Parliament (1935–50) and was knighted in 1954.

Beaton, Cecil (1904–80), photographer and stage designer. Educated at Harrow and Cambridge. Knighted in 1972.

Beerbohm, Max (1872–1956), essayist, dramatic critic, parodist and caricaturist, greatly admired by EW from boyhood onwards. He lived mainly in Italy after his marriage in 1910, but often visited England.

Bell, Clive (1881–1962), writer on art and a member of the Bloomsbury Group, married (1907) Vanessa Stephen, herself an artist and a sister of Virginia Woolf. He was a friend of Roger Fry and a champion of the Post-Impressionists.

Belloc, Hilaire (1870–1953), prolific and once very popular writer, journalist and politician; a Roman Catholic and a close friend of Katharine Asquith (above). EW was introduced to Belloc by Duff Cooper.

Berners, Lord (Gerald Hugh Tyrwhitt-Wilson), 14th Baron Berners (1883–1950), composer, author, painter, aesthete and eccentric, achieved a measure of popularity between the wars for his ballet music and also published fiction and autobiography. EW visited his country home, Faringdon House, Berkshire.

Berry, Pamela, second daughter of the 1st Earl of Birkenhead, married (1936) the Hon. Michael Berry, later Baron Hartwell.

Betjeman, John (1906–84), poet and writer on architecture and topography, was educated at Marlborough and Magdalen College, Oxford. The most popular poet of his day, he was knighted in 1969 and became Poet Laureate in 1972 . He was a friend of EW's at Oxford, and both Betjeman and his wife Penelope remained in close touch with him, Penelope Betjeman serving as a model for the Empress Helena in Waugh's *Helena*.

Boothby, Robert (1900–86), politician, was educated at Eton and Magdalen College, Oxford. He was an MP from 1924 to 1958 and was created a life peer in 1958.

Bowra, Maurice (1898–1971), classical scholar, wit and renowned Oxford 'personality', was first Fellow and from 1938 Warden of Wadham College and served as Vice-Chancellor of Oxford University. Knighted in 1951. He is said to have been the model for Mr Samgrass in *Brideshead Revisited*.

Bridgman, the Hon. Maurice (1904–80), businessman and Chairman of the British Petroleum Company, was the third son of Viscount Bridgman and was educated at Eton and Trinity College, Cambridge. Knighted in 1964.

Bushell, Tony, stage and film actor notable for his good looks. He began as an understudy for Ivor Novello and later worked with Laurence Olivier as associate producer of the film versions of *Hamlet* and *Richard III*.

The Evelyn Waugh Circle   191

Byron, Robert (1905–41), traveller and author, educated at Eton and Oxford, was a close friend of EW in his early years. His books include *The Byzantine Achievement* (1929) and *The Road to Oriana* (1937). He was killed in action while serving in the Royal Navy in the Second World War. See Christopher Sykes, *Four Studies in Loyalty* (1946).

Carew, Dudley (b. 1903) was a contemporary (and hero-worshipper) of EW's at Lancing College and later became a journalist on *The London Mercury* and, from 1926 to 1963, on *The Times*. He also published novels. He is said to have introduced EW to Evelyn Gardner, who became his first wife. His *A Fragment of Friendship* (1974) includes reminiscences of EW's schooldays.

Cecil, Lord David (1902–86), younger son of the 4th Marquess of Salisbury. Educated at Eton and Christ Church, Oxford, he became a don and was Goldsmiths' Professor of English Literature at Oxford (1948–69). He published many works of biography and criticism. His wife Rachel, a daughter of the critic Desmond MacCarthy, was also a friend of EW.

Churchill, Randolph (1911–68), son of Sir Winston Churchill, was educated at Eton and Christ Church, Oxford. He became a journalist and a Conservative MP and served as an intelligence officer in the Second World War. He enjoyed a somewhat tempestuous friendship with EW from about 1930 (for the probable circumstances of their meeting, see the entry for March 1930). There are references to EW in his autobiography, *Twenty-One Years* (1965).

Clonmore, Lord (b. 1902), educated at Eton and Merton College Oxford, succeeded to the title of 8th Earl of Wicklow in 1946. An Anglican priest, he had become a Roman Catholic convert, edited the *Dublin Review* (1937–40) and published a book on Pope Pius (1937).

Cockburn, Claud (1904–81), journalist. Educated at Berkhamsted and Keble College, Oxford. Foreign correspondent for *The Times* (1929–32) and for the Communist newspaper *The Daily Worker* (1935–46).

Connolly, Cyril (1903–74), journalist and critic, educated at Eton (where his contemporaries included Harold Acton, George Orwell, Anthony Powell and Henry Yorke) and Balliol College, Oxford. He worked for the *New Statesman* and the *Observer*, and for many years had a regular book-review column in the *Sunday Times*. In 1939 he was one of the founders of the influential magazine *Horizon* (alluded to as *Survival* in EW's 'Sword of Honour' trilogy), which published *The Loved One*, and remained its editor until its demise in 1950. His novel *The Rock Pool* shows the influence of EW. See biography by David Pryce-Jones (1983).

Cooper, Lady Diana (1892–1986), a daughter of the Duke of Rutland, was a famous beauty and for many years one of the leaders of the London and international social world. She had a close friendship with EW that began in 1932 and (unlike many of his friendships) lasted to the end of his life. In 1919 she married Alfred Duff Cooper (1890–1954), created Viscount Norwich in 1952, politician, diplomat and author, Ambassador to Paris from 1944 to 1947. In the 1920s she was for a time an actress, notably in Max Reinhardt's *The Miracle* (see entry for 16 April 1932). She is said to have been the prototype of Mrs Stitch in *Scoop* and the *Sword of Honour* trilogy. She published three volumes of autobiography (1958–60); her correspondence with EW is full of interest and has been edited by her grand-daughter, Artemis Cooper, as *Mr Wu and Mrs Stitch* (1991).

Crease, Francis, who lived near Lancing College during EW's time there and (though unconnected with the school) gave him private lessons in the writing of illuminated scripts, is described by Michael Davie as an 'unworldly amateur scribe of uncertain origins and effeminate manners'. EW wrote a preface for a book of his designs published in 1928. Later Crease lived at Marston, near Oxford, and EW visited him there.

D'Arcy, the Very Reverend Martin, S.J. (1888–1977), Jesuit priest who gave EW instruction in the Roman Catholic faith, received him into the Church and officiated at his marriage to Laura Herbert. He was educated at Stonyhurst and Oxford and later became Master of Campion Hall, Oxford (1932–45), to which EW was a frequent visitor. He was Provincial of the English Province of the Society of Jesus (1945–50) and published many theological works.

Dawkins, Richard McGillivray (1871–1955), distinguished and highly eccentric classical scholar, became Professor of Byzantine and Modern Greek at Oxford in 1920. The *Dictionary of National Biography* tactfully refers to him as 'an original', adding that 'His taste in men as in books was catholic'. His friends included Norman Douglas (of whom he published a study in 1933) and 'Baron Corvo'. Dawkins' visit to EW at Arnold House, at a crucial moment in the latter's personal life, suggests an earlier acquaintance.

Deakin, F.W. (Bill) (b. 1913), historian, was a tutor at Wadham College, Oxford before the Second World War, in which he served with distinction, leading the first British Military Mission to Tito (1943). Subsequently he served at the British Embassy in Belgrade and later became Warden of St Antony's College (1950–68).

Driberg, Tom (1905–76), journalist, politician, biographer and autobiogapher, was educated at Lancing, where he was a contemporary of EW (and his fellow-sacristan in the College Chapel), and Christ Church, Oxford. He became a popular and successful journalist, creating the 'William Hickey' gossip column in the *Daily Express* (a newspaper for which he worked from 1928 to 1943), and later an MP and Chairman of the Labour Party. Created a life peer in 1975. He was also famous for his homosexual indiscretions. An Anglican, he was the only friend present at EW's reception into the Roman Catholic Church.

Duggan, Alfred (1903–64), born in Buenos Aires of Irish-American parentage and a stepson of the statesman Lord Curzon, was educated at Eton and Balliol College, Oxford, where he was well known for his wealth and his addiction to drink and was a contemporary of EW's. After trying various occupations, he achieved success as a writer of historical novels. His younger brother Hubert (1904–43) was briefly a Conservative MP (1941–3) and was also a friend of EW's; his early death (see entries for 12–13 October 1943) is said to have inspired the description of Lord Marchmain's deathbed in *Brideshead Revisited*.

Dunne, Philip (1904–65), educated at Eton and Sandhurst, became a professional soldier and, briefly (1935–7), a Unionist MP. He married (1945) Audrey Rubin.

Dunsany, Lord (1878–1957), 18th Baron, dramatist, poet and autobiographer, was a friend of Yeats, Lady Gregory and other figures prominent in the Irish literary renaissance.

Elwes, Simon (1902–75), portrait painter, educated at The Oratory and the Slade School. He married (1926) the Hon. Gloria Rodd.

Fagan, Joyce, a friend of EW's during his time at Oxford, was an unconventional young woman who threw herself energetically into the activities of the Bright Young People. She was at one time employed as secretary to the dramatist Clifford Bax, and later married an American diplomat.

Fielding, Daphne and **Xan:** see Vivian, Daphne.

Fleming, Ann (b. 1913), an intimate of EW's in his later years, was three times married: first to the 3rd Baron O'Neill (killed in action, 1944); second (1945), to the 2nd Viscount Rothermere, head of the *Daily Mail* newspaper group, from whom she was divorced in 1952; third (1952), to Ian Fleming, the novelist, who died in 1964.

Fleming, Peter (1907–71), elder brother of Ian Fleming (see previous entry), was educated at Eton and Christ Church, Oxford, and became a journalist and popular travel writer. His works include *Brazilian Adventure* (1933). He married (1935) the actress Celia Johnson.

Fremantle, Anne, née Huth-Jackson (b. 1909), journalist and prolific author.

Fulford, Roger (1902–83), educated at Lancing and Worcester College, Oxford, was President of the Oxford Union in 1927 and became a writer on historical subjects.

Gardner, the Hon. Evelyn (b. 1903), first wife of EW, was a granddaughter of the Earl of Carnarvon on her mother's side; her father, a politician, was created Baron Burghclere. Her marriage to EW on 27 June 1928 was short-lived; after he had divorced her, she married in 1930 John Heygate, who later inherited a baronetcy, but they were divorced in 1936; her third husband was Ronald Nightingale.

Graham, Alastair (b. 1904), educated at Wellington College and Brasenose College, Oxford, was an intimate friend of EW's in the later 1920s. After serving briefly as a diplomat in Athens and Cairo, he retreated into private life. According to EW, elements in the character of Sebastian Flyte in *Brideshead Revisited* were based on Graham, who is also described (under the name of Hamish Lennox) in *A Little Learning*. Lady Circumference in *Decline and Fall* is said to have been based on Graham's mother, who came from a wealthy American family. During the years of his close friendship with Graham, EW was a frequent visit to the Graham home, Barford House, near Warwick, and in the summer of 1926 toured Scotland with Mrs Graham and her son.

Greene, Graham (1904–91), educated at Berkhamsted School and Balliol College, Oxford, became a prolific novelist and dramatist and, like EW, a Catholic convert.

Greene, Olivia Plunket (1907–55), with whom EW was in love in 1924–5, was the daughter of Gwen, née Parry (daughter of the composer Sir Hubert Parry) and Harry Plunket Greene, a well-known Irish singer. Her mother was a Catholic convert, and Olivia's fervent Catholicism may have contributed to EW's conversion. She never married and in later years lived with her mother in a cottage on the Longleat estate in Wiltshire. Her brother Richard (born 1901) was an Oxford contemporary of EW's and a fellow-master at Aston Clinton; in 1925 he married Elizabeth Russell, with whom EW also formed a friendship. A younger brother, David (1904–41), a gifted musician, committed suicide.

Guinness, Bryan, subsequently the 2nd Baron Moyne, was married to Diana Mitford (see below) from 1929 to 1934. EW stood godfather to their son Jonathan, born in 1930, who succeeded to the title on his father's death in 1992.

Harrod, Roy (1900–76), economist, don and government adviser. Educated at Westminster and New College, Oxford. Knighted 1959.

Haynes, E.S.P. (d. 1948), solicitor and prolific author, acted for EW in his divorce proceedings. Educated at Eton and Balliol College, Oxford, he was a friend of Alec Waugh and a well-known gourmet.

Henriques, Robert (1905–67), author and farmer.

Herbert, Laura (1916–73), second wife of EW and mother of his seven children, was the third of the four children of the Hon. Aubrey Herbert, MP, second son of the Earl of Carnarvon, and the Hon. Mary Vesey, daughter of the Viscount de Vesci. The family home was at Pixton Park, near Dulverton, Somerset. She had a brother Auberon (1922–74) and sisters Gabriel and Bridget.

Heygate, John (1903–76), educated at Eton and Balliol College, Oxford, was named as co-respondent in EW's divorce proceedings and subsequently married Evelyn, EW's former wife (the marriage was dissolved in 1936). A news editor for the BBC, he was sacked after his involvement in the divorce case became known. He later published several novels.

Hollis, Christopher (1902–77), educated at Eton and Balliol College, Oxford, and successively a schoolmaster, Conservative MP, author and publisher. EW often visited him and his wife Margaret at their country home in the village of Mells, Somerset.

Howard, Brian (1905–58), of American parentage, was educated at Eton and Christ Church, Oxford. Though he is omitted from the *Dictionary of National Biography* and the *Oxford Companion to English Literature*, his activities as a self-publicizing aesthete and homosexual gave him considerable prominence in the social and literary life of the prewar period. The character of Ambrose Silk in *Put Out More Flags*, and perhaps also that of Anthony Blanche in *Brideshead Revisited*, are said to have been based on him.

Jungman, Teresa ('Baby'), a vivacious young member of London society and a Roman Catholic, to whom EW was strongly attracted in the early 1930s. He proposed to her after his divorce, but was rejected.

Kinross, Baron: see Balfour, Patrick

Knox, Monsignor Ronald (1888–1957), son of an Anglican bishop and himself ordained as an Anglican priest, was Chaplain of Trinity College, Oxford and caused a considerable sensation by being received into the Roman Catholic Church in 1917. He became a Roman Catholic priest two years later, and from 1926 to 1939 was Roman Catholic chaplain to Oxford University. A celebrated wit and preacher, he published works on theology and a translation of the Bible as well as detective stories. In the postwar period he and EW became close friends. EW's biography of him appeared in 1959.

Lamb, Pansy, née Pakenham, a sister of Frank Pakenham (now Lord Longford) (see below), married the painter Henry Lamb. In her early days she was a close friend of Evelyn Gardner, who became EW's first wife.

Lambert, Constant (1905–51), composer and conductor, a friend of the Sitwells; his book *Music Ho!* (1933) stimulated controversy on its appearance.

Laycock, Robert (1907–68), a professional soldier with a distinguished record, was EW's commanding officer for part of the Second World War. He became Chief of Combined Operations (1943–5) and later Governor of Malta, receiving a knighthood and other honours. *Officers and Gentleman* is dedicated to him, and the character of Tommy Blackhouse in *The Sword of Honour* may be partly based on him.

Lucas, Audrey, daughter of the writer E.V. Lucas, was a close friend of EW's in the period between his marriages.

Lygon, Hugh (1904–36), second son of the 7th Earl Beauchamp, was an Oxford contemporary of EW and an intimate friend until his sudden death while travelling abroad. The character of Sebastian Flyte in *Brideshead Revisited* may owe something to him. His elder brother William (1903–79), who had the title Viscount Elmley, was also at Oxford with EW, was President of the Hypocrites Club, and took part in the film *The Scarlet Woman* (see entry for July 1924); he later became an MP and succeeded to his father's title in 1938. EW was friendly both with him and with his sisters, Lady Lettice (1906–73), Lady Sibell (born 1907) ,

Lady Mary ('Maimie') (born 1910) and Lady Dorothy ('Coote'), especially with the last two of these. Lady Mary married (1939) Vsevolode Joannovitch, a Russian prince employed by a firm of wine merchants, Saccone & Speed, but was later divorced from him; Lady Dorothy never married. EW was a frequent visitor to the family home, Madresfield Court, near Great Malvern, Worcestershire, in the period before his second marriage, and in his later years saw 'Maimie' Lygon frequently in London. The Marchmain family in *Brideshead Revisited* may be partly based on the Lygons, and their house may have been one of the prototypes for Brideshead. Like Lord Marchmain, but for different reasons, Earl Beauchamp lived abroad (he had been involved in a homosexual scandal).

Maclean, Fitzroy (1911–96), a career diplomat who enlisted in the ranks in 1939 and became Brigadier in command of the British Military Mission to the Jugoslav partisans (1943–5), in which capacity EW came into contact with him. He later became an MP and also published *Eastern Approaches* (1949), a popular account of his experiences. He is reputed to have been the prototype for Ian Fleming's James Bond.

Marsh, Edward (1872–1953), senior civil servant, man of letters, translator, memoirist and patron of poets and artists, was the executor and editor of Rupert Brooke and the editor of *Georgian Poetry* (1912–22).

Mitford, the Honourable Nancy (1904–73), novelist and biographer, eldest of the six daughters of Lord Redesdale. In her early years she was a close friend of Evelyn Gardner, who became EW's first wife. She married (1933) and later divorced (1958) the Honourable Peter Rodd (1904–68), on whom the character of Basil Seal is largely modelled. During the Second World War she worked in a bookshop in Curzon Street, often visited and mentioned by EW. After the war she lived in Paris. Her sister Diana (born 1910) married first the Hon. Bryan Guinness (see above) and later Sir Oswald Mosley (see next entry); her youngest sister Unity was a friend and enthusiastic admirer of Hitler and a prominent member of the British Union of Fascists, who attempted suicide on the day the Second World War broke out and died in 1948.

Mosley, Lady Diana (born 1910), fourth of the six daughters of Lord Redesdale, and a younger sister of Nancy Mitford (see previous entry). She married (1929) the Hon. Bryan Guinness (divorced 1934) and subsequently (1936) Sir Oswald Mosley, leader of the British Union of Fascists. With her husband she was imprisoned during the Second World War (she in Holloway, he in Brixton) and after the war lived in France.

Nicolson, Harold (1886–1968), diplomat, politician and author, published a number of popular biographies, including the official life of George V, as well as fiction, travel books and *belles lettres*. He was married to the novelist Victoria Sackville-West. His diaries have been published in three volumes.

Pakenham, Francis Aungier (Frank) (b. 1905), educated at Eton and New College, Oxford, succeeded as the 7th Earl of Longford in 1961. He converted to Roman Catholicism, partly under the influence of EW, and has been an Oxford don, an author, a publisher and a well-known social reformer, as well as having a successful career as a politician and government minister, holding among other offices of state those of Colonial Secretary and Lord Privy Seal. Created Baron Pakenham in 1945. Married (1931) Elizabeth Harman. His sister Pansy married the painter Henry Lamb (see above).

Pares, Richard (1902–58), educated at Winchester and Balliol College, Oxford, and an Oxford contemporary and close friend of EW. He became a Fellow of All Souls College, Oxford, and Professor of History at Edinburgh University.

Peters, Augustus Dudley (1892–1973), EW's literary agent, educated privately and at St John's College, Cambridge, began his career as a journalist and established a literary agency in London in 1924. He was also energetic as a theatrical producer.

Powell, Anthony (b. 1905), novelist, began his career with *Afternoon Men* (1931) but is now best known for his postwar sequence of twelve novels *A Dance to the Music of Time* (1951–75). He has also published his memoirs in four volumes (*To Keep the Ball Rolling*).

Quennell, Peter (1905–93), educated at Berkhamsted Grammar School and Balliol College, Oxford, has published biographical and historical works as well as poetry.

Rice, David Talbot (1903–74), educated at Eton and Christ Church, Oxford, became an archaeologist and art historian, specializing in Byzantine art. Watson-Gordon Professor of the History of Fine Art at Edinburgh University from 1934 and author of important studies, some of them in collaboration with his wife Tamara and with his (and EW's) friend Robert Byron (see above).

Rothenstein, John (1901–92), art historian and son of the painter Sir William Rothenstein, was educated at Worcester College, Oxford and was Director of the Tate Gallery from 1938 to 1964. Knighted in 1952. His two-volume autobiography appeared in 1965–6.

Roxburgh, J.F. (1888–1954), a charismatic figure who taught the sixth form at Lancing while EW was there and later became the first headmaster of Stowe School. See biography by Noel Annan.

Russell, Conrad (1878–1947), fourth son of Lord Arthur Russell, was a gentleman farmer and a friend of Diana Cooper and Katharine Asquith as well as of EW.

Russell, Elizabeth: see Greene, Olivia Plunket.

Sackville-West, Edward, music critic and Roman Catholic convert, was a cousin of Vita Sackville-West, wife of Harold Nicolson (see above).

Sitwells, The: Edith (1887–1964), poet, published her first volume of verse in 1915, edited the modernist magazine *Wheels* from 1916 to 1921, collaborated with William Walton on *Façade* (1923), and acquired a well-deserved reputation as a colourful, controversial, often eccentric figure. Made a Dame of the British Empire in 1954. Her elder brother Osbert (1892–1969), novelist, travel writer and autobiographer, inherited the baronetcy and the family seat, Renishaw Hall in Derbyshire, while her younger brother Sacheverell (1897–) published poems, biographies and books on art and architecture, and incurred the displeasure of his siblings by marrying (his wife Georgia being also a friend of EW).

Sparrow, John (1906–94), educated at Winchester and New College, Oxford, practised as a barrister until appointed Warden of All Souls College, Oxford (1952–77). He published widely on classical and modern literature.

Stanley, Oliver (1896–1950), politician, was a son of the 17th Earl of Derby. Educated at Eton, he was an MP, 1924–45 and held various ministerial offices, including those of Secretary for War and Colonial Secretary.

Sutro, John (b. 1904), a wealthy Oxford contemporary of EW and founder of the Oxford Railway Club.

Sykes, Christopher (1907–86), educated at Downside and Christ Church, Oxford, writer and EW's authorized biographer (*Evelyn Waugh: A Biography* (1975)) as well as a close friend. In his later years EW often visited Sykes and his wife Camilla at their home in Mells, Somerset, where they were neighbours of Katharine Asquith and Ronald Knox.

Vivian, the Hon. Daphne (b. 1904), daughter of the 4th Baron Vivian. She married (1927) Viscount Weymouth and, after a divorce, Alexander ('Xan') Fielding, author.

Waugh, Alexander (Alec) (1898–1981), elder brother of EW, prolific novelist and travel writer, achieved early notoriety with *The Loom of Youth* (1917) and, much later, considerable success with *Island in the Sun* (1956). His *My Brother Evelyn and Other Profiles* appeared in 1967.

Waugh, Arthur (1866–1943), father of EW, publisher and man of letters, was for many years Managing Director of the old-established firm of Chapman & Hall, a position from which he retired in 1929. He edited the Nonesuch Dickens and published an autobiography, *One Man's Road* (1931).

Waugh, Catherine, née Raban, mother of EW, married Arthur Waugh (see previous entry) in 1893.

Waugh, Laura: see Laura Herbert.

Woodruff, Douglas (1897–1978), Roman Catholic journalist, author and publisher. Educated at Downside and New College, Oxford, he edited the *Tablet*, a leading Catholic journal, from 1936–67.

Yorke, Henry (1905–73), Birmingham business man and, under the pseudonym of Henry Green, novelist. EW greatly admired his early work.

Index

Abdy, Diana, 83
Abdy, Robert, 45, 52
Acton, Harold, 10, 11, 12, 15, 16, 18, 21, 22, 23, 27, 28, 32, 33, 34, 50, 107, 111, 116, 175, 181, 189
Acton, Lord and Lady, 162, 165
Addinsell, Richard, 13
Alcuin, Brother, 41
Allsop, Kenneth, 169
Anstey, F., 71
Ashton, Frederick, 125, 145
Asquith, Katharine, 49, 50, 59, 86, 141, 155, 165, 184, 189
Attlee, Clement, 84, 89
Auden, W. H., 110, 111
Austen, Jane, 75

Bacon, Francis, 156
Balcon, Jill, 113, 151
Balfour, Patrick, 28, 48, 108, 149, 152, 189
Baring, Maurice, 31, 86, 181
Barzun, Jacques, 123
Bath, Marchioness of, 101, 107
Baxter, Beverley, 91, 189
Beaton, Cecil, 32, 33, 34, 40, 110, 125
Beatty, Peter, 91
Beauchamp, Lord, 39
Beaverbrook, Lord, 151
Bedford, Sybille, 152
Beerbohm, Max, 12, 31, 99, 100, 105, 116, 136, 148, 154, 189
Bell, Clive, 95, 189
Belloc, Hilaire, 31, 126, 134, 190
Bennett, Basil, 105
Benson, R. H., 148
Berenson, Bernard, 116
Berlin, Isaiah, 132
Berners, Lord, 44, 83, 190
Berry, Pamela, 92, 101, 113, 114, 125, 155, 175, 176, 190

Betjeman, John, 32, 33, 34, 36, 45, 52, 63, 71, 81, 92, 93, 95, 96, 97, 98, 101, 104, 119, 142, 143, 186, 188, 190
Betjeman, Penelope, 82, 86, 87, 101, 106, 115, 175
Beveridge, William, 67
Birkenhead, Lady, 34
Birkenhead, Lord, 34, 183
Black, Stephen, 134
Blair, Eric: see George Orwell
Blow, Jonathan, 78
Bonham-Carter, Violet, 45
Boothby, Robert, 84, 95, 181, 190
Bourchier, Basil, 4
Bowen, Elizabeth, 81
Bowra, Maurice, 35, 45, 48, 53, 70, 71, 81, 87, 88, 93, 101, 103, 104, 105, 110, 120, 144, 149, 167, 181, 187, 190
Boyle, Stuart, 104, 105
Bracken, Brendan, 61
Brandt, Carl, 96
Brandt, Carol, 96, 103
Breit, Harvey, 112
Bridgman, Maurice, 108, 190
Brownlow, Lord and Lady, 142
Buchan, John, 34
Bullock, Malcolm, 83
Burghclere, Lady, 27, 81, 93, 167
Burton, Richard, 36
Bury, Lord, 34
Bushell, Tony, 8, 9, 11, 12, 13, 18, 20, 21, 190
Butler, R. A., 91, 154
Byron, Robert, 10, 12, 16, 22, 28, 32, 35, 191

Caine, Hall, 25
Campbell, Robin, 72
Campbell, Roy, 125
Caraman, Philip, 109, 138, 145, 169, 178, 180, 188

203

Index

Carew, Dudley, 7, 9, 184, 191
Carleton-Greene, Hugh, 174
Cazalet, Victor, 34
Cecil, Lord David, 34, 35, 59, 70, 89, 103, 105, 114, 140, 149, 191
Cecil, Lady, 70, 81
Chaplin, Charles, 15, 97
Charteris, Hugo, 171
Chekhov, Anton, 14
Chirico, Giorgio de', 28
Christie, Agatha, 145
Christie, Mr, 41
Churchill, Clarissa, 126
Churchill, Randolph, 32, 33, 34, 40, 64, 65, 69, 72, 76, 77, 78, 80, 83, 84, 85, 88, 90, 92, 98, 100, 101, 109, 118, 129, 134, 139, 140, 143, 145, 149, 152, 158, 168, 179, 183, 191
Churchill, Winston, 61, 70, 84, 124, 158, 185
Clark, Kenneth, 109
Claudel, Paul, 113
Clinton, John and Violet, 45
Clonmore, Lord, 48, 191
Clunes, Alec, 116
Cockburn, Claud, 11, 12, 14, 15, 16, 17, 18, 19, 20, 22, 23, 84, 136, 191
Coghill, Nevill, 149
Colefax, Sybil, 101
Colette, 140
Collins, Wilkie, 79
Comfort, Alex, 56
Compton-Burnett, Ivy, 31, 166
Connolly, Cyril, 28, 32, 71, 72, 79, 81, 85, 91, 100, 102, 103, 105, 113, 117, 118, 126, 130, 136, 139, 141, 150, 165, 175, 178, 181, 185, 192
Connor, William, 174
Cooper, Artemis, 132
Cooper, Diana, 39, 40, 43, 44, 47, 48, 50, 54, 61, 63, 67, 69, 71, 76, 77, 88, 91, 101, 104, 105, 113, 124, 130, 132, 134, 136, 137, 145, 146, 149, 150, 153, 155, 158, 162, 164, 165, 174, 175, 178, 182, 184, 188, 192
Cooper, Duff, 54, 62, 68, 71, 76, 77, 88, 113, 132, 134, 135, 136, 137, 192
Couturier, Père, 113
Coward, Noel, 12, 15, 34, 146
Craft, Robert, 112
Crease, Francis, 25, 179, 192
Croft-Cooke, Rupert, 105
Cunard, Lady, 35
Cunard, Nancy, 35
Curzon, Lady, 127, 130, 165

D'Arcy, Martin, 34, 35, 36, 42, 48, 50, 51, 52, 54, 55, 72, 90, 108, 118, 123, 146, 151, 154, 159, 192
D'Arms, John, 170, 174
Day, Dorothy, 110
Day-Lewis, Cecil, 113
Deakin, F. W., 89, 93, 193
Denham, Lord, 41
Dennis, Nigel, 186
Devonshire, Duke and Duchess of, 160
Dickens, Charles, 49, 65, 80
Disney, Walt, 60, 97, 149
Dobson, Frank, 32
Donaldson, Lord and Lady, 109, 135, 137, 145, 154
Dostoievski, Feodor, 16
Douglas, Lord Alfred, 88
Douglas, Norman, 88, 124
Draper, Ruth, 33
Driberg, Tom, 7, 9, 16, 25, 31, 36, 45, 52, 84, 122, 134, 143, 151, 170, 175, 193
Duggan, Alfred, 17, 42, 126, 127, 129, 130, 137, 165, 180, 181, 182, 191, 193
Duggan, Hubert, 40, 48, 72, 193
Dunne, Philip, 85, 186, 193
Dunsany, Lord, 25, 36, 194
Dutton, Ralph, 141

Eden, Anthony, 126, 127, 157
Eliot, George, 177
Eliot, T. S., 17, 95, 118, 145
Elmley, Lord, 39, 197

Index

Elwes, Simon, 97, 100, 194
Fagan, Joyce, 9, 194
Fairbanks, Douglas, 132
Fielding, Daphne, 141, 151, 174, 176, 201
Fielding, Xan, 151, 201
Firbank, Ronald, 177
FitzHerbert, Giles, 178, 181
Fitzwilliam, Earl, 72
Fleming, Ann, 125, 132, 140, 142, 143, 145, 146, 148, 149, 151, 152, 159, 167, 174, 175, 178, 179, 180, 181, 183, 185, 188, 194
Fleming, Ian, 3, 125, 132, 139, 142, 171, 175, 178, 181, 194
Fleming, Peter, 32, 40, 194
Ford, Ford Madox, 124
Forster, E. M., 64, 84
Francis, Saint, 149
Freeman, John, 170
Fremantle, Ann, 110, 111, 114, 119, 194
Fulford, Roger, 22, 52, 194

Galsworthy, John, 180
Gardner, Erle Stanley, 78, 112, 170
Gardner, Evelyn (the Hon. Mrs Evelyn Waugh), 23–30 *passim*, 47, 194
Garrett, John, 94
Gathorne-Hardy, Robert, 115
Gerhardie, William, 113
Gerson, Mark, 165
Gertler, Mark, 5
Gilbert, W. S. & Arthur Sullivan, 21
Gill, Eric, 68
Girouard, Mark, 143
Gracias, Cardinal, 143
Graham, Alastair, 8, 9, 10, 11, 12, 14, 15, 16, 17, 18, 21, 22, 24, 25, 29, 36, 195
Graham, General, 74
Green, Henry: *see* Henry Yorke
Greene, Graham, 54, 69, 75, 105, 107–8, 109, 116, 117, 118, 119, 120, 121, 122, 127, 131, 132, 133, 139, 140, 142, 144, 145, 149, 150, 153, 161, 166, 167, 172, 175, 183, 187, 188, 195
Greenham, Peter, 177
Grenfell, J. S. G., 4
Griffin, Cardinal, 75, 93
Grossmith, George and Weedon, 95
Guinness, Alec, 146, 159, 169, 173
Guinness, Bryan and Diana, 30, 31, 32, 33, 34, 195, 198
Guinness, Jonathan, 31, 44
Guthrie, James, 10

Hailes, Lord and Lady, 176
Harling, Robert, 130
Harrod, Roy, 10, 22, 24, 181, 195
Hart-Davis, Rupert, 132
Haynes, E. S. P., 9, 23, 31, 63, 196
Hayward, John, 23, 108, 109
Head, Anthony, 144
Heard, Gerald, 34
Heenan, Archbishop, 180, 184
Heller, Joseph, 174
Hemingway, Ernest, 118, 125, 174, 186
Henriques, Robert, 86, 103, 196
Heppenstall, Rayner, 93
Herbert, A. P., 35
Herbert, Auberon, 42, 53, 88, 99, 118, 143, 196
Herbert, Gabriel, 42
Herbert, Laura: *see* Laura Waugh
Heygate, John, 29, 30, 196
Hill, Pamela, 126, 127, 196
Hodges, Lucy, 106
Hollis, Christopher, 15, 17, 20, 23, 35, 36, 42, 48, 49, 50, 51, 52, 55, 58, 59, 131, 132, 137, 141, 149, 150, 173, 196
Hollis, Mary, 50
Hollis, Roger, 19
Howard, Brian, 10, 18, 24, 162, 196
Howard, Lord, 57
Howe, Helen, 97, 102
Hughes, Richard, 35
Hunt, Holman, 166

Index

Huxley, Aldous, 27, 129, 146, 180
Huxley, Julian, 88

Inge, W. R., 7
Ionesco, Eugène, 170
Isherwood, Christopher, 88, 139, 148, 177

Jacobs, Barbara, 5
Jagan, Cheddi, 176
James, Henry, 93, 94
James, Robert Rhodes, 179
James, William, 22
Jebb, Gladwyn, 119
Joad, C. E. M., 67
John, Augustus, 81
Johnson, Edgar, 135
Johnston, Edward, 166
Joyce, James, 34
Jungman, Teresa, 39, 40, 44, 196

Kennedy, Ludovic, 153
Kennington, Eric, 9
Kermode, Frank, 172
Kinross, Lord: *see* Patrick Balfour
Kipling, Rudyard, 145
Knight, G. Wilson, 151
Knight, Laura, 87
Knox, Ronald, 67, 70, 93, 100, 101, 103, 108, 109, 116, 117, 119, 123, 137, 149, 150, 155, 157, 158, 159, 160, 161, 165, 197
Korda, Alexander, 51, 52

Lamb, Henry, 25, 26, 33, 34, 197
Lamb, Pansy, 25, 26, 27, 33, 34, 35, 93, 135, 197
Lambert, Constant, 78, 197
Lancaster, Osbert, 71, 116, 154
Lawrence, Christie, 96, 103
Lawrence, D. H., 29, 171, 173, 177
Laycock, Robert, 75, 104, 197
Lehmann, John, 138
Lehmann, Rosamund, 113
Leigh, Vivien, 125, 147, 159
Lejeune, C. A., 109
Linklater, Eric, 129
Lloyd, Harold, 15, 17, 20, 21

Lloyd George, David, 145
Longford, Lord (d.1961), 173
Longford, Lord (b.1905): *see* Frank Pakenham
Lonsdale, Frederick, 126
Lothian, Marquess of, 152
Loyola, St Ignatius, 123
Lucas, Audrey, 31, 33, 34, 35, 197
Luce, Clare Booth, 110, 112, 115, 129, 149
Luce, Henry, 110, 112
Lutyens, Edwin, 70
Lygon, Dorothy, 39, 77, 79
Lygon, Hugh, 10, 39, 44, 48, 197
Lygon, Mary ('Maimie'), 39, 48, 50, 57, 59, 62, 67, 70, 71, 73, 87, 91, 93, 96, 99, 102, 104, 147, 167, 169, 197–8

Macaulay, Rose, 95, 155
MacCarthy, Desmond, 104
McCarthy, Mary, 182
MacDonald, Ramsay, 34
McEwan, Jock and Bridget, 153
McIntyre, Alfred, 110
Maclean, Fitzroy, 72, 76, 80, 82, 198
Macmillan, Harold, 179
Maillol, Aristide, 28
Mannin, Ethel, 33
Maritain, Jacques, 111
Marlborough, Duke and Duchess of, 33
Marsh, Edward, 32, 101, 125, 198
Martin, John, 69
Martin, Kingsley, 89
Marx Brothers, 101
Matisse, Henri, 5, 85
Matthews, W. R., 67
Maugham, Lord, 91
Maugham, W. Somerset, 98, 124
Melba, Nellie, 33
Merton, Thomas, 108,
Messel, Oliver, 23, 40
Meynell, Francis, 32
Minton, John, 157
Mitchison, G. R. and Naomi, 10
Mitford, Jessica, 169
Mitford, Nancy, 29, 30, 32, 33, 34, 70, 71, 83, 84, 86, 88, 102,

109, 113, 116, 120, 121, 132, 139, 153, 161, 165, 171, 172, 187, 198
Mitford, Unity, 149, 198–9
Monsell, Viscount, 113
Monro, Harold, 35
Moore, George, 35
More, Sir Thomas, 121, 123
Morgan, Charles, 141
Morris, May, 25
Mortimer, Raymond, 28, 132
Mosley, Lady Diana, 187, 198, 199
Mountbatten, Lord, 71
Muggeridge, Malcolm, 131, 143, 144, 159, 167
Myers, L. H., 19

Nabokov, Vladimir, 164, 165, 177
Newby, P. H., 142
Newman, Cardinal, 101
Nichols, Beverley, 142
Nicolson, Ben, 91
Nicolson, Harold, 76, 88, 91, 95, 130, 151, 176, 180, 199
Noel-Buxton, Lord, 143, 144, 145

Ogilvie-Grant, Mark, 28
Oldmeadow, Ernest, 45
Olivier, Laurence, 108, 147
Onslow, Teresa, 173, 174
Orwell, George (Eric Blair), 84, 88, 107, 112, 113
Osborne, June, 109

Pakenham, Elizabeth, 96
Pakenham, Frank, 33, 34, 35, 36, 48, 58, 59, 67, 71, 72, 81, 91, 93, 94, 101, 105, 108, 121, 122, 125, 126, 133, 148, 159, 172, 173, 199
Pakenham, Thomas, 143
Pakenham, Pansy: *see* Pansy Lamb
Pares, Richard, 10, 141, 199
Patten, Susan, 133
Peck, Winifred, 165
Peters, A. D., 32, 36, 49, 54, 59, 102, 129, 172, 188, 199

Picasso, Pablo, 85
Piper, John, 68
Pirandello, Luigi, 13
Plato, 15
Plomer, William, 142
Plunket-Greene, Elizabeth: *see* Elizabeth Russell
Plunket Greene, Olivia, 10, 11, 12, 13, 15, 16, 18, 23, 24, 26, 28, 32, 33, 34, 35, 49, 52, 107, 125, 107, 125
Plunket Greene, Richard, 15, 16, 17, 18, 19, 22
Porter, Cole, 140
Poussin, Nicolas, 10
Powell, Anthony, 25, 81, 85, 137, 141, 142, 145, 149, 154, 161, 162, 169, 170, 173, 177, 188, 199–200
Powers, J. F., 112
Priestley, J. B., 160, 184
Pritchett, V. S., 118
Proust, Marcel, 106

Quennell, Peter, 10, 12, 88, 143, 200

Raphael, 91
Rathdonnell, Lady, 99
Rathdonnell, Lord, 101
Rattigan, Terence, 169
Ravensdale, Irene, 36
Rayner, John, 77
Redgrave, Michael, 133
Reed, Carol, 109, 125, 137
Revnolds, Graham, 133
Reynolds, Sir Joshua, 10
Rhys, Stella, 3
Ribbentrop, Joachim von, 87
Rimbaud, Arthur, 36
Richards, I. A., 21
Robeson, Paul, 32
Rodd, Peter, 198
Rossetti, Dante Gabriel, 23, 24, 25
Roosevelt, Mrs Kermit, 96
Rothenstein, John, 12, 14, 70, 200
Rothermere, Ann: *see* Ann Fleming
Rothschild, Barbara, 113

Rousseau, Henri, 21
Rowse, A. L., 166
Roxburgh, J. F., 6, 200
Rubens, Peter Paul, 10
Ruskin, John, 134
Russell, Bertrand, 12
Russell, Conrad, 50, 58, 99, 119, 200
Russell, Elizabeth (Mrs Richard Plunket Greene), 15, 16, 17
Russell, Maud, 117
Russell, 'Tusky', 98
Ryan, Thomas C., 160

Sackville-West, Edward, 115, 117, 118, 132
Sackville-West, Victoria, 176, 199
Sadleir, Michael, 64
Salmen, Stanley, 130, 137
Sargent, Malcolm, 99
Saunders, Joan, 140, 168
Scarsdale, Lord, 152
Schaffer, Peter, 175
Scott, Charles, 72
Scott Moncrieff, C. K., 13
Selassie, Haile, 36
Selznick, David, 117
Shakespeare, William, 14, 15, 21, 32, 133, 147, 151
Shaw, G. B., 8, 11, 150
Shearer, Moira, 151, 153
Silk, Bill, 11, 17
Sitwell, Edith, 32, 33, 35, 68, 110, 119, 144, 145, 146, 163, 180, 200
Sitwell, Osbert, 27, 29, 35, 59, 68, 83, 91, 98, 106, 110, 114, 118, 119, 160, 200
Sitwell, Sacheverell, 23, 29, 33, 34, 35, 40, 95, 180, 201
Smith, Logan Pearsall, 32
Smith, Maggie, 175
Sorensen, Virginia, 180
Spain, Nancy, 143, 144, 145, 152
Spark, Muriel, 156, 158, 160, 164, 171
Sparrow, John, 52, 177, 180, 201
Speaight, Robert, 32
Spencer, Stanley, 148, 149, 169

Spender, Stephen, 176, 180
Stanley, Oliver, 101, 201
Stark, Freya, 129
Stendhal, 159
Stirling, William, 69, 75, 76
Stokes, Richard, 93, 149
Stopes, Marie, 88
Stopp, Frederick J., 136–7, 161
Strauss, E. B., 138
Stravinsky, Igor, 112
Sturgis, Howard, 79
Sutro, John, 10, 12, 18, 23, 24, 27, 34, 153, 181, 201
Swift, Jonathan, 186
Sykes, Camilla, 99
Sykes, Christopher, 32, 48, 71, 85, 95, 96, 99, 102, 104, 105, 108, 113, 120, 122, 133, 145, 148, 163, 172, 174, 181, 188, 201

Talbot Rice, David, 14, 153, 200
Talbot Rice, Tamara, 153
Thesiger, Ernest, 9, 14
Thomas, Dylan, 185
Thomas, General, 74
Thomson, Roy, 180
Thorndike, Sybil, 21
Tito, Marshal, 127, 131
Trevor-Roper, Hugh, 100
Tucker, Sophie, 34
Turner, Reginald, 28

Vechten, Carl van, 33
Velasquez, Diego, 10
Vivian, Daphne: see Daphne Fielding
Vsevolode, Prince, 91, 198

Wain, John, 151
Waley, Arthur, 35, 175
Wallace, Edgar, 37
Walpole, Hugh, 81
Walston, Catherine, 109, 118, 122, 126, 154
Walton, William, 34, 35
Warner, Rex, 113
Waugh, Alec, 3, 4, 5, 10, 11, 12, 13, 15, 18, 19, 23, 24, 31, 34, 58, 63, 66, 84, 96, 110, 119,

131, 137, 139, 143, 151, 152, 158, 174, 180–1, 183, 201
Waugh, Arthur, 3, 4, 5, 20, 28, 71, 131, 201
Waugh, Auberon, 59, 66, 84, 99, 101, 104, 114, 125, 130, 134, 142, 143, 145, 146, 147, 149, 151, 163, 164, 166, 167, 168, 171, 173, 174, 185
Waugh, Catherine, 3, 5, 16, 71, 76, 81, 84, 95, 103, 105, 106, 130, 137, 141, 202
Waugh, Evelyn, works of:
Balance, The, 14, 15, 16
Basil Seal Rides Again, 179, 181
Black Mischief, 39, 40, 42
Brideshead Revisited, 73, 74, 75, 76, 78, 79, 82, 83, 84, 85, 86, 92, 94, 97, 116, 117, 118, 170
'Curse of the Horse Race, The', 3
Decline and Fall, 12, 25, 26, 27, 28, 43, 56, 121
Edmund Campion, 45
Handful of Dust, A, 41, 43, 45, 117
Helena, 82, 85, 86, 87, 88, 89, 109, 113, 114, 115, 116, 117, 118–19, 120, 123, 169
Holy Places, The, 130
Labels, 28, 31, 35
Little Learning, A, 13, 177, 178, 180, 182
Little Order, A, 88
Love Among the Ruins, 129, 131, 132, 133, 134
Loved One, The, 97, 99, 100, 102, 103, 104, 105, 106, 108, 111, 112
'Man Who Liked Dickens, The', 41
Men at Arms, 121, 122, 123, 124, 125, 126, 127, 141, 146, 166
Mr Loveday's Little Outing and Other Stories, 47
Ninety-Two Days, 43
Noah, 21, 23

Officers and Gentlemen, 130, 131, 136, 137, 141, 143, 144, 146, 166
Ordeal of Gilbert Pinfold, The, 146, 155, 156, 157, 158, 159, 169–70, 173
Put Out More Flags, 65, 67, 118
Remote People, 36, 38, 39
Robbery under Law, 56, 57
Ronald Knox, 159–64
Rossetti, 26, 27, 94
Scarlet Woman, The, 8
Scoop, 50, 51, 53, 55, 159
Scott-King's Modern Europe, 90, 93, 94, 103, 104
Sword of Honour, The, 112, 186
Temple at Thatch, The, 8, 10
Tourist in Africa, A, 171
Unconditional Surrender, 168, 169, 170, 171, 172, 173, 175
Vile Bodies, 29, 30, 31, 39, 43, 169
Waugh in Abyssinia, 50, 51
When the Going was Good, 95
Work Suspended, 57, 58, 66, 69, 187
World to Come, The, 4
Waugh, Harriet, 75, 150, 188
Waugh, James, 90, 141, 153
Waugh, Laura, 42, 43, 45, 47, 48– passim, 196
Waugh, (Maria) Teresa, 55, 74, 104, 149, 150, 151, 152, 155, 170, 174, 176
Waugh, Margaret, 68, 106, 132, 141, 153, 155, 159, 168, 169, 175, 176, 177, 178, 180, 186–7, 188
Waugh, Michael, 117
West, Rebecca, 33, 156
Wheeler, Monroe, 138
White, Terence de Vere, 98
Whittemore, Thomas, 36
Wicklow, Earl of, 151
Wiggin, Maurice, 123
Wilde, Oscar, 34, 84, 90, 130, 177
Williams, Tennessee, 111
Williams-Ellis, Clough, 34

Williamson, Henry, 28
Wilson, Angus, 125, 126, 175
Wilson, Edmund, 91
Winterbotham, Hiram, 106
Wodehouse, P. G., 107, 124, 136, 141, 151, 174
Wong, Anna May, 32, 97
Woodruff, Douglas, 34, 35, 36, 50, 51, 54, 58, 71, 89, 90, 93, 96, 99, 101, 102, 104, 105, 108, 118, 159, 163, 165, 168, 202
Woodruff, Mia, 52
Woods, William T., 10

Woolf, Leonard, 15
Woolf, Virginia, 28
Worsthorne, Peregrine, 171
Wycherley, William, 22

Xavier, St Francis, 127, 128

Yorke, Henry, 10, 22, 29, 32, 33, 35, 40, 48, 52, 53, 59, 81, 93, 117, 202
Young, W. R. B., 12, 13, 18, 182, 184

Zelten, Hubert van, 161